LAUNDERED

Nice Weekend Publishing Ltd

Published by

Nice Weekend Publishing Ltd

P.O. Box 322, Bridgend

niceweekend@hotmail.com

Laundered

ISBN 978-0-9564957-0-9

First published in Great Britain in 2010

A CIP catalogue record for this book is available from the British Library.

Cover design by Matthew Tyson

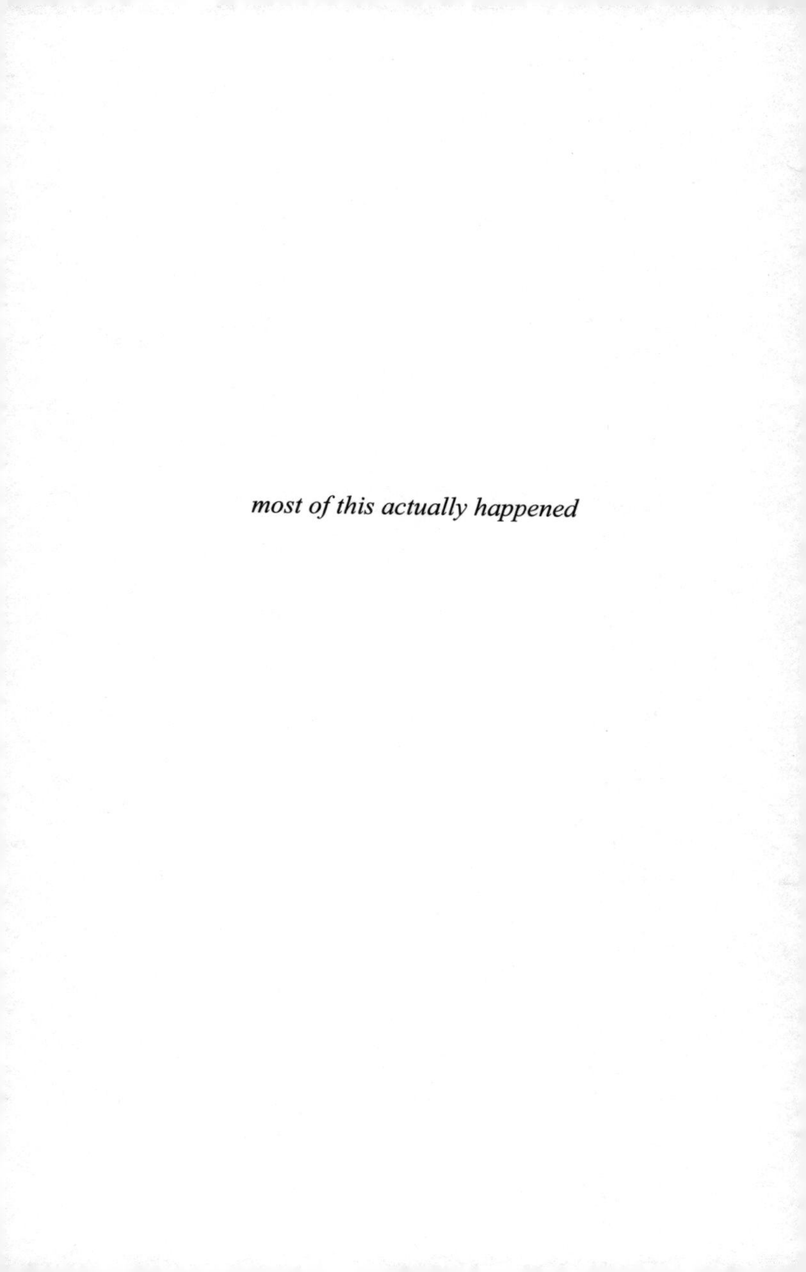

most of this actually happened

1

'Get up!'

No response.

'Ben! Wake up. Now!'

Ben Taylor opened his eyes a fraction. The side of his head remained firmly pressed into the pillow. The morning light was painful. The naked, bulky woman's eyes were bloodshot and glassy. He closed his again.

'Ben! I slept through my alarm. Jason's going to be home from nightshift any minute. Ben!'

'Huh?' He made a determined effort to stay conscious, though his eyes stayed shut. 'You said he'd moved out.'

'Yeah, well, we're still finalising the arrangements.' The woman's tone changed. '*Please*, Ben?'

'Alright, I'm up. I'm up.'

He raised himself into a sitting position, his legs draped over the side of the bed, and found the carpet with his feet.

Then he tried opening his eyes again. It felt like a nail was being driven in through the left one. The aroma of stale alcohol was hanging in the unmoving air.

A small child, maybe two years old – he was

hopeless at estimating ages - was standing next to the bed, staring at him. Ben watched as a flow of snot crept, like wax dripping down a lit candle, between the toddler's nose and emerging tongue. In no mood to see it reach its destination, he stood up and manoeuvred the child towards the door.

'Thanks Ben, I'm so sorry. I'll make it up to you. Buy you a coffee at lunch? I'll probably be on twelve or twelve-thirt…'

The woman's hand flew up to her mouth and he heard her trying, unsuccessfully, to stifle a loud retching sound. She turned and scampered, feet pounding heavily, out of the bedroom. Presumably in the direction of the toilet, as shortly thereafter came the sound of explosive, hangover-fuelled, hopefully accurate vomiting.

He bent and levered himself into his clothes, then followed her out.

As he reached the landing he could vaguely discern her wide silhouette through the gloom, huddled against the bath.

'See you at work, then,' he called, as he started making his way down the stairs, feeling obliged to be as polite as possible. 'I'll let myself out.'

'Yeah, yeah, see you at the bank.' She sat up and curled herself over the toilet bowl.

Then vomited again.

2

He didn't like to wake them.

He had no idea, whatsoever, as to the required etiquette. They'd arrived at seven o'clock and it was now approaching midnight.

Were they expecting to stay until morning? Was that the accepted protocol? He wished, now, that he'd asked more questions 'up front'.

He stayed out on the balcony. It was still nice and warm.

He'd made himself another espresso from the complicated machine – the girls had shown him how to work it – and he had a spectacular, panoramic (was that the right word?) view of the city lights to his left, and of the aeroplanes landing at the airport to his right.

He'd watched the sun set over *Santa Monica Bay* earlier, and he intended to watch it rise over the *San...something* mountains in the morning. Two of those '*things to do before you die*', as he'd heard some people say.

He'd thought, at considerable length, about whether to stop over in Las Vegas instead, but the prices there for anything upmarket were astronomic. He'd worked too long and too hard to start squandering his cash now.

The girls were the exception.

He'd been promising himself *that* particular treat for months, since he realised that his lucrative little operation was drawing to an end.

Twenty thousand dollars.

He'd negotiated the price with the 'agent' without the slightest clue as to what he was doing. The agent clearly knew this within the first five seconds of their meeting.

Still, it had been worth every penny. Or rather, every cent. They were achingly, almost unbelievably, attractive. A Latina girl and an older woman – a 'genuine soccer mom' as the agent had referred to her.

He had no idea what that meant.

He wasn't sure he liked this espresso. It was very strong, tasted bitter. Perhaps he wasn't working the machine right. He'd order a pot of tea with his breakfast – he was confident the hotel would be able to accommodate that. With some toast and cereal – in the absence of a '*full English*' from the room-service menu.

Maybe he'd be adventurous and try the '*Eggs Benedict*', whatever the hell that was.

For the price he'd paid, the agent had thrown in a cocktail of little pills, to '*keep the party rockin' bro*'. He'd been highly dubious about swallowing them, but at around ten o'clock, when fatigue had been setting in, he decided that there was nothing to lose. The girls had assured him they were safe and this was a once in a lifetime thing, so…

…the burst of energy they'd given him was incredible (there was also an instant physical side effect that had startled him and amused the girls). Problem was, he was still buzzing, two hours later. He wondered if he'd get any sleep before his Qantas flight departed at nine. The espresso wouldn't be helping, it dawned on him, so he placed the cup, and its remaining contents, down on the table.

The air was still warm out on the balcony, and he watched the planes for a while.

It all felt a world away from Henleys Bank.

Four years of living and working in stress (and disbelief that it was all so easy to do), unnoticed and unmonitored. Despite the precautions he'd taken though, his nerve had eventually, finally, started to go. Recently he'd become convinced that the authorities, or someone, had started following him. He'd even moved out of his house, in case he was being watched. When the bank announced that it was commencing some official investigations, he knew he had to get out.

His last deal came at just the right time.

Watching the planes landing was hypnotic. You could actually see them circling, queuing up, in the cloudless night sky.

He wondered when he'd go back. It would be, at least, a couple of years before it would feel safe – and he certainly wouldn't miss Henleys and its comedy-incompetent managers. Except maybe Taylor and

Moran, he conceded. He was a decent enough bloke and she was nice to look at, at least.

Not as nice as those two in the room, though.

He quietly snuck back in and sat down, on the suede tub chair, next to the bed.

They were spectacular.

Their skin was flawless.

No excess weight on any part of either of them.

They looked fantastic, sprawled across the white sheets, their bodies gently reverberating from the deep breathing of slumber.

The older one, lying on her taut stomach, slowly opened her eyes and looked at him.

'Come back to bed, Scotty.' Even her voice was perfect. 'You need some rest before your flight.' She smoothed the sheet with the palm of her hand. 'That is your real name, isn't it? *Scotty*?'

He smiled and shook his head.

'In that case,' she replied, immediately and without the slightest hint of any surprise, 'come back to bed, *Honey*.'

3

The Canary Wharf office of Henleys Bank's new Retail Operations Director was plain and simply furnished. Businesslike and efficient.

To Greg Lamb, Operations Manager (*HenleyEast* office, near the M25, north of London), it was something of a disappointment. No executive toys, no flatscreen on the wall, no leather sofa. Not like he had expected.

(What Greg, or 'Lamby' as he liked to be called by peers and superiors, hadn't yet realised was that Marc Smyth didn't actually have an office. A permanent office was old-school thinking. The latest buzz from the US was all about peripatetic management – being out with the teams, *in their faces, hot-desking*, working on the move. It kept things *energised.*)

As his eyes wandered around the minimalist decor, the door was flung open and Marc Smyth bustled his way in, mildly startling Lamby who wasn't sure whether to stand up or remain seated, and so hovered momentarily somewhere in-between the two.

They had met before. Not for a couple of years though, since Marc had relocated himself and had been 'working out of' *HenleyWest*, near Cardiff (close to the M4 motorway, hence *logistically efficient* as a *base office*).

Lamby noted the apparent results of the spoils

enjoyed by Marc since his well-publicised promotion to Level Ten – he was now much weightier around the middle and his jawline had disappeared under the side effects of a couple of years' worth of corporate lunches.

The effects of Henleys *AlphaManagement* training (available exclusively to Level Tens and above) were also very apparent.

'Lamby! Long time no see.' Marc boomed, offering a painfully firm handshake. 'How the fuck is business?'

Lamby smiled. He had acquired enough second-hand knowledge of the *AlphaManagement* course to spot a rhetorical question when thrown out. It was invariably easier to allow *Course Completants,* as Henleys referred to them, to finish their *Dominance Establishment Phase* (or '*DEP*') without interrupting.

'What can I get you? Coffee, yeah?' Marc strode, without waiting for a reply, to the coffee machine in the far corner and continued with his monologue for, actually, even longer than Lamby had anticipated. Maybe there was a new course out now – *AlphaManagementTwo?*

Marc continued speaking. He was outlining the parameters of the discussion that they were about to commence. Lamby tried his best to follow the stream of words that Marc directed at him.

...glad you could spare the time...as you know we've been asked to provide a couple of secondees to assist the Financial Crime Agency with the Money Laundering investigations...knew you had some strong candidates out at HenleyEast...would value your input...

Lamby wondered which type of coffee Marc was preparing. He quite liked the powdered latte sachets that were available from the machines used in most Henleys premises.

'Lamby?'

'Yes, Marc?' Lamby was hoping that Marc was about to repeat whatever it was he'd last said.

'The CVs? For the candidates I asked for? Do you have them?'

'Of course.' Lamby was pleased with the job he did of concealing the relief in his voice, as he retrieved the documents from his case. 'I thought we could start with Alison Carter? She's very capable and…'

'Do you have the file for that chap Taylor? Let's start with him.'

'Err…okay, here it is…'

Marc snatched the papers from Lamby's hand.

'This guy is supposed to be good, then?'

'*Really* good guy actually.' Lamby responded, using the standard Henleys Bank compliment. (The clerical staff heard management say 'really good guy actually' so often that they abbreviated it to '*RGGA*', though this hadn't yet made the official acronyms list in the *HenleyStaffManual*). 'Ben manages a Payments and Processing team. He's been at *HenleyEast* about six or seven years.'

'A first, eh? Economics?' Marc flicked through the file. 'Made decent bonuses in the City early in his career. Always had strong appraisals by the look of it. Why's he been slumming it out with you for so long?'

'Just seems to enjoy the quiet life, I guess. Decent house on the Broadlands development, where a lot of the staff are living. He can walk to work. Company car, no real pressure and free membership of the *HenleyGym*.'

'Lacks ambition then? The killer instinct?'

'Not, really sure about, that.' Lamby couldn't imagine a scenario where a *killer instinct* would be required in Payments and Processing. 'He's popular with almost everyone, works long hours and is easy to manage. Never causes any issues.'

Marc glanced at the copy of the photo ID on the file, an enlarged duplicate of the security tags worn by all employees in the *HenleyHubs*.

'Popular with the female staff? Does he shag around? Would he spend all his time trying to get the knickers off the girls in my team?'

'No. I mean, I couldn't really say. He has a *bit* of a reputation, but no worse than any other single guy at the bank. It's pretty tedious stuff - they need a release outside the office. Taylor's professional, never seen it affect his work.'

'What's this note here, about rugby? Back when he joined the bank?'

'He played professionally when he was at university. Kept getting injured or something though, gave it all up when he joined Henleys.'

'Whatever.' Marc closed the file and tossed it back to Lamby. 'Next?'

'You asked to see this one? Samantha Moran?'

'Yeah! One of my mates knows her ex-husband. Reckons she has a fabulous little arse on her. Marc grabbed the file from Lamby and turned to the photo ID page.

'Huh.' Marc paused and assessed the picture. His

expression changed. He looked as if he'd been caught off guard, almost like he'd been handed something he wasn't expecting.

'What?' Lamby was curious.

'She looks a bit…a bit like the wife.' Marc stared at the photo ID. Lamby got the impression that he rather liked it. 'Around the eyes anyway.' Marc eventually continued. 'Older though, dirtier looking. Wouldn't mind hanging out the back of her, eh Lamby? Does she fuck around?'

'I…err…no…not at all.' Lamby wasn't sure how much detail he was expected to go into on these sort of matters. 'She was married to a Commercial Manager, had a couple of kids, he started an affair with his PA and they ended up getting divorced. Her and her ex have one of those new 'four days on four days off' routines – sharing the childcare. Absolute nightmare when you're trying to manage the holiday list. She *was* seeing some IT technician, a year or so back, but mostly just socialises with Taylor when she hasn't got the children.'

'Bangin' him?'

'Nah. It's not like that.' Lamby shook his head with a degree of authority. 'Been mates for years, that's all. Think they met when they both worked for Tomas Vladic, in the City. May even have been at university together, can't remember.'

Marc paused, as if dredging something from deep in his head.

'Tomas Vladic? That guy that left the bank to start a property company?'

'That's the chap. Multimillionaire now, apparently he's…'

'Whatever. This Moran bird looks fit-as-fuck, fair play!' Marc continued to gaze at her picture before eventually bringing his attention back to the matter being discussed. 'So these two are your best, yeah?'

'Head and shoulders above the others. Only thing is…'

'What?'

'Well, Taylor's okay to work with. I mean, it's like he's bored all the time, no challenges for him, just going through the motions and all that, but he seems content. I don't think he's going to be happy about being nominated for a secondment.'

'And this little cracker?' Marc analysed Samantha Moran's photo again.

'Ah, well, that's the thing. Don't let the pretty green eyes fool you. Sam's clever, at least as bright as Taylor, but horrendous to work with - always challenging things, looking to do stuff differently, improve processes. If she wasn't so super-accurate and good at her job, well…anyway, I don't think either of them would be what you're looking for.'

'And, Lamby old chap, you're not just saying this to retain your best people?'

'By all means interview them, if you like, but I don't want to waste your time, that's all.'

Marc pondered for a while, stroking his tie. Lamby was pretty sure that Marc was trying to read his body language, or something like that, so he sat very still. Then Marc glanced down at his gold Rolex. 'Sorry Lamby, I'm going to have to push this along a bit. I'm meeting with *HenleyAudit* and some bloke from the Financial Crime Agency shortly. Who else do we have then?'

Lamby suppressed a sigh and retrieved the next CV from his case.

4

Abigail Smith watched, slightly embarrassed, as her nine-month old twins attempted to destroy one of the softplay items from the *HenleyTots* nursery toy collection.

She was even more embarrassed when it became clear that Suzy Webb, owner of this franchised outlet at *HenleyWest* (most of the large Henleys buildings now had day/evening care facilities for pre-schoolers, outsourced to independent, qualified managers operating under the *HenleyTots* brand name), was walking over to say hello. Suzy was one of those women who always looked immaculate, even, in her case, after the occasional fifteen-hour shift. Her blonde hair invariably perfect and her expensive make-up applied with pinpoint precision. Abi always felt slightly gangly and untidy around her, particularly when she hadn't yet done her own make-up, like now.

'Abi, *darling*! You wanted to see me?' Suzy greeted her with a kiss on both sides.

Her poised manner with parents (or 'clients' as she liked to call them) remained on the right side of annoying, because Abi knew she was a genuinely sweet person. Sweet, very petite, wasp-waisted, with huge boobs, it wasn't difficult to see why most of the dads, when picking their kids up, were always keen to hang around to try and chat with Suzy. Although, as

Abi was one of the select few to have been let into the secret that Suzy's business partner, Karen, was also her 'life partner', she doubted whether she would be impressed by their amateurish flirting. Completing today's vision of loveliness was a perfectly tailored, pinstriped waistcoat and trouser combo, over a crisp, blindingly white blouse.

'Yes.' Abi replied, pushing her unbrushed hair out of her eyes. 'I was wondering if I could arrange some extra hours for the twins? I'm asking Dan, my team leader, for some more flexi hours in the evenings.'

'Of course, darling! We're pretty much at full capacity, but it wouldn't look good if I turned down a request from the wife of the new Retail Director, would it?' She smiled. 'Not good for business, you know!'

Abigail smiled back.

'How is Marc getting on in the new job?' Suzy continued. 'I haven't seen him down here at *HenleyWest* in simply ages.'

'No, he's out and about all the time now, setting up these corporate *Roadshow* things. *Tomorrows Bank*, and all that? I think he's in Canary Wharf or Lombard Street, or somewhere, today. Don't see much of him at the moment. That's why I thought I'd take the opportunity to do some extra hours, you know?'

Suzy gave her a look that seemed to query why the wife of a Henleys Director would be coming back to work at all.

'Nice to be able to treat yourself to the occasional new pair of Italian shoes – you know how it is, Suze?' Abi offered up a gentle laugh, and was glad when Suzy's quizzical look dropped and she laughed too.

They watched Abi's twins as they continued to take turns in smashing the toy kangaroo, or whatever it was, against the floor. It was becoming quite brutal.

'Sorry about them. They're getting rather lively these days! I'll pay for any breakages, of course.'

'Don't be silly!' Suzy reassured her. 'That stuff is the latest technology, heavy duty, virtually indestructible and anti-bacterial too. Henleys give us a very generous toy budget. If I can persuade them to let me change that ghastly *HenleyTots* brand name, they'd be the perfect franchisor! Gosh, you really are lucky, Abi, they are the most beautiful children. They take after you, don't they!?'

'Oh, I don't know - I hope they won't be as scruffy. Look at the state of me, no make-up, in my lovely *HenleyWear* uniform. Haven't had chance to do my hair yet!' She wanted to reinforce the fact that she didn't usually look so unkempt. That she'd just been in a rush this morn…

Suzy was suddenly standing up on tip-toe and starting to adjust the front of Abi's hair. The aroma of her expensive perfume drifted around them. Abi didn't like people in her 'personal space' and this felt odd.

'There, that's better.' Suzy said, a moment later, as she pushed Abi's temporarily unruly fringe to the side and swept some hair back behind her ear. 'Gosh, you really have the most stunning colouring, you know. When I first met you I thought you wore green contact lenses and dyed your hair!'

'Oh, don't be silly!' Despite the protestation, it did feel nice to be paid a compliment, Abi decided.

Suzy spun back down off her tiptoes and returned

her attention to the children and staff in the nursery. Everything there seemed to meet with her approval – and Suzy resumed the conversation.

'You know?' she continued, 'I simply hate girls like you – that can look so good with no effort! This…' she pointed at herself, up and down, 'takes more and more effort as the years go by. *Particularly* when you pass to the wrong side of forty. You just wait, Mrs Smith!' With that she turned and glided her way back to the office at the other end of the nursery.

Abigail glanced at her watch. She'd just stay a few minutes more. She was surprised by how good the compliments from Suzy made her feel. Suzy undoubtedly played all the parents in a similar way; she was the consummate schmoozer, but so what? If it made you that little bit better prepared to face the day, then a little falseness did no harm.

She glanced at the time again. Just a couple minutes more, then she'd head upstairs - Henleys Premier customers wouldn't be going anywhere.

They'd be waiting. With their endless queries about PIN numbers, balances, misplaced gold *HenleyCards*…

They were always losing their gold cards.

Last glance at the watch. One more minute, then she'd go.

5

The walk from the far end of the Broadlands estate was clearing Ben's head.

He'd covered half a mile or so before pausing at one of the many, seemingly identical roundabouts that were scattered around this sprawling residential area of the development.

From here, close to the top of the hill, he could see over the top of what must be thousands of red-bricked houses, all the way to Broadlands Business Park, a mile or so further down to the south, and the M25 motorway beyond it. There were dozens of units on the business park - but only one was identifiable from this distance.

Slap bang in the middle, standing proud and dwarfing all those around it, was the colossal *HenleyEast*, one of four similar complexes that Henleys Bank had built around the UK.

Known unofficially as the 'Hubs', each centre housed more than a thousand staff, managing everything from Corporate Mortgages to Premier Banking, Payment Processing and Cash Handling.

Ben's place of work for the last seven years.

He started walking again as the drizzle began falling a little heavier. He debated whether he should bear off to the right, to go home and change, or just head on to the Hub. He'd gone straight out from work to the Red Lion last night (someone had been having yet another 'leaving do') and then to Helen's house.

He gave himself a glance over – his overcoat was keeping out most of the damp and his trousers weren't looking too crumpled.

Ben decided to head for work.

He could freshen up with a quick rinse in the gents when he got there.

6

Maxine Macgregor sat in the featureless corporate office, staring at the Henleys director bloke, Smyth, and his enormous gold watch.

She'd only been here five minutes and was bored. She suspected that her boss, Jon Greenwood, would not tolerate Smyth's stream of management-speak for much longer, and interject. She'd start paying attention when he did.

She didn't know the other guy in the room. They'd been introduced only a few minutes earlier. Ryan Willis, from *HenleyAudit*, apparently. He looked about fourteen, but she assumed he must be late-twenties, maybe a bit younger than her, but not by much. She'd heard decent enough reports about Henleys' audit team during her two-year secondment from the Met to the Financial Crime Agency, but was also aware that they were fighting an uphill battle – and losing. The volume of money-laundering activity at the bank was such that it was impossible to do anything meaningful about it, given the meagre resources at their disposal.

Smyth was still talking.

'…if we can build a framework of trust, develop some win-wins…'

'Marc,' Greenwood finally spoke, looking at his watch as he did so, 'I'm sorry to interrupt, but I have to get across town to a meeting with the Home Secretary.' Macgregor smiled as Smyth's eyebrows leapt skywards. 'There are similar collaborations between your bank and the Agency being initiated at branches and offices all over the South East today. Lots going on. I just need to quickly brief you in line with the Treasury directive, then I'll leave you in the most capable hands of Max here. Okay?'

Macgregor watched Smyth nod in agreement, apparently fighting the unfamiliarity of taking orders. Greenwood, though, was in the fortunate position of not having to listen to the opinions of anyone outside Government or Whitehall. She found herself enjoying Smyth's obvious discomfort.

'It appears,' Greenwood continued, 'that the Treasury is rather keen to smooth the path of the takeover of Henleys by the Commercial Bank of China.'

'Henleys is still a strong brand, despite the recent…'

'Yes, I've read the press releases, Marc. They are not directly relevant to us at this stage - they are for the public and the media. I'm afraid that *we* have to deal with the reality of the situation. The reality which is, of course, that Henleys has, rather unfortunately, found itself in a precarious financial position due to, err, how did the Financial Times describe it? *Somewhat aggressive* overexposure to risky overseas investments? The whys and wherefores do not concern us. That is between your Board of Directors and the Bank of England. At our level we just have to work the machinery. Okay?'

Smyth's facial expression belied his displeasure at

having the status of his Regional Director role downplayed, but as it was being done in a self-deprecating way by the Head of the Financial Crime Agency, and in the global scheme of things it was perfectly accurate, he had little choice but to take it on the chin.

Smyth nodded and Greenwood continued the brief.

'So, the Treasury are evidently most reluctant to use a taxpayer bailout. Not popular amongst the public any more, or so they tell us. The solution is, so we are advised, the CBC takeover. But, it would appear that the Chinese are not at all impressed by Henleys Bank's rather, how should I put it? *Horrendous* record on money laundering? The criminals '*Bank of Choice*' as the media are fond of saying?'

'Most cases are historic, there's little evidence to suggest that…'

'I've *read* the press release. Unfortunately, Marc, Henleys Bank's systems are so archaic that we have no idea what the evidence suggests. The other banks are way ahead of you in terms of their systems and their anti-money-laundering processes. Now, the Agency appreciates that there is no way on earth of uncovering more than a handful of cases in the timescale that we've been given, BUT , the Treasury is very keen to ensure that we do manage to find ourselves that handful. And, that the subsequent prosecutions are *very* high profile - well publicised.

Thus, Henleys can claim to be taking a serious approach to anti-money-laundering issues.

Then, we will offer a post-merger support package to continue the investigations when the CBC owns everything. Thus they are reassured and all parties are happy bunnies. Have I summarised effectively?'

Before anyone could respond, he continued, 'Now, Marc could you give us a few minutes please?'

'Pardon?'

Macgregor thought Smyth's eyes were going to pop out of his head.

'A few minutes. I need to have a quick word with these two.' Greenwood smiled then, without waiting for any additional response from Smyth, turned his attention to Macgregor and Willis, leaving Marc to shuffle out. Greenwood waited until Smyth closed the door behind him. Then he spoke to the two of them.

'Okay. I do really have to dash, unfortunately, but is there anything you need to check with me at this stage?'

'Yes, actually, sir.' Macgregor spoke up. 'How much time is likely to get taken up by this hunting down of a few Henleys cashiers that are taking backhanders, or whatever, to turn a blind eye? Rubbish cases like that? You know I only agreed to this on the understanding I could use the time to get more information on Tomas Vladic?'

'That's between you and Willis here. If the two of you succeed in quickly uncovering some cases that can progress to the courts, then I'm not bothered about micromanaging how you spend the rest of your time. But the 'quick wins', sorry for sounding like a banker here all of a sudden, *must* be the priority. *Not* a case that you've been working on for two years and, to be frank, haven't uncovered anything of interest on so far.'

'But sir, Vladic is ex-Henleys staff! He used to

hold all his business accounts here and…'

'I know Max. You've explained the whole damn case to me on numerous occasions!' He smiled. 'And, I'm happy for you to continue your investigations, subject to assisting Willis here first. Okay?'

She nodded. Decided to keep her mouth shut. He was giving her some scope here, at least.

Her boss turned to the *HenleyAudit* guy, Willis.

'Exactly how much trouble is Smyth likely to present?'

She watched Willis shuffle nervously in his seat for a moment, but when he spoke his voice carried the immediate authority of someone who knew his subject matter well. Macgregor liked people like that.

'None, actually. Retail Ops may not possess the most intellectually gifted managers but they know better than to do anything that could be perceived as obstructing an audit. I report directly to our Assistant Director. It's a completely different business line to Marc Smyth and Retail.

'Good. If he gives you even the *slightest* issue though, then you let me know, okay? Now, if Max here helps you out on these prosecutable, if that's a real word, cases that your bank wants to find, I'm sure you can show her one or two things that will help her research her Vladic case?' Greenwood stood to leave.

'Of course, I'd be delighted to.' Willis replied.

'Good.' Greenwood shook Willis' hand. 'Just try and keep Max out of too much trouble?'

'Sure.'

'One last thing,' Greenwood looked at them both, in turn. 'This case is important from many perspectives, I know you appreciate that. I'm particularly sensitive about the ordinary staff working for this organisation. There are a lot of honest, hard-working people at this bank and it's not their fault that the company ended up being run by imbeciles with no banking credentials. If we can do something to smooth the path of this merger then we could help safeguard a lot of jobs, understand? It's important to me.'

Macgregor nodded and Willis said 'Yes, sir' in reply, even though Greenwood was Macgregor's boss, not his. They watched Greenwood leave, then Macgregor stood up, walked over and closed the door again.

'You agreed to help me?' She sought some immediate clarification.

'If *you* help me. That's what your boss said.'

'Good, let's go somewhere for a coffee. I'll tell you what I need.'

'Aren't we supposed to wait for Marc Smyth? We can have a coffee here. I'll just…'

'No. Not here. This place depresses me. We can see Rolex Boy later.'

She reopened the door and strode out.

Willis let out a little sigh. Then followed her.

7

'Fancy a coffee? I'm getting some from the machine.' Ben asked.

'Well, well!' Samantha Moran replied, swivelling around in her chair to make the most of this opportunity. 'Still wearing yesterday's clothes, you vile tramp? You obviously spent the night at Helen Hippo's?'

'Do you want a coffee? Or not?' To enter into any form of banter with her in this mood was doomed to failure. Keep changing the subject. That was the key.

'Her husband still hasn't moved out, you know?'

'Yeah. That came up. Colombian Mountain or powdered latte sachet?'

'Don't think we have time, sorry loverboy. Lamb just got back. Wants us in his office "*ASAP*".'

'Oh, wonderful. Has anyone heard from Steve Scott yet?'

'Don't think so. This will be, what, his third day absent without explanation? Perhaps he's dead? Pulled Helen Hippo a couple of nights ago in the Red Lion and she sat on his face for a minute too long!' She started chuckling at her own joke.

'That's…disgusting.'

'You'd know. Come on, we'd better go. We can ask him what he wants to do about Scotty's disappearance when we're up there.'

She jumped out of her chair and directed herself towards the stairwell at the end of the department. Ben followed.

Sam waited for him at the doors. Then they started climbing the stairs together, side by side.

'You read the FT this morning?' She asked.

'Yeah, of course, I stopped off at Mr Patel's shop in the Square and quickly leafed through it.'

'Benjamin, sarcasm is *not* a good colour on you! Anyway, it reckons that the bank's audit team is going to work alongside the Financial Crime Agency to stamp out money laundering once and for all. You know, to oil the wheels of this Commercial Bank of China merger thing.'

'*Stamp out* money laundering?'

'Well, I suppose that's spin for *'find an unlucky few and prosecute the shit out of them'*. Full fourteen-year prison terms, the works.'

Ben shrugged. 'Do you think that's what this briefing is all about?'

'Don't know. Isn't it terribly exciting though, darling?'

'Yeah. Thrilling.'

'If the merger happens, do you think we'll be able to transfer to, you know, Shanghai, or somewhere!?'

'No.'

'Buzzkill.'

'*Buzz*kill?'

Ben raised his hand to tap on Lamby's door, but Sam pushed straight past, walked in and sat down, so Ben followed. The Centre Manager had his back to them, taking framed pictures down from the walls.

'What's up, Greg?' Sam shouted.

He almost dropped the frame he was holding.

'Ah, Sam, Ben, thanks for sparing the time.' Lamby spun around and placed the frame on the floor, as he regained his composure. 'Just wanted to *touch base*. What can I get you, coffees, yeah? Had a breakfast meeting in Canary this morning…'

'Why's he talking so loud? Sam leaned across, whispering to Ben, who gave a little shrug, as Lamby headed for the coffee machine.

'Don't know. He sounds like one of those *AlphaManagement Course Completants*.'

'…looking to complete the cascade and…'

'What's going on with your pictures, Greg?' Sam asked, evidently bored with the new style.

'What?'

Sam was adept at interrupting his train of thought. It often embarrassed Ben, who would sometimes try and curtail her. This time though, he was happy to let her do her thing. His head was starting to hurt again.

'Your pictures. Why are you taking them down?'

'Just trying to mix things up, Sam. Keep things fresh. *Leverage* a new look here. I'm going to be spending more time out with the teams, *hot-desking*, getting in their faces, raising the profile of…'

'Oh, Greg, not the *Determination* poster! Please! You *have* to keep that one. It *is* the size of someone's will that determines their success.'

'I'm just relocating them to other parts of the building, Sam, I'm not throwing them…'

'No!' She got up and retrieved one of the other frames, taking it back to her seat with her. '*Synergy* is my favourite, I'm keeping this one! It's going up next to my desk. I *always* embrace harmonious working to achieve more.'

'Okay, Sam, fine. You can have the poster.'

'Thanks Greg. I'll treas …'

'How did the meeting go, Lamby?' Ben decided it was time to move things along. Lamby was making his headache worse.

'Huh? Yeah, good. Very productive. Marc Smyth is a really good guy, actually. Likes the management-speak but basically a really good guy.'

'Marc Smyth?' Sam tore her attention away from her newly acquired print. 'Is he the guy that used to be Mark Smith, with a 'K' and an 'I', but changed it when he started getting a few promotions, because there were too many other *Mark Smiths* on the internal directory?'

'Yep.' Confirmed Ben. 'That's the chap. Wanted to differentiate his *Personal Brand*, so they say.'

'Did he?' This was evidently news to Lamby. 'Well, shrewd move 'cos he's definitely the right guy to take Retail Ops forward as part of *Tomorrows Bank. Really* impressive guy actually.'

'Sounds like a twat.' Suggested Sam.

'Anyway, Marc and I discussed the *Tomorrows Bank* programme at the breakfast meeting. He's looking to …'

'Will there be any job losses? When does it start?'

'Sam, I'll take questions at the end of the cascade.'

'Sorry, have you started? Is this the cascade?'

'Sam!' Whispered Ben under his breath.

'Sorry, Greg, I got confused. I'll be quiet.'

'Thanks. Anyway, as I discussed with Marc Smyth earlier…'

'At the breakfast meeting?'

'Yes. Marc Smyth is looking for…'

'Who's Marc Smyth again?'

'She knows who he is. Carry on Lamby.'

'Lost my…where was I?'

'*Tomorrows Bank* programme.'

'Oh yeah. Well Marc Smyth is looking for a couple of *secondees* to assist with technical support to the Financial Crime Agency and …'

'I can't Lamby.' It was Ben's turn to interrupt now. 'Far too much on I'm afraid and Scotty is still AWOL, so we're covering his …'

'No way *I'm* doing it.' Sam cut in. 'Can't possibly work with someone who can't spell his own name properly. Don't care how good a guy he is, actually.'

'Calm down guys. Alison and Pete are going to be doing it.'

'What! I'm way better than either of them!' Sam protested.

'You just said you didn't want to do it!'

'Yeah, well. It would have been nice to be asked, at least.'

'Look, we're getting *off message* here, Sam.' Lamby was making a determined effort to reshape the meeting to his own agenda. Ben had seen this attempted many times. If Sam was present then it invariably failed. 'The point is we're going to be two team leaders short on the rota, so there'll be some redistribution of work.'

'We'll do the workload plan.' Ben said.

'Thanks Ben. If you need my input just…'

'It's okay. We'll do it.'

'Is that it? Cascade over?' Sam smiled.

'Well, yes, I suppose.'

'I'll be off then. See you downstairs!' She jumped up out of her seat and bounded from the room.

'Keep an eye on her, will you Ben?'

'She doesn't need to be kept an eye on.' Ben replied as he left, breaking into a jog to catch Sam before she reached the stairs.

'Why, Sam, why?' He laughed as he caught up with her.

'Because he's a moron. How can he possibly manage us when he's never actually done any of the jobs here himself? Honestly, the day this bank started promoting in unqualified sales-puppets from other departments, that was the start of the rocky, slippery slope to…ruin!' She narrowed her eyes at him, as she often did to emphasise her point and compensate for her semi-deliberate, clunky metaphors. Then she shook her head in frustration - then changed the subject. 'Red Lion after work? Swift one?'

'Kids with your ex tonight then?'

'Well, yes, obviously. I don't just leave them with a tin opener and a can of tuna chunks. They're with Tim until Thursday.'

'Can't get my head around your four days on, four days off,routine. I'd lose track if they were mine.'

'No, it's brilliant! Best thing we ever did.' Her children were pretty much all Sam ever showed genuine enthusiasm for talking about during the working day. The transformation when she did so was quite marked and often caught Ben by surprise, even after all the years he'd known her. Her face would almost literally glow with pride – she even smiled sometimes. 'It's much fairer, because you get to see them at different weekends and stuff – and at the kids' ages it doesn't matter exactly what the routine is, as long as there is one.'

'Fascinating. Sounds like something made up to sell books to middle-class divorced people to massage their feelings of guilt?'

'Fuck off Taylor!'

'Sorry. Glass of Rioja on me later?'

'Huh! You wouldn't know a Rioja from a Ribena. No working late tonight. I want to be in the Lion by half-five, okay?'

'Yeah, okay. I might be a bit late, though – need to use the gym first. I'll get there as early as I can.'

'Hey, you forgot to ask Lamb about Scotty.'

'Oh, yeah. Well, no matter, he wouldn't have known what to do anyway. I'll take a wander over to Scotty's house later on. See if he's laying in bed with flu or something, before we start filling in a dozen different unexplained absence forms.'

'Good plan, Benjamin!' She flashed him one of the rare smiles, then apparently decided it was time to actually start doing some work.

8

Abigail tapped on the door of her team leader's office and popped her head around.

'Any chance of a quick word, Dan?' She enquired.

'Sure, Abi. Come on in. Wouldn't do my career any good to send the wife of our new Retail Ops Director away! Haha!'

Abi gave a polite laugh as she sat down.

'I think Marc will be an awesome *ROD*.' Dan continued. 'Just the guy to take us into the *Bank of Tomorrow*. Can't wait for the *Roadshows*. When do they start?'

'Erm...not sure, next week I think? He's in the City over the next few days.'

Dan looked slightly puzzled, maybe by her lack of awareness of the details. She felt she should provide some extra information.

'The schedule changes all the time and he's had to postpone some stuff because of this Crime Agency investigation into the money-laundering issues. Everything's a bit topsy-turvy. When he starts talking about it, I just switch off, to be honest! Ha!'

Apparently Dan couldn't see the humour in this. He still looked puzzled.

'Anyway, I won't keep you,' Abi continued, 'I just wanted to put my name down for extra flexi hours, when available? I was hoping to start working most evenings, if that's okay?'

'Extra hours?'

'Yes. I was full-time before the twins were born. I'm trying to get myself back in the swing of things!'

'Yeah, okay, sure.' Dan appeared to still have his mind on the forthcoming *Roadshows*. 'Plenty of work to be done here in Premier Banking! I'll sort out some amended contract papers from Human Resources?'

'Thanks Dan, I really appreciate it.'

'Can I just ask though, why evenings?'

'It's the best time. The twins are asleep, in one of the best nursery facilities in the county. Marc is tied up with his new Director stuff and will be away from home on the *Roadshows* for a month. Chance to finance some new outfits for myself, you see!'

'Fair enough.' Dan smiled, his curiosity evidently satisfied. 'I should have a response from HR within forty-eight hours.'

'Thanks again Dan, you're a star.' Abigail said as she left the room.

'No problem. Any time. My door's always open!' He called, after her, down the corridor.

9

The Red Lion pub, the nearest licensed premises to the *HenleyEast* site, was packed.

Must be another leaving-do, concluded Ben. There were two or three a week at the moment, as people responded to the insecurity surrounding the Henleys balance sheet 'issues', and rumoured merger, by jumping ship. Barclays and HSBC were currently taking on experienced Henleys staff all over the country at bargain salary prices.

In a modern building, but designed to look like a traditional village pub (except twice the size) the Lion was a weird mix of quaint features; fireplace, dartboard, 'traditional' pub-grub, contrasting with other little gems that belied its Corporate ownership; *three for two* offers on food, plastic menus, spotlights in the ceiling. Nobody really liked the place much.

But, it was the nearest licensed premises to the *HenleyEast* Hub.

Ben picked his way through the crowd, looking for Sam. He found her at the far end of the bar, two filled wineglasses ready and waiting in front of her.

They shared a bottle. Then they ordered some food. Ben went with the same as what Sam was having, rather than risk receiving a detailed critique of his selection. Then they started a fresh bottle.

For the early part of the evening, they managed

quite a decent job of avoiding work-talk. Eventually, though, the conversation swung around to Steve Scott's unexplained absence. After several theories proposed by Sam, including running off with a wealthy customer, being trapped under a fallen wardrobe and having been kidnapped (but the ransom note not yet having made it out of the post-room), Ben decided it was appropriate to suggest something more plausible.

'He's probably just mixed up his holiday dates. He thinks he booked this week off, has gone away to Magaluf or wherever – and doesn't realise. That's all.'

'Oh.' Sam looked disappointed. 'I suppose that *is* reasonably likely. You still should go round his house, to check.'

'Check what?'

'That he's not lying on his kitchen floor. You know? Dead, or something.'

'Dead or something?'

'Yeah. Why didn't you go earlier today?'

'Because I don't think he's dead and…well…he lives near Helen.'

'Helen Hippo?'

'She's not *that* big, Sam. Anyway, I didn't want to be seen hanging around over that end of Broadlands, if you must know.'

'The shite end?'

'Sam. Not nice!'

'Whatever.'

'I'll go first thing tomorrow, okay? Might be a few minutes late in to work.'

'Good boy. So, do you think this anti-money-laundering drive is going to convince the Commercial

Bank of China?'

'How would I know?'

'Maybe if you read a newspaper once in a while? Show an interest? Then you may just have an opinion on the matter?'

'Well, if you really want my *opinion*, I think the Treasury, the Government, the Bank of England, whatever, will make it happen. They'll do anything to avoid another collapsed bank scandal. Or, then again, maybe they won't! Who cares?'

'Benjamin! That's not the sort of talk I'd expect from a professional banker of your calibre. Are you lacking in motivation? Are you!? I could give you a couple of Lamby's inspirational posters?'

'That'd be nice!' He smiled. 'It's just, well, everyone is getting stressed at the state of the bank, liquidity issues, blah de blah. But it's not the staff's fault, it's not even the fault of our ancient systems, or the products and services, which by and large are okay. The whole problem was engineered at board level by execs signing off on complicated investments that they didn't understand. That no-one understands. This whole mess was completely avoidable. The bank should never have been allowed to mess around with depositors' money, investing in that rubbish. You want to be an investment bank, be an investment bank. You want to be a retail bank, be a retail bank.'

'Thatcher's fault! Deregulation of the financial system. All them years ago!'

'Wow! You remember something from our course!'

'That, and you trying to sleep with every girl on it. They loved the rugby star!' She fluttered her eyelashes at him.

'Yeah, well. Long time ago.'

'So,' Sam changed the subject back, 'you think that the anti-money-laundering initiative is an irrelevant thing?'

Ben shrugged. More interested in how much wine remained in this bottle rather than sustaining a prolonged debate.

'Pretty much. One way or another, the merger will happen. The anti-money-laundering initiative, the *Tomorrows Bank* roadshows – they are just window dressing. To create an illusion that Henleys is a solid institution again. With the timescale they are quoting, they couldn't possibly clean up even a fraction of one percent of what's going on in branches and Hubs all over the country. I guess the window has to be dressed, just enough, to make the sale. That's all.'

'Lot of fuss over nothing then. Typical Henleys, eh? Maybe we should start applying to HSBC?'

'Yeah, maybe.' Ben smiled at her, started to say something else, then stopped.

'What?' She poured out the remaining drops of wine.

'Well, you know I said it's just window dressing, an irrelevance…?'

'Yep?'

'Well, that won't be as true for the unlucky few that they manage to find – and decide to make an example of. For them, it will be seven to fourteen years in prison.'

10

'What are you still doing here? I thought you'd gone hours ago!' Willis had popped back to the office to collect his jacket. He'd been working upstairs most of the afternoon and evening.

'You told me you'd help me when I finished these tick-backs. I want to finish them before I leave – so I can start my own work in the morning.' Macgregor replied, whilst keeping her head down, concentrating on the printouts on the desk.

'I…err…thought this would take you a week?'

'That timescale doesn't work for me.' She glanced up and threw him a quick smile. 'Oops, sounded like a banker just then!'

'Okay. I'm officially impressed, as bankers say. You'll have to leave now though, 'cos I'm going home.'

'It's alright. Other people are still here. I'll be fine.'

'I'm afraid you're not authorised to stay on Henleys premises without my supervision. Sorry.' Willis shrugged apologetically.

Macgregor dropped her pen onto the desk, reclined in her chair and had a good stretch.

'Fair enough. I *am* getting tired now. You'll help me tomorrow though?'

Willis found himself feeling relieved that she

wasn't giving him a mouthful of complaint.

'Yeah, sure. Sure thing.'

She sat in her chair, stretching her arms above her head. Willis didn't feel like trying to rush her, as she seemed less tightly wound than she had been earlier in the day. He was also impressed that she was working late.

'This case is pretty important to you, then?' Willis sat down in the chair opposite her.

'Tomas Vladic?' Macgregor narrowed her eyes slightly. As if choosing her words carefully. 'Been on it for two years on and off, since I joined the Agency. I've done other cases as well, of course, you don't always just stick with just the one.'

'You were in the Met?'

'Yep. Still am, technically. I can go back any time I want.'

'I've worked with a few people from the Agency. They're not all police officers?'

'Nah, they have all sorts. Professional types, accountants, researchers and the like, some ex-forces, some graduate-scheme entrants straight out of college. There are quite a few coppers though. It helps because a lot of the cases, sooner or later, require joint operations.'

'Sounds like interesting work.'

'I absolutely love it, to be honest. Not that I would ever admit that to Greenwood! I enjoyed the Met, but it often felt like a losing battle. At the Agency, you may only be uncovering a small percentage of what's going on, but it's getting more sophisticated all the time and, when you do get hold of something, you can follow it through from start to finish, use your initiative. It's like you're trusted, you know?'

'So, what's the deal with this Vlasic guy?'

'*Vladic*. He used to work for Henleys. That's the reason I agreed to this little "attachment". I thought I could maybe dig around in the systems and find some new information on him.'

'When was he on the staff?'

'He left a decade ago. Set up a property company, buying up repossessed properties cheap then letting them out. Lot of student houses, multiple occupancy stuff, BUT, always at the higher end of the market. Since then he's diversified out into manufacturing, recycling, storage, all sorts.'

'Does he still bank with Henleys?'

'He used to do all his banking with you. Gradually, over the years, he's switched accounts, gone elsewhere.'

'Still – shouldn't be a problem. Henleys completed the transfer of all its old paper records to the database a couple of years back. He'll be in the system somewhere, even if the accounts are closed now.'

'Good news!' She smiled.

'I don't understand though.'

'What?'

'Well, property, manufacturing, recycling, all that stuff. Why is the Agency investigating him?'

Macgregor sighed and slumped forward in her seat. She, momentarily looked very tired.

'That's the frustrating part with Vladic.' She peered into her coffee cup, which had evidently long since been drained of its contents. Willis took the hint and got up to get her a fresh one from the machine. 'On my very first case at the Agency, I was working on an investigation into a group that laundered some narcotics proceeds through branches of various banks in south-east London. It was all pretty straightforward and I didn't think anything more of it, until on my fourth case one of the guys we were investigating turned out to be a former business partner of a guy that was also the landlord of a luxury apartment occupied by the financier running the group in my first case.'

'Vladic?'

'Yep. I remembered the name. I thought I'd cracked something huge, but after digging around for weeks afterwards, it was clear there was no connection whatsoever between the groups we'd investigated. Had never met. Had no common business interests. Just did not know each other at all. The only thing was this Vladic connection. Greenwood gave me a bollocking for wasting so much time on it, getting too personal with a case, looking for things that weren't there, all stuff like that.'

'And Vladic was clean?'

'Totally. All his bank accounts were perfectly conducted, his financials were all submitted to Companies House, they were all legitimate businesses. I even drove round to have a peek at his premises. His manufacturing business manufactures things and his recycling business recycles things. The turnover of his businesses is in line with what you'd expect.'

'But you continued with the investigation anyway?'

'I actually dropped it for a while after that, but his name kept cropping up. Mostly larger cases, in the

South East, but all sorts of stuff, proceeds of drugs, prostitution, theft, counterfeit cash. Somebody would live in a Vladic apartment, or have worked for one of his companies, or have had his contact details in their files. Eventually, Greenwood let me pursue some lines of enquiry again.'

'It's not just coincidence? Not just some rich guy who knows a lot of dodgy people?'

'Well, that's the point. Who would know so many people that are involved in money laundering in some shape or form? It's beyond weird. Anyway, it's not just that. You see, he's also *wealthier* than he should be.'

'Wealthier? Wealthier how? In what way?'

'He's never actually sold a property or a business. Everything he's acquired and built, he's kept.'

'So?'

'The businesses are good, profitable, some are very profitable. The dividends, drawings, rental surpluses, everything he earns, it's reasonably easy to identify and calculate. I've been through it dozens of times but it never balances out with the personal wealth he's accumulated; the bank balances, the share portfolio, the big house, the fucking hotel, the yacht, the cars. It's like, there's another source of income that I can't find.'

'What if…you know…after all this – you find it and it turns out to be just another legitimate enterprise?'

'Well, Willis, (a) I don't think it is and (b) I will be devastated that I've spent so much time on a wild goose chase.'

'That doesn't sound good. You should, at the least,

be content that you did such a thorough investigation.'

'Spoken like a true auditor! I like it. From now on, option (c) is what you just said. Come on, we'd better go if I'm not allowed to stay here on my own. Mummy will be getting worried about you, Ryan.'

Willis grabbed his jacket and followed her out.

'I don't live with my parents, Max, I have my own…' He paused, realising she was teasing.

'So. You'll help me?' She asked.

'Of course. It'll be a nice change from ticking back audit prints. Just don't be disappointed if it turns out to be nothing, OK?'

'Yes, Ryan.'

11

Ben looked around for Sam. She'd disappeared earlier, to go and have a gossip with some of her team. He eventually spotted her, at the far end of the bar, still deep in animated conversation.

It was getting pretty late and he couldn't see anyone else worth talking to, so decided to call it a night.

The crowd had thinned out a little, but it was still a painstaking process to duck and weave his way through to the front door, bumping into people as he shuffled along – and Ben found himself getting irritated when a figure seemed to deliberately block his path.

He realised a moment later, however, that he knew this person.

'Ben Taylor! How are you, gorgeous?' She shrieked.

'Hi Grace.' He smiled. No reason not be polite. 'Nice to see you. What…err…brings you back here?'

'I was good friends with Nicola, silly! Wouldn't have missed her leaving do for the world!'

'Right.' Ben glanced up at the door, a few yards ahead. He had no idea who Nicola was. Grace didn't look like she was going to get out of his way though. 'Where are you these days?' he asked.

When Ben had last seen her, three or four years

ago, she had been sleeping her way up the rungs of the promotion ladder at Premier Banking. Her long legs and short skirts had proved popular with the management there. 'I'm in Business Banking now.'

'Really?'

'Ya! Felt I'd achieved all my goals at Prem. Biz are *sooo* customer focussed and you really get the chance to exceed clients' expectations. Plus, the company car list is *sooo* much better than at Prem.'

'Going well, then?' Ben kept his eye on the door, hoping a clear path would open up and he could resume shuffling towards the fresh air.

'Ya! The targets are really challenging, particularly new deposit monies, but that helps us be the best that we can be.'

'*jesuschrist*'. Ben muttered. It was lost in the surrounding ambient noise near the bar.

'The bonus structure is awesome! On target bonuses are thirty grand.'

'Seriously?' She had Ben's attention with that one.

'Ya! Although …' Her confident shell seemed to crack a fraction. 'I am way behind on my deposit target.' Then the shell healed itself. 'I'll still make five or six grand though!'

Ben smiled and started to move in the direction of the door. Then she spoke again.

'Buy me a drink?'

Ben gestured at the crowd waiting to be served.

'It'll take a while.' He shrugged.

She flashed a distracting smile. Not the best looking girl in the bank, by any stretch of the imagination, but alright. 'Fancy getting out of here? Your place is close by, isn't it?' She suggested.

Ben glanced at the exit route, then back to Grace Millar. Her long legs, short skirt and her white teeth. He thought that maybe if he tried to keep the conversation away from work and, in particular, how much bonus Business Banking management were paying their staff, then she may be tolerable company.

She took his arm and they pushed their way through to the door.

An hour later, Grace stood up from Ben's sofa and placed her emptied wine glass on the table.

Very slowly, she bent over to slip her shoes off, giggling as she gave Ben a flattering view of her bottom and legs. Then she decided to stop teasing him, turned around, expertly slipped her skirt down over her thighs, let it drop to the floor around her ankles, stepped out of it then, very gently, eased herself into a sitting position astride his lap.

12

'Abi, I told you to wake me at six! A car is picking me up later.'

'It's okay.' Abi placed the iron down on the board and switched it off at the plug. 'I've got your overnight bag ready, all your toiletries. It's all done.' She took her own *HenleyWear* suits that she'd also ironed, and started heading out of the spare room to hang them in the closet.

'Good girl.' Marc's tone changed. 'The Retail Ops Director is impressed! Remind me to instruct your boss to give you a good performance appraisal at your next review.'

'Thanks.' She smiled. As she tried to edge past him through the doorway, though, he grabbed her arm. It hurt a little.

'I…err…don't suppose, you could slip one of those suits on, could you?'

'Marc, the twins will be awake soon and …' She stopped as she saw the look on his face. It would be quicker and easier just to play along. 'Okay, Marc. Give me two minutes?'

She went to the closet, hung two of the suits, put the other on over a *HenleyBlouse*, slipped on her work shoes, he liked her to wear the shoes, and then made her way along the upstairs hall to the bedroom suite.

He was waiting for her, already naked, grinning

and touching himself, on the bed. 'Mmmm, hot!' he breathed, as he looked her up and down.

She lay down next to him and hitched her skirt up around her waist. It was quicker than waiting for him to do it.

He rolled himself over onto her and tried to push himself in.

'Ouch.' She winced and wriggled out of range. 'Just a second, Marc.' She reached up to her mouth, daubed some saliva onto her fingers, then applied it neatly to the relevant spot. 'There, ready now.'

'Yeah, you like that, don't you?' He grunted at her.

'Uh-huh. Just a little slower, please, I…' He was really going for it already, oblivious to her request. She suppressed another 'ouch'.

'You like doing it with a Director, you little slut?' He was using his dirty words and thrusting rapidly – this would be concluded shortly. To speed things along further, she wrapped her legs around his back and moaned.

A few moments later she was taking off the *HenleyWear* and lobbing it back into the laundry basket.

'Marc, I meant to tell you, I've requested some extra hours at the…'

'Did you pack my Ralph Lauren shirt, the blue one?'

'No. About my hours, I…'

'Why not?'

'I…pardon? It's in the closet if you want it. Right-hand side.'

He went into the closet, then re-emerged two seconds later.

'I said the fucking blue one!'

She went in and got it for him.

'So, I've asked for some extra hours. I'll be doing a few more evenings, but I'll take the twins to the nursery so that…'

'I don't think so.' Marc interrupted, watching himself in the mirror as he tried on the shirt. 'I have enough on my pad at the moment without worrying about domestic arrangements.'

'You don't have to worry about them. I've sorted everything out so…'

'I said *no*, Abi! The Retail Ops Director position is very politically high profile. I'm not sure how it would look to the Board if people started discussing the issue of my wife doing additional hours. It may get misinterpreted. I've worked too hard at my brand to have distractions like this now.'

'I don't see the relevance to my…'

'I said NO! For fucks sake!'

She paused for a moment, decided further comment was futile, then headed for the en suite shower as he carried on getting ready.

She turned the water on, slipped out of her underwear and walked in.

The water felt fantastic.

She put shower gel on her arms and legs, enjoying the hot power-spray.

He'd hurt her a little, by rushing things and being rough. She sifted through the bottles of lotions and soaps on the shelves and in the shower tray. Eventually she located the aloe gel. She oozed some out onto her fingers and applied it gently to the affected area. It felt instantly cool and soothing.

'Abi! My yellow, silk, Armani tie?'

'Middle drawer.' Why did he now mention the brand name along with every item? He never used to do that.

He needn't have been so rough. She daubed and applied another generous dollop of gel. Eased some inside, then a little deeper. The cooling sensation started to radiate out through her stomach and legs. It felt lovely.

She stopped, then peeked around the shower screen. She could see his reflection in the bathroom mirror as he scurried around, not finding things. She put her hand back and resumed. She often finished off like this nowadays, after he'd satisfied himself and fallen asleep. She'd nip downstairs or to the spare room to do it.

But she'd never tried it like this, with him wide awake and in the next room. She was pretty sure he wouldn't understand if he knew. *Lots* of raising of the voice would ensue. If she was very quick and quiet though, maybe …

'Abi!'

'Yes?'

'My cufflinks. The Mont Blancs?'

'Kitchen drawer, with the pens and keys.' She knew they weren't there, but it would give her a couple of minutes while he went all the way down and had a look around.

She thought back to when they'd first met. When Marc was transferred down from London to *HenleyWest*. He'd been very different then, very sweet. Sex had been fun. Although, and she suddenly felt *very* guilty about thinking about this, not as much fun as with Paul, her only serious boyfriend before she met Marc. He'd been lovely. Nice looking boy. She had *loved* doing it with him. She thought about how tender and gentle he always was with her. Started moving her fingers faster, getting into it more. Maybe she would have time after all. Recalled Paul slipping her out of her favourite summer dress, slowly kissing her down her neck, chest and stomach, easing her underwear down and…

'ABI!'

Shit! She almost fell out of the shower.

She stood motionless for a moment, trying to hold her balance, her eyes still shut and her hand between her legs. Mortified that he may have seen what she was doing.

'Yes?'

'They're not there. And one of the twins is crying. Hurry up please.' He was out in the bedroom. He hadn't seen her.

Not surprised they're waking up with you shouting your head off. Can't you see to them, just this once?

She tried to finish, but started rushing it, not getting the feeling right. Reluctantly, she turned off the shower and reached for the towel.

'On my way!' She called.

No response. She couldn't hear any crying and she couldn't hear Marc bustling about. Perhaps he'd actually ventured into the twins' room. She stepped out of the shower and started towelling herself dry. From here, she could see her bedroom door in the reflection in the bathroom mirror. By keeping her eye on it, she'd know if and when he re-entered the room.

Almost subconsciously, she put her hand back. Decided that she would feel much better for finishing off - but was also doubtful that she had time. She'd give it a quick thirty seconds, though, just in case.

Her fingers moved faster and her breathing quickened as she kept watch in the mirror. It wasn't quite right though – there wasn't going to be enough time.

Then, something popped into her head.

It was, on the one hand, a rather disturbing thought, but, on the other hand, it made her stomach drop and churn in such a way that she felt there was no harm in borrowing this mental image for just a few moments.

Expensive clothes, that body, absolutely gorgeous perfume. How soft and gentle would it be with Suzy from the nursery?

Oh. Oh dear me…this…could do the trick.

She dropped the towel and, with her free hand, gripped on to the edge of the bath for balance. Bent over slightly, she could no longer see the door in the mirror, but was past caring.

In her head, Suzy had ventured upstairs at a deserted *HenleyWest*, late in the evening, to discuss her hours, or something, that part didn't really matter…

concentrate Abigail!

…she gently swept Abi's hair behind her ear, but instead of stepping back, moved in closer, pushing against her, then put her arms around Abi's back, tilting her head up and touching her lips to Abi's. Abi wouldn't pull away, but wrapped her own arms around Suzy, locking the two of them together. Then

Suzy would softly ease her tongue into Abi's mouth and…

oh…thank god…finally…

her hand moved furiously and she let herself collapse against the side of the bath, her knees buckling.

A few moments later, when her husband stormed into the en suite, shouting that both twins were now crying, he saw his lovely wife, her face flushed from her hot shower, tying up her bathrobe and breezing past him, her eyes sparkling as she smiled.

'I'm on my way, darling.'

13

Ben woke up and tentatively stretched an arm across to the other side of the bed.

The duvet was really heaped up over there, but he found no-one underneath it. He sat up, rubbed his eyes and looked around. There was no evidence of his visitor from last night. Maybe she'd left a note in the living room or kitchen, but he very much doubted it.

He got up, used the bathroom, wandered downstairs. The empty wine bottles were on the table, next to two used glasses.

Ben made himself some toast, ate it, and then went back upstairs for a shower and shave.

He got dressed at a reasonably leisurely pace, after remembering that he had to go across to Steve Scott's house this morning. He didn't want to be wandering around over there before Steve's neighbour, 'Helen Hippo' as Sam liked to call her, had gone to work. If she saw him it would look odd, need an explanation. Be a bit awkward. There were sometimes drawbacks to so many staff all living on the some housing development.

It took about half an hour. Ben fancied another walk and strolled over, taking his time. The drizzling rain wasn't too heavy. Scotty, and Helen H, lived on the inexpensive corner of Broadlands. Scotty was in a Henleys corporate let. The bank owned several around the estate, they were intended for staff on short-term contracts or who had been recently transferred in. Scotty had moved in to one five years ago, originally on a three-month arrangement, and never moved out.

When Ben reached Scotty's end-of-link house, he realised he'd solved the 'mystery' of his disappearance. A large, black Range Rover, with enormous black alloy wheels was parked outside.

Scotty had been looking at other job opportunities for ages – and he was a very competent worker. He'd obviously found somewhere willing to pay the 'top dollar', and had treated himself to new transport. Not yet had the courage to tell anyone at Henleys that he was going elsewhere. His new employer, HSBC maybe, may even have given him a *golden hello* to start there immediately.

It was a *very* impressive vehicle, Ben thought, as he wandered past. HSBC, or whoever, must have offered a *really* good salary package. Maybe he could ask Scotty if he could get him an interview too.

The front door was slightly ajar.

Ben tapped the door and pushed it open.

'Scotty! It's Ben.' He stepped inside, but then paused. Didn't feel comfortable just striding into someone's house.

He heard Scotty shuffling about in the kitchen. Probably had his earphones in, listening to music.

'Scotty! Hello? I'm coming in.'

Ben walked through the small living room and poked his head around the kitchen door.

It wasn't Scotty.

It was two, very large, very casually nonchalant, strangers. They were standing, leaning back against the counter, sifting through letters and paperwork. The kitchen drawers were opened and much of the contents had been laid out neatly on the work surface.

The taller of the two was enormous, as large as anything Ben had encountered during his rugby days. At least six and a half feet tall, his plain blue t-shirt was straining to fit around gym (and probably chemically) enhanced shoulders and chest. His arms were even freakier than the rest of him, with rope-like veins tracing their way over the muscles from bicep to wrist.

The other guy was shorter, maybe a shade under six feet, but if anything appeared even stronger, more naturally powerful. His arms looked heavy and bulky, and his chest seemed to jut out almost horizontally from under his chin, like two slabs of meat had been stuffed under his t-shirt.

They both wore dark, canvas trousers and hiking-style black boots. Despite, or maybe because of, their size and builds, they looked slightly comical squeezed into Scotty's miniscule kitchen.

'Scotty isn't here.' The shorter one eventually said. His build did not really match his voice, which was quiet, softly spoken, sort of posh, or educated at least. They both carried on leafing through the pile of papers.

Ben debated, at some length, what to say in reply. He was confused by the unfamiliarity of what was going on here. *'Who are you? Do you know where he is? Why are you looking through his stuff?'* Nothing sounded very adequate in his head.

‘Are you from Henleys?’ asked the shorter one, evidently the leader of this duo – perhaps sensing Ben’s awkwardness and wanting to move the conversation along.

‘Yep.’ Ben replied.

They both continued their sifting.

‘We were concerned for him.’ Shorter One said. ‘He wasn’t answering our calls.’

‘O…kay…’ Ben considered telling them about how the bank had also been trying to contact Scotty, but then decided not to. He was still very confused by who these two could be. ‘…well, I suppose I had better leave you boys to it.’ Ben was keen to not hang around any longer. ‘I’ll maybe just call round later? See if he’s back this evening.’ He turned to leave.

‘He’s not coming back.’ Shorter One stopped sifting and looked up at Ben.

‘What do you mean?’ Ben’s confusion wasn’t clearing.

‘We think he’s left the country. We’re also pretty sure his name isn’t Stephen Scott.’

Ben watched the shorter man for a few seconds. It was difficult to gauge his mood or intentions. He continued to appear very ‘relaxed’.

‘Sorry, gents, I’m being a bit slow here.’ Ben found himself feeling distinctly uneasy, but also curious at the same time. He stepped back, ever so slightly. If, for any reason he needed to, he’d sprint for the front door. They were still leaning back against the units. Given their bodyweights, Ben was pretty sure they’d be slow off the mark. ‘Who *are* you, exactly?’

Shorter One placed the papers he was holding

down on the worktop, then looked up at Ben. Ben shifted his weight onto his toes - he could be through that front door in no time - before *Muscles* here would get anywhere near him.

Shorter One, though, remained relaxed, smiling slightly, almost appearing friendly now.

'We're a private consulting firm.' He responded.

'Oh? What sort of things do you consult on?'

'Well, that depends. We've done work for many clients, mostly corporate, including Henleys Bank.'

'I see.'

Did that mean that *this* was Henleys work? Or that they'd just done some occasional work for Henleys in the past? Ben concluded that this was probably as detailed an explanation as he was going to get.

Shorter One picked the papers back up and started working his way through them again.

Ben decided that he didn't really fancy hanging around here any longer – and turned to leave. Shorter One said nothing more – and paid him no further attention.

It was something of a relief to be back out in the fresh air, despite the persistent drizzle. He wasn't sure what to make of the encounter.

He was keen to tell someone, i.e. Sam, about it.

Ben decided to cut across the bottom road back to *HenleyEast*. It was a few minutes longer but he fancied a change of scenery. This way took you past the shallow, fenced, pond and some trees.

He was pretty sure that he remembered Scotty had first come to Henleys on a temp contract from one of the agencies, he couldn't recall which one. It was odd that he'd never moved out of the temporary accommodation, but maybe he never thought he'd stay very long. Maybe he'd never even changed to a full-time contract, just every three months he had his temp contract renewed.

The pond looked picturesque in the rain – and the trees were a nice change from the endless lines of red-brick houses.

When he got to *HenleyEast*, Ben didn't go straight to his Payments and Processing department. He headed instead for the Premises Manager's office and requested the duplicate key to Scotty's desk. Scotty's disappearance was common knowledge throughout the Hub now and the Premises Manager handed over the key without any further questions or paperwork.

At Scotty's workstation, Ben first glanced over the items on the surface of the desk. There were some sticky notes, reminders to call customers, one to stop and buy petrol on his way home. An assortment of pens and other stationery. It was pretty untidy. The contents of the desk drawers were just as uninteresting; some car magazines, old printouts, an ancient packet of mints, an invitation to a Corporate Charity Ball and some old payslips.

Ben slumped down in the chair. Although the chances of finding anything had, of course, been slim, he was disappointed. Part of him had wanted there to be some obvious clues to solve the *Mystery of the Missing Scotty*, so he could go round telling people how he'd cracked the case. He slipped the Charity Ball invitation into his pocket though, as it was for the best one of the year - goodness knows how Scotty scammed an invite. He started closing up the desk, but then had a thought.

He picked up the phone and pressed pre-set number five. A few moments later a distinct accent crackled down the phone line.

'Henleys IT support, Alan speaking, how may I help you?'

'Hi "Alan". This is Ben Taylor at *HenleyEast* Hub in the UK. One of our team has left the bank without notice and I need to log into his workstation. Can you give me access please?'

'I am afraid not Ben. Such requests must be emailed in from the Head of Department. Is there anything else I can be helping you with today?'

'No thanks.' He replaced the handset. Then picked it up again and redialled. A few moments later it was answered.

'Henleys IT support, Trevor speaking, how may I help you?'

'Hi, this is Steve Scott at *HenleyEast* Hub in the UK. I've forgotten my password.'

'What is your staff number please, Steve?'

Ben retrieved one of the payslips from the drawer and read out the staff number.

'You are reset.' Trevor advised him a few seconds later. 'Please use *password123* to log in and then change it when prompted. Is there anything else I can be helping you with today?'

'No thanks.'

Ben hung up and then logged on to the workstation PC. The screen took ages to go through the various log-on stages; these workstations were a decade obsolete now, and Ben hit the 'OK' box whenever prompted. Eventually he arrived at the menu screen.

First, he looked at Scotty's personal bank account. He had just the one, which was unusual for staff, where multiple accounts were the norm. It showed his monthly salary going in, a few entries going out, with the balance gradually increasing over time. By last week, it had reached a credit balance of nearly ten grand, which was then cashed, in full, at the Henleys branch in town.

Ben scrolled back up through the entries and saw one unusually large debit - a card payment to British Airways. Perhaps Shorter One may actually have been onto something with his theory. Ben wondered how good the rest of his information was.

He brought up the credit search screen and entered Scotty's name and postcode. The process only took a few minutes and would generate everything relating to an individual: bank accounts, credit cards, mobile phones, car loans. Even for the most prudent spendthrift there would be dozens of entries on their credit search. Ben glanced across at the printer to make sure there was paper in it – he'd take Scotty's search back to his own desk for a proper analysis.

The result came up on screen – and it was immediately obvious that neither a printout, nor further analysis, would be required. The only thing on it was Scotty's Henleys account. No phone contract, no personal finance whatsoever. This was weirder than meeting strangers in Scotty's deserted house.

Ben made a couple more phone calls, then powered down the workstation and walked down the department to Sam's desk.

‘Where have you been?’ She demanded. ‘*Loads* of people have been looking for you. Lamb hasn’t turned up this morning, what the hell is going on around …’

‘Never mind about that, listen.’

Ben told her about the encounter at Scotty’s house and how his account had been cleared of funds. ‘And,’ he finished up, ‘it didn’t look like anyone had lived there for a while, and I don’t think his name was Steve Scott. I think he was just *Steve Scott* here at the Hub.’

Sam had listened fairly intently; it was the longest sustained period of quiet she’d managed in ages. But she remained unconvinced.

‘I don’t know about all this, Ben. HR would have needed ID from Scotty, for a start.’

‘Thought of that. I phoned HR, spoke to Charlie. There’s nothing on the file for him. She confirmed he started here on an agency contract and back at that time, Henleys assumed the agencies were IDing new staff and the agencies assumed Henleys were doing it. They changed the system eventually, but never did retrospective IDs.’

‘Are you serious?’

‘That’s what Charlie told me. Now I’m thinking that Scotty, or whoever he really was, knew exactly what he was doing all along. Knew our systems were shite, knew he could get on the staff without proper ID, probably came here to launder cash for a few months, couldn’t believe how easy it all was and that no-one ever got suspicious – stayed for four years.’

‘Like - some kind of professional?’

‘Perhaps. Then, one day, he gets a great opportunity, too good to pass up, to clean up on a big deal and disappear with the cash instead of paying it in?'

'That's a bit of an assumption.'

'I know, but those two at his house, they were serious, high-price something or others. They could be 'consulting' for the people that Scotty was laundering cash for?'

Sam shrugged. She liked facts rather than speculation.

'You know, it's a real shame.' She eventually replied.

'What is?'

'Scotty was a really good processor.'

Ben laughed. Then remembered the ticket.

'Almost forgot, you fancy going to this Charity Ball with me?' He retrieved it from his pocket and pushed it across the desk to her.

'Ben Taylor, are you asking me out?'

'No. I thought it would be a change from The Red Lion, that's all. To go into the city for a night?'

'Are you sure you don't want to ask Helen Hippo or Grace Millar instead?'

'What? How do even know about Grace Mi …'

'Wow. You don't mess around!' Sam blurted out as she read the details on the ticket. 'I've never been to one of *these*. You're certainly moving up to a higher social circle.'

'Actually, I found it. In Scotty's desk.'

'How the hell would *he* have gotten himself one?'

'Well, knowing what I know now, maybe he stole it?'

'Still, I'm impressed. Our first date and…'

'It's not a date.'

'Our first date and you're taking me to Tommi Vladic's annual Charity Ball!'

14

Greg Lamb waited patiently in what was, he'd now realised, a bookable meeting room, rather than Marc Smyth's personal office.

'I've postponed a conference call for this.' Marc announced as he rolled in through the doorway. 'What is it, that is so urgent?'

Greg waited for Marc to sit down opposite him before responding.

'I have a revised plan for Retail Ops. Wanted to run it by you.'

'Isn't this something you could have implemented on your own, Lamby? You need a Level Ten to hold your hand through the…'

'This is something that will affect us both, Marc.'

Something in Lamby's tone convinced Marc to go and get them a couple of coffees and grant him a few minutes *One to One* time.

'What is it then?' He asked as he returned to his seat.

'The word is the investigation team for the South, Ryan Willis from audit and some Agency girl, are shit-hot. And they're taking this all *very* seriously.'

'And?'

'And? And, they are getting through audit tick-backs at a hell of a rate. Worked late into the night, already way ahead of schedule. They're not looking to find just a few high-profile cases – at the rate they're going they'll find dozens before the secondment is over. It looks like they're trying to take this opportunity to make names for themselves.'

'So what?'

'So, it doesn't look particularly good, does it? It highlights the fact that a fleet of buses could have driven through the gaps in anti-money-laundering procedures at the Hubs.'

'How do you know they're working so hard on it?'

'I have my contacts too, Marc.'

'Doesn't make no fucking difference to me.' Marc shrugged. 'Let 'em carry on.'

'Really? You don't think it's a bad reflection on our department that dozens of our staff have probably been taking backhanders to assist money launderers.'

'It's a systems issue. Henleys has never thrown any resources behind it. No way of policing it. Nothing we could have done about it.'

'Yeah, I know the official policy line. But, nothing? Nothing at all? You could have at least implemented some form of system, even if it was just for show. But since you've taken over as Director, you have blatantly buried your head in the sand when it comes to these issues.'

'Don't you *dare* speak to me like that!' Marc bawled, saliva spitting out of his mouth. 'Remember the fucking differential in our grades, Greg.'

Lamby though, remained calm. He'd thought this through in some detail – and was pretty sure of his ground.

'Point is, Marc, I'm wondering whether the Board will look at the results of this investigation and decide that the icing on the cake, the thing that will really convince the Chinese bankers that Henleys are taking money-laundering issues seriously, is to also downgrade, or even displace, the Retail Ops Director and the Hub Managers?'

Marc opened his mouth to respond, then paused, sipped some coffee instead.

'Wouldn't happen. No way.' He eventually muttered.

'Are you absolutely sure of that? Are you really so highly regarded that the Board would completely rule out the possibility of replacing you with another Ops Director? From all the perfectly competent candidates that would be clamouring for the role?'

They sat in silence for a minute or so. Lamby wanted Marc to speak next, and eventually he did.

'Run this idea by me then? Make it quick. I have things to do.'

'We close the Hubs.'

Marc stared at him for a while. Then asked him to repeat it.

'Shut the Hubs. Or, rather, propose a *Phasedown Plan* with immediate effect. They could realistically be closed within six months.'

Marc was searching around for a reason to shoot this proposal down. But he found it immediately appealing.

'Is it workable?'

'Totally. We already have a detailed business plan, with full logistics. Taylor and Moran put one together for your predecessor last year, as a theoretical emergency plan. Cash handling is first to go, outsourced to one of the security companies, they already do it for some of the other big banks and they can do a process *cut and paste* to take on Henleys. They have spare capacity and the process can be completed in three weeks.

'After that, departments would get phased back into the buildings they came out of in the first place - a decade ago. There's plenty of surplus space around. Most of the original buildings have upgraded IT now, so everything should work better too. There's no downside to it, apart from job losses, but that saves money for the bank anyway. It's extra icing on our cake. Maybe they'll even bump us each up another Level?'

'Ah, but, the Board isn't going to just let the Hubs lie empty.'

'Henleys doesn't *own* the buildings. The leases all expire over the next eighteen months. Moving out and not renewing them will save the bank millions in rent over the next few years.'

'You certainly have thought this through, haven't you, Lamby?'

'Can't really take all the credit – Taylor and Moran did. The plan is very detailed though, covers everything. I'll send it over to you later.'

'Yeah, do that. Something on this scale though, with job loss implications, it'll have to be signed off at board level, with full union involvement, all that shit.'

'Of course. Doesn't matter though. I spoke to a friend of mine in audit. He said that if a closure, or *Phasedown* plan, had been put before the Board for consideration, then the investigations would be postponed pending the sign-off. They're stretched paper-thin and there's plenty of branches to investigate instead. They won't allocate any resources to departments that are under a *Phasedown* proposal. It's in their guidelines.'

'Willis and that Macgregor girl would be reassigned to some crappy little branch investigation elsewhere?'

'Exactly. And, they wouldn't be replaced.'

Smyth slurped the remaining contents of his cup and pondered for a while.

'Let's have some more coffee and run over this again,' he responded after a while, 'I want to put something together for the Board by COB tomorrow.

'Don't forget your conference call.'

'Doesn't matter. It was to discuss staffing levels at the Hubs. With any luck they won't exist for much longer.'

15

She tapped on the open door.

'Come on in, Abi.'

He seemed subdued, almost uneasy, which was unusual.

'Everything okay, Dan?'

'I've had a response from HR.'

'Great!'

'I'm afraid it's not good news…this is…this is so awkward Abs.'

Abs?

'What's awkward? Dan?'

'They've said…I mean, what it is - your request has been declined.'

'What? But I…that doesn't make any sense? Workload is increasing, you said it would be no problem, I don't understand what…'

'The problem is with *you* doing extra hours, Abs.'

She paused for a moment, digesting the information, then said 'What!?' again.

'I phoned HR and asked for a clarification.'

'What did they say!?'

'They said that…this is really awkward Abs…they said that Marc's office had vetoed the request.'

'I don't…' She could almost feel tears of frustration welling up. But she never cried. And was definitely not going to start in front of Dan.

'HR were advised that the Retail Ops Director did not want any disruption to his routine while the *Roadshows* and audits were in progress.'

'I can't believe it…he doesn't have any authority to do this…send it back and tell them I need to do extra hours. Sign it off? *Please*, Dan?'

'I'm afraid it's not that straightforward, Abs. Forget the personalities involved, this is effectively a direct request from the Retail Ops Director. I can't ignore that, I have my own issues to think of. My Performance Review is coming up soon and…'

'*Your* Performance Review is affecting *my* hours?'

'Abs, please!'

'Don't use that tone! I've done nothing wrong.'

'I'm sorry, but there's very little I can do here. I can't have this hanging over me at the moment. I'd be happy to review the situation when the Retail Ops Director's *Roadshows* are concluded.'

She couldn't recall when she'd last lost her temper - probably not since she was at school - but she felt very close to it again now. She took a couple of deep breaths, calculating her words carefully. She didn't want to be unprofessional and in any way justify this unbelievable decision.

'Okay. Thank you. I understand the bank's position. *My* position is that I am giving you formal notice, as my team leader, that I am invoking stage one of the *Henleys Staff Grievance Procedure*. I will confirm this in writing, as required under the guidelines, as soon as I get back to my desk.'

The colour faded from Dan's face.

'Abs, please don't do this. My performance review…I…I said I'd be happy to revisit this after the…'

Abi stood up and calmly, deliberately, left the room.

She took a slow walk back to her desk. She wanted, more than anything, to go down to the nursery, collect the twins and take them home to spend the rest of the afternoon with them. Her anger, however, had done a rather decent job of focussing her attention on some practical matters of personal business – and she wanted to sort out a few things.

On her return to her workstation, Abi logged on and made sure all her hours, her current quota, were all up to date and fully booked, starting with as many evenings as she could squeeze out of her existing allocation. She didn't want Marc to get any ideas about trying to get HR to *reduce* her hours.

Then, she composed a concise email to HR, copying in Dan and the union rep, confirming, as required under the rules, her invocation of stage one of the grievance procedure.

Lastly, she started reworking her budget planner, based on the income from her existing hours only. It made her calculations very tight, and she wouldn't accumulate enough for the deposit for her own place at a particularly speedy rate. Without the extra hours it was going to make saving any cash a long and gradual process.

The meeting, the (near) loss of her temper, the concentration on the rota and memos, it all suddenly hit her. She felt exhausted, fatigued and frustrated.

She hadn't cried, properly, since childhood, since

her parents were killed in the car crash. She was aware of the self-control and sense of perspective it had instilled in her. Since then, everyday problems seemed trivial by comparison.

Until now. This whole situation was starting to get to her. She felt lower and more alone than at any time since the accident.

16

'You said you'd help me look up some information on Vladic.'

The statement was said with a note of such authority, that Willis pushed aside the printouts he was looking at.

'Come on then. Pull up a chair.'

She gave him a genuinely warm smile, grabbed a thick, well-thumbed notepad from her bag, hurled a swivel chair across the room, bumping it into Willis, before dropping herself down on it.

'Okay.' Willis said, rubbing his arm. 'Name and address?'

'Tomas Vladic, there's the spelling, there – and there's his residential address.' She pointed to the immaculately handwritten notes. Willis was slightly surprised by the neatness of her notepad, despite it being absolutely covered in handwriting. She wasn't paying him any attention though, she was staring at the screen waiting for him to hurry along here.

Willis keyed in the appropriate details. The Vladic entries came up on screen a few moments later.

'That's him!' her eyes widened.

'I know. Now, what sort of thing are you looking for?'

Macgregor looked at him, chewing on her bottom lip. Her earlier enthusiasm was dimming slightly, as if she didn't know exactly where to start.

'Connected accounts?' Willis prompted. 'Entries on the accounts? Previous addresses? Err… properties…?' he suggested.

'Properties. Properties!'

'Alright-y. This will bring up a list of all the properties that used to be charged to the bank.'

'Charged?'

'Mortgaged.'

'Oh. But he doesn't have any commercial loans.'

'Maybe he used to? Let's have a quick look?'

'Okay, so, this will show us any property that Vladic used to secure any borrowings in the past?'

'Exactly.' Quick learner, obviously, thought Willis.

The list rolled up on the screen and Macgregor grabbed the notepad back, then started comparing her list to the Henleys database.

'Capital House…Millennium Towers…the Parkway portfolio…I know all these.'

'I'll scroll down?'

'No! Hang on, what's that one, at the bottom?'

'Doesn't detail it. Just says 'agri land'. Bit weird. Hang on, I'll try this other link…'

'Agri? That means agricultural? Vladic never owned a farm.'

'Err, yes he did. Look.'

'L – L – Y – S – Y…what the hell is that?'

'Sounds Welsh.'

'What? He's never owned *anything* in Wales! You sure this is accurate?'

Willis started following various links, occasionally typing something, then clicking on other screens.

'Well?' Macgregor enquired after a minute's

silence.

'It's definitely a Vladic entry, but there isn't much else here.'

'What do you mean?'

'Well, these records would have been originally inputted by data collectors taking the details from the old, handwritten ledgers. They're only as accurate as the original inputter was at the time. And this inputter was obviously confused by the Welsh language thing – only completing partial details. There are dates though, see, that's when he acquired the land originally, then the security was released a year later.'

'He was still working for Henleys back then.' Macgregor was staring at the screen. 'He ran a team that dealt with repossessed commercial properties, amongst other things.'

'The old Debt Management Team? I've seen them mentioned in the archives. One of those wild departments, pretty much operated unsupervised for years. There isn't much else to go on though, I'm afraid. What do you think?'

'I don't know what to think.' Macgregor's brow was etched with visible levels of concentration. 'I've never found any reference to him owning a farm or of anything to do with Wales. I'm certain he doesn't own a farm *now*…'

'Sorry, Mac, there's plenty of other things we can look up, though. His accounts, other companies, maybe there are some other things you've missed and…'

'Ledgers!'

'Pardon?'

'You said something about ledgers. The records

that were originally used to compile these databases?'

'The original files would have been handwritten in big ledgers. So?'

'They'll have all the details of this property? Of the loan?'

'Yes.'

'Where are they?'

'Oh, I see what you mean. Well, they'll probably have been archived into the strongroom of the account-holding branch at the time. Hang on a sec…'

Willis followed a couple of links and typed some additional detail. 'It would be Lombard Street branch, in the city. Makes sense if he was staff at the time. It was an old head office building back in the day. I suppose…what…what are you doing?'

Macgregor had stood up and was putting on her coat.

'Going to Lombard Street. I'm way ahead of schedule on your tick-backs and I really want to see those ledgers.'

'Why the rush, Max? They're just ledgers in some vault. They're not going anywhere.'

'Ryan, I've been investigating Vladic on and off for two years. There hasn't been the slightest indication of any agricultural link. He bought this land before he'd left Henleys. What does that even mean? Was it some kind of laundering activity, way back then? An integration of funds via a property purchase, more than a decade ago? If it was, that's the only direct link I've found to Vladic himself. If he *was* laundering while at Henleys, is he still using the same contacts now? This could open up all sorts of new lines of enquiry. I might actually get somewhere with this case at last.' She turned to leave. 'Are you coming, then?'

'Max, you can't just turn up there and ask to start nosing around in the vaults. I'll have to set it up with their Service Manager first and…' He stopped.

She was handing him the phone.

17

'Oh, *my christ*! This is, without doubt, the most glamorous first date I've *ever* been on. In *my life.'*

'It isn't a date.'

They walked up to the steps in front of The Barclay, a boutique hotel in this year's trendy part of the city. Ben double-checked the invitation. To make sure they were at the right place.

'I suppose you're right.' She finally conceded. 'On the basis I've known you for more than ten years, I don't suppose it counts, does it?'

'Exactly.'

'I'm going to pretend, though, just for an hour or two? This dress cost a fortune!'

'Alright. On the condition that you *don't* call it a date again.'

'Deal. Do I *look* pretty?' She clicked open her compact thing and checked her make-up.

Ben wasn't immediately sure what to say. She never asked him questions like this.

'The girl in Debenhams said that she wouldn't normally recommend green eyeshadow for someone with green eyes' Sam continued 'but I think it looks cool. What do you think?' She stared straight at him, then slowly blinked her eyelids.

'I don't know Sam, I…actually…you do look rather nice.' He watched her perform the same move again, then she smiled.

'Come on, let's get inside. It's going to rain any minute.'

Ben followed her in.

He was no expert at these sorts of things, but imagined that this was what would be described as a 'lavish' event. There were people walking around with trays of drinks, you didn't have to go and get your own from a table, or the bar, like at a Henleys party. The women appeared, generally, ridiculously glamorous, *not* like a Henleys party – and there were some guests that Ben recognised from having seen them on television and, in one case, from films. It all felt very wrong to him. Sam seemed to be in her element though and, in fairness, looked suitably 'glam'. Like, at first glance at least, she was accustomed to mixing in this sort of company. Probably one of the most naturally attractive, i.e. not surgically enhanced, persons in the foyer of this hotel, Ben thought.

Sam breezed over to one of the drinks carriers, acquired two glasses of champagne and returned with them, handing one to Ben.

'We really should do this sort of thing more often, don't you think?' She suggested.

They watched the gathering of guests for a while, Sam passing comment on most of them, then Ben pointed out someone they both recognised.

'Ooh! There he is!' Sam breathed.

Tomas Vladic was looking suitably impressive as host of the event, holding court with a group of fat cats at the far end of the room. His long-term wife, Ben recalled her name was something like Marcia or

Marissa, was on his arm. Looking at her, Ben revised his earlier opinion. Sam was the *second* most naturally attractive person here.

They watched as Vladic apparently stopped listening to the conversation around him and stared straight across the room at them. Then he said something to his wife, ignored the others, and headed over.

'Is he coming to talk to us?' Sam asked, as she sipped her champagne.

'Not sure. Looks like.'

Vladic stopped directly in front of them. Tall and lean, with longish, swept back, stylishly greying hair, he was an imposing figure, particularly in his no doubt astronomically expensive, dinner jacket.

Ben and Sam both smiled.

'What the *fuck* are you two doing here!?' Vladic's handsome features creased into a huge smile. He gave Ben a two-handed handshake and Sam a kiss on both cheeks.

'There was a ticket going spare.' Ben explained, apologetically. 'Hope you don't mind?'

'Don't be stupid, Taylor! I would have invited you before, if I'd thought that you two would have been the slightest bit interested in this sort of thing. How does this place compare to the Red Lion?'

'What do you know about the Red Lion?' Sam almost shrieked, surprised and in awe. Like she was talking to a celebrity, or something.

'I still have many friends at Henleys, Samantha!'

'Nice place, Tommi.' Ben said, looking around. 'Classy. Perfect for these sorts of events, I suppose?'

'Oh, yeah, yeah.' Vladic nodded. 'Creates the right

"ambience" and "vibe". All that shit. It's also the only hotel I own, so I have to hold it here, ha!'

'You *own* this?' Sam gasped. Ben thought for a moment that her jaw was going to dislocate itself.

'Don't get too excited, the place barely breaks even. The wife likes it though, so, you know…'

He turned and gave Marcia/Marissa a little wave.

'I'd better go and rescue her, she hates your City banker colleagues. I'll catch up with you later? I'll get someone to bring a couple of the best wines to your table, okay?'

'He's still gorgeous!' Sam advised Ben as Vladic walked away.

'Pardon? Our first date and you're lusting after other men? Are you saying he's better looking than me?'

'What?' She snapped.

'Tommi Vladic is more handsome than me? Is that what you're saying? How charming!'

'Grow up Ben. You're being silly.'

'I just want to know who you find the more attractive? And there's no need to blush so much, he's gone now so…'

'Fuck off, Ben. Seriously.' She pushed past him and joined the first guests venturing through into the dining room.

'Jeez, Sam …what did I…?' He watched her walk away.

They enjoyed a fantastic dinner, with Ben doing his best not to upset her again, perhaps she was sickening for something, and even he could tell that the wine that Vladic had arranged for them was a notch or three above supermarket fare.

After dessert and coffee, Vladic came over to see if they'd enjoyed the dinner.

'It was lovely, thanks Tommi.' Sam was more like herself now, finally.

'Excellent. Sam, do you mind if I borrow Ben for a short while? Just need to pick his brains?'

Sam smiled at Vladic, but didn't look at Ben as he got up and accompanied Vladic back to the foyer.

'Come with me, Ben. I've just opened a private games room, thought you might like to see it? Didn't think it was Sam's sort of thing.'

Vladic showed Ben through to a side door, which opened into a spacious area, with a snooker table in the middle. Some of the guests were already enjoying a game. The oak-panelled walls were decorated with old black and white photographs of various historic sportsmen and events: Muhammad Ali's Sonny Liston fight, Pele, Bradman, Bobby Moore, the 1968 Black Power salutes. It was the probably the sort of room that business associates would find impressive, thought Ben. He doubted whether it was to Vladic's own personal taste, more a place for him to have meetings in town.

'*Really* nice here, Tommi.' Ben said, sensing that Vladic was waiting for him to speak. Vladic smiled, as if he knew what Ben was going to say before he did.

'Come on, I'll give you a game.'

'I'm not very good.' Ben replied.

'Not to worry – you should see these clowns.

They've ripped two cloths already this week.'

Ben and Vladic played a game, badly, with Vladic staying on as winner to play a second game against a small man with a goatee beard, so Ben chatted with some of the other guests. Some seemed nice enough, others seemed to be a long way up their own arses, thought Ben. He was about to go and rejoin Sam when Vladic suddenly addressed the room.

'Gentlemen. I'm afraid I have to talk a little business here for a while. Apologies, but if I could ask you to give me a few minutes.'

Everyone complied with the request and Ben joined the line of men filing out of the room as Vladic held the door for them. When Ben reached the door, though, Vladic placed a hand on his arm, holding him back as the last of the others exited.

Vladic closed the door behind them.

'I'd like to ask a favour.' Vladic said, quietly, his hand still on Ben's arm.

Ben just looked at him. Couldn't think of anything to say. Couldn't think what possible favours he could afford Tommi Vladic.

'Come on, let's play another frame. I'll explain.' Vladic smiled.

Ben reset the snooker balls and Vladic broke off. The standard of play proved to be even worse than before, as neither of them had their mind focussed on the game.

'What is it, Tommi?' Ben asked, his curiosity getting the better of him after a few minutes.

Vladic stood up without completing his shot and leaned on the edge of the table. He appeared to be choosing his words very carefully when he finally spoke.

'One of my, how should I say, closest associates, has recently encountered some difficulties with Henleys Bank.'

Ben breathed a huge sigh of relief.

'Tommi, if you need me to chase up a complaint for you, just give me the details. I'll submit a six-two-eight form first thing in the…'

'It's not that *straightforward*, Ben. The service being provided was not one of Henleys', how should I say, *advertised* services. And the banker dealing with my friend has suddenly dropped off the radar. Disappeared. As I personally introduced him to my friend, this is proving extremely embarrassing.'

Ben felt the blood draining out of his head. He placed the snooker cue on the table and sat down on one of the chairs against the wall. He was fairly certain that he could already see where this conversation was leading.

'The banker that was dealing with your friend. What was his name?'

'Stephen Scott.'

Ben just nodded.

'He had done some excellent work for my friend on several occasions.' Vladic continued. 'My friend thought that he could be trusted to handle a larger transaction. Unfortunately neither my friend nor I are evidently as clever as we thought. My friend appears to have been, quite significantly, ripped off.'

'Tommi, I have no experience in this kind of thing. I'm not the man for that sort of work, honestly.'

Vladic smiled. 'I just need your advice, that's all, Ben.'

‘I’m really not comfortable with…’

‘Look, just advise me on how easy would it be, these days, to place a moderately large cash deposit, through, say, one of the Hubs instead of a branch.’

Ben looked up at Vladic. He wondered whether that was what Scotty had been doing for Vladic’s ‘friend’. Placing funds through branches was probably the best way to do it, as long as the placements were relatively small. You could use different branches, move around. Most cashiers were now given very stiff sales targets to worry about – the last thing they’d want to waste time on would be completing a *Suspicious Activity Report,* even if they did spot an unusual transaction. It would only work up to a certain amount though. There was a limit as to what they would feel comfortable ignoring.

‘How much are you talking about when you say, “moderately large”?’

‘Let’s assume, say, two point five.’

‘Two and a half million pounds? In cash? That isn’t “moderately” large, Tommi.’ Even the most innumerate, cack-handed, short-of-target cashier would notice that sort of amount being shoved across their till. You weren’t honestly going to try and get that through a branch?’

Vladic smiled again. ‘How would *you* do it then?’

‘The Hubs are the only option. It would have to go through a Cash Centre. But regular Hub staff have no access to cash handling, so you’d either have to…’

He stopped, pondering over how easily Vladic had played this situation to get the information he wanted. Oh, what the hell.

‘…you’d either have to book a visit in, make it

look like a genuine transaction, or be working with someone in the Cash Centre.'

'Booking an appointment will prove difficult, I suspect. Unfortunately, my associate has already closed his Henleys accounts. He was aware of their crackdown on certain activities, to appease the Commercial Bank of China board.'

'He's closed his accounts?'

'Yes, any transaction will have to go through the Henleys internal accounts. Then an electronic transfer to a nominated account at the National and Commonwealth Bank. From there, my associate will undertake his usual *layering* of transactions, I believe he calls it.'

'Anything going through the internals will leave a trail a mile wide. Staff numbers will be all over the audit.'

'With all the transactions that go through a Hub, it's unlikely to be noticed, though?'

'Not on an internal account. That could be picked up quite easily. Way too risky. What's the timescale on this "deal" of your friend's?'

'It has to be completed within the next three days. Or my friend will lose a very significant capital investment.'

Ben laughed and shook his head.

'Three days! Completed and funds sent? I'm afraid your friend should be prepared to write off that investment.'

Vladic sat down next to Ben and rubbed his right eye gently with the tips of his fingers. Like he had a headache coming on.

'How much did Steve Scott disappear with?' Ben

asked.

'Ninety thousand, or thereabouts.' Vladic rested his head back against the wall and massaged his face with his hands. He suddenly sounded, and looked, older.

'How much does your friend pay for this service?' Ben was wondering how much Scotty would have been making.

Vladic sat upright again and sighed. Then the youthful energy returned to his voice as swiftly as it had left, although he still looked distracted, glancing at the door, like he had somewhere else to be.

'Ten percent is the going rate. Scott did ten or twelve transactions this year for my associate, totalling maybe five hundred grand in cash deposits.'

'Scotty made fifty grand in a year! Just for taking cash to the bank?'

'Well. There *is* a little more to it than that. The cash has to be collected from site first, then delivered to the appropriate branch. It's more of a courier, door-to-door type service, rather than just queuing up in a bank.'

'What's the site?'

'My friend rents some land from me. Land that is useful, you might say, as a means of gaining entry to the country. So useful that he pays a very generous rent for the use of the property.'

'Like an airfield?'

'Not exactly. More of an unofficial port.'

'Really? Where?'

'Ben, I've probably given enough details?' Vladic looked serious for a moment, but then smiled and stood up.

'Come along, let's finish the game and get back to the party.'

They played for a few minutes, taking turns at missing easy shots. Ben spent the time debating, in his head, as to whether he should give Tommi one last bit of assistance.

'You know,' he said, as Vladic lined up a pot, which he proceeded to make a complete hash of, 'if you could find someone, say, a Business Banking Manager, to open a new account for you, you could book a deposit, via a Hub Cash Centre, that way. You'd need someone to transfer the money out as well, but it would mean that the cash would get deposited, at least.'

'The Business Banking Manager would need ID.' Vladic shook his head. 'We don't have time to arrange such things. Your friend Scott has left him in a bit of a situation.'

Ben paused again. There was an obvious way around this. Should he tell Vladic? He decided it wouldn't harm - this was just conversation.

'Thing is, though, Tommi, Business Banking are desperate for new accounts, deposit monies in particular, because of the bank's funding gap – with the Henleys balance sheet looking so bad at the moment, and all that.'

'So?'

'So, this isn't public knowledge, but a while back the business account managers were told that they didn't have to wait for ID to get the accounts open. They could do it there and then, as long as ID got faxed through to the Account Opening team before close of business same day. It meant that if managers were out at customer premises, or working from home that day, there wouldn't be delays in getting the account numbers sorted.'

'You can open accounts without ID now?' Vladic looked incredulous.

'Hey, Sales Managers call the shots now, not the bankers. Besides, it's only for deposit monies, not transactional accounts with cheque books and the like, and it's only temporary. If the ID isn't forthcoming the accounts are closed off and funds returned from whence they came, as it were. But, the bizarre bit is that the Business Managers are still allowed to claim any money paid in against their targets, even if the account closes. The systems aren't good enough to distinguish between long-term money and single-day money, so the Sales Managers gave up and let it *all* count.'

Vladic started slowly pacing back and forth at the end of the table. 'So, the money could be paid in, credited, and then sent out again, all before the account closes?' He clarified.

'As long as it's transferred out by half-past three, the cut-off time for electronic transfer. If it's still stuck there after that it will cause a hell of a mess, because the account will try and close with funds still in it. Error messages will go off all over Account Opening. Like alarms.'

'But, if you get it right, the whole transaction is completed in one day, with no ID required.'

'It's even better than that, from your friend's perspective. If the account closes same day, it doesn't show up on the daily account audit print. It's like it never existed, as far as the tick-backs are concerned.'

Vladic continued pacing around, another smile gradually spreading across his face. After a minute or so, he leaned on the table again and looked across it.

'One last question, Ben?'

'What?'

'Will you do it for me?'

Ben shook his head. Didn't even need any time to consider the offer.

'Two hundred and fifty thousand pounds, Ben. A quarter of a million! In cash and tax free. You can finish in that shithole Hub and go and do something worthy of your intelligence. Your talent.'

'Hey, I'm happy Tommi. It's a decent job, no pressures. I don't need the "rush" that entrepreneurs like you live for!' He smiled. 'That's why I had no interest in staying in the City.'

Vladic pondered for a moment, then returned the smile.

'Benny my boy, no pressure! If you're not interested, we'll conclude our discussion. It's still been great catching up with you.' Vladic set his cue down on the table, walked over and gave Ben a warm, friendly handshake. 'You must promise me one thing, though?'

'Yeah, sure Tommi.' Ben replied, assuming that Vladic was going to ask him to keep their conversation a secret.

'In ten years, when you've just been overlooked for the third time for an overdue promotion to *Senior Assistant Hub Manager, South Region*, you don't ring old Tommi Vladic up and say you'd wished you'd taken me up on the offer I made that night we played snooker at The Barclay. Okay?' He grinned and let go of Ben's hand. 'Come on. Let's go and be sociable.'

They emerged from the games room and started to wander back across the foyer.

Ben's eye was caught by the figure of Sam, standing near the front doors, looking out through the glass. He pointed her out to Vladic – and let Tommi return to the dining room on his own. Ben walked over to her.

'What's up?' Ben tapped her on the shoulder.

'They've called me a taxi.'

'Oh, why? Are you feeling okay?'

'No, I am not. I've been on my own for *ages*. Where the *hell* have you been?'

'I'm so sorry, Tommi wanted to play snooker and…'

'What!? How fucking old are you?'

'I'm sorry, Sam, I lost track of…'

'Forget it. I'm tired of your apologies.'

'Wha…that's a bit harsh isn't it?'

'I don't believe you anyway. You've probably been upstairs somewhere with some tart. That would be more your style.'

'Sam! What's this all about?'

She turned to him, looked like she wanted to cry but that the anger was holding it back.

'I really dislike you sometimes.'

'What's brought this on? I don't underst…'

'You used to be such a nice bloke. Everyone liked you. But now you just drift along, doing a job that everyone knows you're way too talented for. And these days you're so bored with your own life that you spend all your time sleeping around, with fucking absolutely *anything*, just to try and find some variety to it all. Do you know how much it hurts me to watch this, year after year? Do you? Do you have any idea how much it upsets me?'

'Sam, I don't know what to say, I…'

'You never fucking do any more, do you? You would *never* have left me alone at a party before. You've *always* looked after me. *Always!* After the divorce and everything, when I was in bits. It's like you don't give a shit about anyone now. We used to be best friends.'

'We're still best friends.' He tried to give her a hug, but she pushed him away.

'Don't you dare…Fuck off…just fuck right off…that doesn't make up for anything. We're not friends. I don't even *like* you anymore.'

As a taxi pulled up she ran down the steps, opened the rear door and got in. Ben watched the car pull away.

18

Macgregor was enjoying her cappuccino and croissant breakfast at the coffee shop opposite the Lombard Street branch, in the City.

'Better than Henleys coffee?' Willis wondered.

'Mmm.' She responded, between mouthfuls of French pastry.

'Well, eat up, they're opening any minute and I arranged to meet the *Branch Host* first thing. You said you were keen to get in there.'

'Woulda been more impressed if you'd sorted it for yesterday.' Macgregor swilled the remnants of the croissant down with the last of her coffee and followed Willis out and across the street to the branch, where they joined the end of the queue of customers filing through the opening door.

Willis seemed to know his way around, so Macgregor fell in behind him as he strolled casually over to the reception area. The branch was much more old-fashioned than Macgregor had expected. There was a lot of antique wood and the floor was authentic looking marble. It contrasted with the bright blue 'Henleys' signs and the steel and glass screens of the counter area at the end of the banking hall. This is what banks *should* look like, Macgregor thought, even though there was a distinct feel that this place had seen better days.

Willis was talking to a very tall, very glamorous,

very young-looking girl sporting an immaculately pristine *HenleySuit*. Her *HenleyBadge* said *'Stacey – Branch Host'*. She was playing with a lock of her long, jet-black, *very* straight hair as she spoke. Something about her demeanour suggested to Macgregor that the things that Willis was saying to her were taking a while to travel successfully between ears and brain. She was very pretty though, Macgregor had to concede.

Eventually she stepped out from behind the reception desk, said something to her colleague and started leading Willis and Macgregor across the banking hall. Macgregor noticed that she wasn't actually that tall - at least five inches of her was heels. Which she was an absolute expert at gliding along on.

Stacey got them to sign the visitors' book, reminded Willis to keep his photo ID visible, then, after looking around to check no members of the public were near them, punched in a code number on the keypad and opened a heavy looking door. They went through and stood in a tight space, Stacey close to Willis, she noted, while the outer door was closed and Stacey repeated the keypad process to go through an inner door.

Once through the 'airlock', as Stacey referred to it, she retrieved two keys from a wall-safe. She gave Willis the one with a red tag, Macgregor the one with a blue tag. Macgregor glanced at hers; on the blue tag was engraved *'SR 7'*.

Stacey strode through the back office, the male members of staff watching every stride of her tanned legs as she passed, to which she remained apparently oblivious. Willis was staying close behind her.

Macgregor touched his arm and brought him back closer to her as they walked.

'Where are we going, exactly?'

'Oh.' Willis replied. *Almost as if he's forgotten I'm here*, Macgregor thought. 'We're going to the back vaults. These aren't like the chrome-doored safe deposit rooms you see on the films - the ones customers can rent. The quickest way to the *old* storage vaults is actually through the branch itself.'

They followed Stacey down a narrow flight of stairs, through a longish corridor, then down some more steps. The whole feel of the place changed here – as they went below street level, Macgregor assumed. This felt like it was an even older part of the building. The temperature dropped appreciably. They went through more corridors and down another flight of steps. Macgregor started to get a bit bored, although she remained fascinated by how fast Stacey could cover the ground in her heels.

At long last, the corridors and passageways opened out into a spacious, if badly lit, stairwell, complete with iron staircase, winding its way down – Macgregor estimated by leaning over the handrail – another two flights.

'Can't go wivvya no further.' Stacey giggled. 'Not in these shoes, ha! Go down all the way to the bottom. Strongroom number seven is right in front of ya. Waders on your left, the old branch ledgers you're looking for is probably down the back somewhere.'

'Thanks Stacey, you've been marvellous.' Willis cooed. Macgregor gave her a quick smile.

'Gimme a shout on ya way out, willya?' Stacey pirouetted and clip-clopped her way back down the corridor.

'Lovely girl.' Willis was still smiling.

'She's gone Willis. You can stop swooning. Did she say "waders"?'

'We're below the level of the Thames here. Strongrooms and vaults in this part of the city can be a bit leaky.'

'How leaky?'

'Only one way to find out.' Willis started down the stairs. Macgregor reluctantly followed.

Strongroom seven was awaiting them at the bottom, as Stacey had promised. There was a lock with a red-painted circle around it and a corresponding blue version below it in the metal grill door. The system had to be this simple so that people like Stacey could figure it out, Macgregor felt slightly guilty for thinking, as she unlocked the blue one after Willis had done the red.

'Better put a pair of those on.' Willis pointed to a rack of waders and wellington boots as the door swung open.

They proved to be a wise precaution, as the ramp inside the strongroom sloped down into murky water at least a foot deep.

They shuffled along, testing the floor with their feet as they slowly progressed. The lighting was pretty inadequate, but Macgregor could just about make out the far end of the room, maybe fifty feet ahead, as her eyes adjusted to the gloom. The side walls were lined with metal shelving, on which was an assortment of seemingly random boxes. The room was narrow enough so that, with arms fully outstretched, Willis could almost touch both sets of shelving at the same time, as she paddled through.

'What's all this…stuff? None of it is labelled.'

Willis stopped, a few feet ahead of her, and gazed around.

'Looks like unidentified customer items, UCIs, things that got left here years, decades ago, and have gone unclaimed. After, say, twenty years, if boxes haven't been visited, they'll often get shifted out to make room for newer stuff.'

'I don't understand. These belong to Henleys customers?' She looked closer at some of the items. There were metal cases, small wooden chests, even a few old suitcases with padlocks. As she gave them closer scrutiny she could see on some faded labels with a bank stamp and names.

'Yeah. See, you get the safe deposit boxes, the flashy ones, upstairs where the customer has one key and the bank keeps the other – but these here are things that the customers just locked up themselves and dropped off at the bank for safekeeping. Much cheaper than a safe deposit facility.'

'Banks do that?'

'Most used to, if they had the space. It's dying out now as banks move into smaller, modern buildings and retail units, with little or no vault space.'

'What's the difference between a strongroom and a vault?'

'Different letters in the words.'

'Funny!' But she did find herself suppressing a laugh. 'So, there could be absolutely *anything* in these boxes and cases?'

'Customers were asked to sign disclaimers that there would be nothing illegal or potentially dangerous – combustible materials, for example. But the bank has no way of knowing. Unless the lock falls off or the box falls apart.'

'Why would people just abandon them here though?'

'People forget, move house, die, go senile, whatever. I calculated once that at least seventy-five percent have worthless crap in them, documents and junk. A few will have something worth nosing at though. It used to be quite the trend amongst staff apparently, to have occasional raids on their UCIs, break them open and see what fell out.'

'Seriously?'

'Back in the day, when these old buildings were bursting at the seams with staff and you could hide out in places like this for an afternoon and not be missed. My boss told me once about these two chaps that were rumoured to have found gold coins – sovereigns or Krugerrands or whatever. A huge investigation was undertaken, but nothing could be proved because the box, if there was one, had been there so long – and the records were so inadequately kept. Only way the case could ever be progressed would be if a relative, descendant or whoever, came forward with a deposit receipt. Even then, they couldn't prove what was actually inside the case.'

'Doesn't the bank make any sort of effort to find the people that these belonged to?'

'No resources. Which department would pay for the man hours required? Besides, it's mostly junk.'

'Jeez, all this stuff just abandoned? That's sad. Hey, have you ever looked in one?'

'Of course not. I'm an auditor. Come on, you

wanted to see the ledgers.'

Willis turned and continued paddling towards the benches at the end of the strongroom. Something, though, made him turn around after a few paces and he was horrified to see Macgregor wielding a small metal box, about to smash it against the particularly feeble-looking padlock on a bulky, battered suitcase.

'Max! No!'

It was too late.

The old padlock split open and then disintegrated, its component parts falling down into the water.

Macgregor looked at him with an exaggerated, naughty, expression on her face.

'Oops!'

'Max, what the…'

'What's the problem? You said they were abandoned.'

'*Probably* abandoned. And that's not the point. You can't go smashing peoples' property like that!'

'Why? I haven't damaged anything. Apart from that old lock, obviously. Was practically falling off anyway. Besides, I'm not going to take anything, am I? I'm an officer of the law. I just wanted to see what was inside.'

'Max, that's not the…'

'Do you want a look in there or not?'

'No. I can't do things like this, I'm an…'

'Auditor, I know. You didn't do anything. I did. Shall we have a look? Maybe it's gold coins!'

Willis shrugged. 'Oh, go on then.' He walked back to her as she unclasped the lid and flicked it open.

'See? Junk.' He confirmed, following a quick glance at the contents, before making his way towards the benches holding the ledgers.

Macgregor paused though, and leafed through the papers and photographs in the case. They looked like they were maybe thirty or forty years old. There were photos of a couple getting married and others of the couple, with small children, then others as the children and the family grew. There were also handwritten journals, airline ticket stubs, unused postcards from New York, the Far East, India. She looked over at Willis. He was examining an untidy pile of huge ledger books, peering at the branch codes and wording on the sides.

She rummaged deeper in the case, pulling out some newspaper cuttings, more photographs and an old, expired passport belonging, she confirmed by looking at the photograph, to the man in the other pictures. *Mr John Collard.*

'Max! Put that back and give me a hand?'

Macgregor put the passport into her pocket as she tiptoed her way over to him.

'Max, what are you doing? You can't keep that!

'Don't wet your panties Willis. I'm just going to borrow it and try and trace the family that it belongs to, okay?'

'What?'

'That stuff shouldn't just be left to rot down here. It might mean something to somebody. And don't pretend to look so surprised, alright?'

'I had no idea you were sentimental! You're not going to fool me with your hard-as-nails act any longer you know.'

'Piss off. Have you found the right ledger yet?'

'Err…yeah, it's this one, I think.' Willis levered a

particularly thicklooking binder onto a clear area of the wooden bench. He leafed through the pages until he got to the 'V' section, then slowed down to pinpoint the Vladic page.

'Should these really be down here in a room like this, all damp and everything?'

'Most certainly not.' Willis had a stern look on his face. 'I'll be drafting a memo later to the manager here. These are still live documents, they should be moved immediately to a more appropriate storage facility. Now, here we are, *Tomas Vladic…*'

'Where? Let's have a look.'

Macgregor budged him over slightly so they could both get a good look at the page. Vladic's records appeared to almost fill one side of one page in the large ledger. Macgregor pored over the details as Willis confirmed some of the handwritten notes.

'See, here are the original records corresponding to the database we looked at yesterday. There are the investment property entries, relating to the ones you said you already knew about, but here, this first entry – see where it still says "staff loan" in the margin? – is the agricultural land.'

Macgregor took her notepad from her pocket and started transcribing the information from the ledger, the Welsh spelling slowing her down slightly.

'He had a staff loan to buy the land?' She asked as she wrote.

'Yeah. Probably sanctioned it himself, such was the unofficial policy of the Debt Management team back at that time. Looks like he bought it following a repossession by the bank. Farm must have gone bust owing Henleys money.'

'He gets a staff loan, buys some land on the cheap, then repays the loan less than a year later?'

'Yes. You can see the note in the third column. "Security Released".'

'So the deeds wouldn't be held by the bank any longer?'

'The note says they were released to customer. Which means he didn't remortgage it – he paid it off.'

'In less than a year?'

'Must have come into money pretty quickly.' Willis shrugged.

'That could also explain why he left the bank around that time, I suppose. Maybe he turned the farm around, made a success of it?'

'Not sure about that.' Willis was scrutinising the handwritten notes at the bottom of the page. 'See, almost immediately after acquiring the land, he let it to a company, Inspirational Vision, then just before he repaid the loan, it was let again, to another company, Visionary Inspirations. Then the entries stop, when the deeds were returned to him.'

'Rental income from a farm of that sort of value must have been fairly modest, though?'

'Certainly not enough to repay the loan within a year.'

'This doesn't tell us much does it?' Macgregor didn't bother trying to not look, and sound, pretty dejected.

'Well, you've established that he definitely owned a farm in Wales. Possibly *still* owns it. And around that time, he left Henleys and embarked on some sort of meteoric rise towards…what's the matter?' Willis paused. Macgregor was staring at him. Or, rather, through him.

'I'm going down there.'

'Where?'

'Llwyn-y-whatever.'

'When?'

'As soon as Greenwood will authorise it.'

'Why?'

'What's with all the soddin' questions? Because I want to see what goes on at that farm, get on the land there, ask some questions locally. See if there's any evidence that it's still his. The acquisition of this farm was some sort of catalyst to his leaving Henleys and building his little empire.'

Willis shrugged again. It seemed a reasonable plan. The Agency probably did stuff like this all the time. He was quite envious of the variety that they seemed to have in their…

'Want to come with me?' She asked, smiling.

19

They both sat in Lamby's, now sparsely furnished, office. She was avoiding eye contact with him, just staring straight ahead at the wall.

Lamby brought coffees and sat down behind his desk.

'Now, I have a rather important announcement to cascade.' Lamby reclined in his chair and smoothed his tie. Neither Ben nor Sam noticed his attempts at refining his delivery style. 'For logistical reasons this cascade has to be treated with the utmost confidence. There's an embargo on issuance to staff until the union has responded.' He looked delighted to be discussing something that had union implications.

'Sure.'

'Whatever.'

Lamby paused. He had been expecting more interrogative feedback. It was like they weren't even listening to him properly.

'Good, well, anyway, Marc Smyth and I have been working closely on a special initiative.' He waited for a response but, not getting one, decided to just tell them. 'We will be implementing a *Phasedown Programme* for the Hubs.'

It took a moment, but Ben and Sam gradually came out of their apparent stupors.

'Subject to sign-off, the first closure will be

HenleyWest at the end of next quarter, followed by…'

'Hold on Greg.' Ben was the first to respond. 'Where the hell has this come from?'

'Marc thinks the cost benefits are so significant that an immediate proposal to the Board was appropriate – in time for a full review before the expiration of the leases on the…'

'This is a load of absolute bollocks, Greg.' Sam interrupted. 'This hasn't been discussed at all.'

'Yes it was. Last year. The two of you wrote the business plan!'

'Don't talk shit, Greg. Sam and I did that following a direct request from the previous Ops Director. It was theoretical only, as a short-term contingency if the ancient IT in the Hubs completely broke down. Nothing to do with permanently shutting the Hubs. Nothing whatsoever.'

'Marc feels the plan can also be adapted to support full closure. He was most impressed with your work, you know.'

'What are you and Smyth trying to do?' Sam snapped at him. 'Is this some ridiculous overreaction to the money laundering investigations? This isn't about cost-cutting. You're trying to cover your own arses?'

'I think we need to keep the cascade in perspective.'

'Sorry, Greg.' Ben shook his head. 'There's no legitimate business case for this at the moment. You're suggesting to the Board that we displace thousands of staff on what appears to be a whim. The union are going to jump all over this. The timescale just isn't workable. You'll never close *HenleyWest* within six months, it just isn't…'

'You don't care, do you?' Sam was glaring at Lamby – the penny had dropped. 'You and Smyth know that putting a proposal like this to the Board will automatically postpone the money laundering investigations. What are you so afraid of, you scheming fucker? I knew you were a shit manager, but this? Just so you and that arsehole with his misspelt name can worm your way up another Level on the payscale? This is just…absolutely…'

She shook her head, got up and walked out. Even Lamby recognised it was best to leave her go.

'Is that true?' Ben asked. 'What she just said? You're doing this as some sort of smokescreen? So you and Smyth don't get dragged into any job-shedding as part of the restructuring?'

'Many factors have been factored in, Ben.' Lamby had an odd, cocky smirk on his face.

'What if the Board don't realise how stupid it is? The union has no teeth any more, what if they can't stop it? What if you set this thing in motion and it gets too big?'

'So, the bank saves a few million a year in rent. No big shakes.' He continued smirking.

'All the *staff*, Greg? They'll displace people – everyone will have to apply for jobs in new locations, wherever the work gets relocated. Even if it doesn't get signed off, people are going to be even more scared about job security than they are now. It'll be chaos, Greg.'

'Hey. Marc and I are running a business here. Entrepreneurs have to look at the…'

'You're not running a business. You're a mid-level

Hub manager. Why the delusions of…'

Ben looked at the weird smirk that Lamby still wore, then decided he couldn't be bothered with this conversation any longer.

He turned and followed Sam out of the room. As he walked away, he thought he heard Lamby saying something about there being 'more to cascade', but he had heard more than enough of this.

Ben went back to his desk, but Sam wasn't there. He asked a couple of people if they'd seen her, but got negative responses.

He had a tangible sense of disbelief. The proposal was unlikely to get signed off, but just submitting it was unbelievably reckless. He started thinking about the years he'd wasted here at the Hub – doing the same job for most of them.

Appealing or interesting job roles elsewhere in the bank were going to be few and far between in the 'current climate'. He may even have to accept a downgrade to get a job in another department. Maybe it wouldn't take long to work his way back up again – but he found himself feeling utterly indifferent to the prospect, without really knowing, specifically, why. Maybe he should…

'I'm going home.' A voice advised him.

Ben looked up. Sam had her hat and coat on.

'Will you cover my phone.' Her voice was monotone. It was not phrased as a question.

'Yeah, of course I will. Look, I know this is all a bit sudden – I haven't thought through all the implications myself yet. You want to get a coffee? We can have a chat and…'

'I'm going home because the boys have the flu.

My life doesn't revolve around Henleys. Or you. I just need to go and look after my sons, okay?'

'Sorry, I…just thought that…'

She turned to go, then looked back.

'Oh yeah, almost forgot. I've just been to tell Lamb that I'll be covering Scotty's work for a while, until we know what's happening. I'll be basing myself over there. Janet's going to pick up most of my stuff here. I told Lamb that you'd help her. I do hope that's okay with you.'

She didn't wait for an answer.

20

Ben looked down at his daily task-list.

Then he started working his way through it, making occasional telephone calls and referring to on-screen information as appropriate.

The same sort of processes that he had done every working day for seven years.

He thought about going home for a break but ended up working through his lunch hour. He thought about phoning Sam to see how her boys were doing, but then decided against it.

The afternoon wasn't particularly busy and it wasn't particularly quiet. It was average. Like almost every other day.

He found himself looking around at the staff, most of them with their heads down, working diligently. In a while the daily rush would commence. They'd start bringing him payments to sign-off, queries to resolve, instructions to check – and he would take over some of the payment instructions himself to ease the workflow. It had been a solid, workable system since he'd taken over this particular desk three years previously. A 'robust' process, as the bank liked to call it. It meant that the daily rush lasted no more than twenty minutes to half an hour – and never caused any real issues.

He wished that he knew more about the people around him. About how they'd react when news of the

Phasedown proposal started to make its way along the grapevine. The ones with families would, of course, be worried. One or two would panic, he was sure. If the proposal somehow made its way through Board and union approval, which was unlikely but by no means impossible, then there'd be huge disruption as staff tried to apply for redeployment to other sites, others put their names down for redundancy, many looked for jobs elsewhere…

When he'd joined the bank, just a decade previously, Henleys had been a very different place. A proud banking institution, the oldest clearing bank in the country, the largest network of branches – it was quite a prestigious company to work for. Over the years, though, as the old-style professional bankers had been pensioned off to be replaced as department heads by an influx of over-promoted salesmen, the Henleys brand had, quite rapidly, been tarnished by one scandal after another; mis-selling of pensions and other products, then a raft of court cases on unfair bank charges, then penalty interest rates on credit cards, then self-certification of mortgages, then the big one – the money laundering scandal – that still hadn't gone away.

None of the issues were unique to Henleys Bank, but what *was* unusual was that the bank seemed to have had its fingers in *every* scandalous pie that the banking industry had stuffed its face with. All the other banks appeared to have just dabbled with one or two questionable business lines, but Henleys, due to, presumably, insatiable greed had gone for *everything*. When the bank's balance sheet suffered in the global downturn it hadn't stood a chance, so the media had reported.

Now, with the real bankers long gone, the bank was in such a state that two 'team leaders' as intellectually challenged as Lamby and Smyth could put forward a proposal potentially putting dozens, if not hundreds, of the staff here out of work. A few short years ago they would have been sacked for gross idiocy. Now, even if the plan was declined, they'd most probably get a promotion for demonstrating *entrepreneurial downsizing flair.*

What made it even more sickening was that his and Sam's names were linked to the plan, as they had designed it. People wouldn't want to hear when all hell was breaking loose that Lamby and Smyth had completely disregarded the whole intended purpose of the original plan.

It wasn't the fact that he would be suddenly unpopular that bothered him so much, although he was concerned for Sam, but the fact that it was all so fucking senseless. That people now had jobs, senior jobs, with the bank that amounted to nothing in terms of actual productivity, providing a service for customers or whatever, but just playing games in the shadows, looking after their own career interests. Ben acknowledged that this was probably a naive attitude in this day and age, but it still left a vile taste in his mouth.

At four o'clock, the workload rush over, staff started drifting out of the office, then at five the mass exodus began. By five-thirty, the place was pretty much deserted. Only four or five people were left, dotted around the far end of the department.

Ben killed some time by taking an hour over completing the end-of-day section of his task-list. It normally took fifteen minutes.

He couldn't be bothered to walk home just yet. He thought about going to the Red Lion, but couldn't be bothered to do that either.

After he'd dragged the end-of-day out for as long as he possibly could, he started playing on the computer, glancing through random searches and articles, not really reading anything. He pondered over getting himself a coffee from the machine, but on his way over there, he remembered something that Sam had kept in her desk for ages – two bottles of red left over from some office party – and wondered if they were still there. He kept a spare key to her desk in his top drawer – and after a bit of a rummage he finally located the bottles. The fact that they had corks rather than screw-tops slowed him down a bit, as he had to go and retrieve a corkscrew from the kitchen, but he was pouring a paper-cupful soon enough.

It tasted better than a coffee would have.

He took a walk around the pretty much deserted floor.

Only one or two people, not on his team, remained. In the semi-distance. Some of the other areas of the Hub; Premier Banking, IT, would still be reasonably well populated, but they were in other sections of the building. Payments and Processing would be deserted until morning.

Still not in the mood to go home, he went back to his desk and poured himself a refill. He took his time over drinking it, playing around on the computer, before pouring another.

A long while later, after sipping that one down, he drank a fourth, then a fifth, draining the first bottle.

He opened the second, determined to make it last longer.

He was often the only one left in this part of the Hub. The eerie quiet didn't bother him. It actually felt welcome tonight, after all the things he'd had to listen to recently. And the wine was doing a good job of taking his mind off things.

After some time, the sound of an industrial-power vacuum started drifting in from the distance.

He'd forgotten the cleaners would be around. He wondered which one would be doing this section tonight.

A minute or so later he saw it was her. She glanced over, apparently noticing him as she moved the vacuum head over the carpet tiles in large, sweeping arcs.

Ben watched her as she worked around the desks, between the chairs and the wastepaper bins. Her miniature frame moved quickly and efficiently, with apparently no wasted effort. He watched the prominent muscles of her lean calves flex and relax beneath the skin as she bent over to extend the vacuum under the desks. The colourful, floral tattoos around her ankles contrasted with the grubby pink trainers on her small feet.

She avoided eye contact as she worked her way methodically towards his end of the department. Her short-sleeved overall-shirt revealed the perspiration beading around the tribal designs on her upper arms as the vacuum started to arc faster around the floor. Nearly end of the shift.

Ben watched the back of her shirt starting to cling to a damp line that ran down her spine, from just below another tattoo on the back of her neck (butterfly?) to where he imagined the waistband of her short denim skirt was resting.

She finished up and walked over to sit down opposite him.

She asked how come he was working late and he just shrugged. She asked if he'd been waiting for her and he said that he hadn't. She asked if she could have some of whatever he was drinking so he filled another paper cup and handed it to her. As her delicate fingers encircled it, he glimpsed the black lines beneath her unvarnished nails and wondered if she had to clean that out after every shift.

She asked if she could have a lift home again, because of the rain, but he shook his head and held up the empty wine bottle by way of explanation and apology. She shrugged and curled her lip, saying that it didn't matter, she'd just catch the Broadlands circular instead. It went the long way round but a stop was right outside the Hub, so she wouldn't have to walk far.

Ben watched her as she spoke. Her dirty pink trainers, toes pointed to touch the floor, the smooth skin of her legs. She sat with her knees pressed together as she drank, her eyes watching his as they traced their way up her. She took another mouthful of wine and relaxed enough to let her legs open slightly, maybe mindful of the fact that there was nothing of hers that he hadn't seen before.

She held her now empty cup out and Ben refilled it, before topping up his own.

She took a packet of gum from her overalls pocket and popped one in her mouth, wiped her nose with the back of her right hand, then continued chewing. Didn't offer Ben one before secreting them back into her pocket.

The odour of bleach, disinfectant, office grime and sweat was starting to waft as far as Ben's chair. He started estimating her age in his head, but then decided against it. He'd never been bothered about that before. She probably had to be an adult to be on the permanent cleaning staff, he assumed.

She gulped down the contents of her cup and Ben refilled it again with the last of the second bottle. All gone. She drank that one slightly more slowly, as if evaluating something, then asked if he was going to walk her to the bus stop on his way out. He declined, explaining that he had to finish some work.

She smiled at him as she chewed, drank the last of her wine, then stood up and walked out through the doors to the back stairs.

Ben watched her go. Then he drank the last of his wine. Then he followed her.

The stairwell was gloomy and smelled of the fusty damp of unused spaces. The only time anyone ever walked these stairs was during the quarterly fire drills.

She was leaning back, one leg bent up so that the sole of her foot was against the wall. She asked him to come closer, and he did. She swung the knee of her bent leg outwards so that he could stand against her. She undid his shirt and he felt her warm breath against his chest. She undid her overalls and he reached in, enjoying the feel of her tiny waist – almost as though his fingers could completely encircle her.

The smell of bleach and sweat caught in his throat.

He ran his fingers up over her prominent ribs - and kept going. It was impossible to discern any noticeable shape, other than rake-thin. Skin and bone. She hadn't anything on beneath her shirt, presumably because she didn't need anything. He could feel her heart racing as he pressed his palms against her body. He continued, running his hands around behind her clammy back and stooped down so that he could place his mouth near a flower tattoo on her neck. Her breath smelled of chewing gum, wine and takeaway food. Her skin tasted like salty dust. She turned her head slightly, nuzzling him for a split second in a way that was almost tender, then he felt the stud in the side of her nose scuff his skin as she started giggling and reaching for his wrist, grabbing it and pushing his hand down between her legs, squeezing, wriggling and laughing as she pressed her legs together around his fingers.

Bleach, sweat and takeaway.

She started breathing faster, hot and moist against his chest, started fumbling with his belt, unbuckling it, opening his trousers and reaching in with her tiny hands.

Then, suddenly, she was on her knees in front of him, as she'd done on previous occasions, quickly and efficiently easing his trousers down and opening her little mouth wide to…

Ben reached down and grabbed her shoulders.

Lifted her up so suddenly that he feet came almost completely off the floor. Her eyes were wide and wild with surprise and excitement – he hadn't done *this* before. He could hear her heart pounding in the silence of the stairwell.

'I'm sorry…I can't do this anymore.' He watched her expression change as he spoke. 'I'm sorry. I like you. I just…'

He turned and started down the stairs, adjusting his clothes as he went, re-buckling his belt. He started rushing and nearly stumbled, startling himself. But he kept moving quicker, he didn't want her to hear him if he was going to be sick.

Reaching the ground floor, he pushed the release handle on the fire door and emerged into the fresh air. He slammed the door shut behind him. The alarm probably wouldn't go off if you did it quickly enough – which he managed to accomplish.

He leant against the wall next to the door, arms outstretched, hands against the wet brick, trying to take as deep breaths as possible.

It wasn't working – the odours were stuck in his nose and mouth. On his clothes. He gagged, but managed to hold it.

His head was spinning from drinking too much wine too fast. He took his hands off the wall, stood up and started rubbing his head, trying to get some of the cool rain from his hair to his face.

After some time, it started to have some effect, and the nausea gradually subsided, the smells in his nose and mouth less overwhelming now.

He started pacing around – it helped keep his head clear and his stomach calm. He walked for a long time, completed an entire lap of the building – before going back around in the opposite direction.

Then, when his head and stomach felt a little more normal, he slumped down, sitting with his back against the wall, looking up, enjoying the cool rain on his face.

He retrieved his phone from his pocket, looked down and started scrolling through the numbers. He stopped at Sam's. He wanted to phone her, see how the boys were. See how she was. After deliberating for a while, he decided against it – he didn't want to make the situation any worse. He hated the fact that he had upset her.

So he scrolled a little further and without pausing – in case he changed his mind – dialled.

A few moments later the call connected.

'Tommi? It's Ben Taylor.'

21

The landlady, Mrs Richardson of the Harbour B & B, brought another rack of toast and a fresh pot of tea.

'Better get a tidy breakfast down you, if you're going walking the coastal path. *Terrible* weather forecast on the radio, blowing in off the Irish Sea.'

'Thank you.' Willis smiled at her.

'Thanks.' Macgregor grabbed another slice and refilled her cup. 'You wouldn't have any more of this lava bread, by any chance?'

'I'll do you another plate, luv. You want some more bacon and eggs too?'

'Oh, yes please!'

'And you, luv?' She smiled at Willis.

'No thank you. I am stuffed full.' Willis patted his stomach to emphasise the point. 'Do you honestly like that lava stuff, Max?' he asked after Mrs Richardson had returned to the kitchen. 'It tastes like mud.'

'It tastes gorgeous.' She dolloped the remainder onto some toast and started devouring big chunks in single bites.

Willis watched her for a few moments then looked out of the window instead. There were some seriously dark clouds in the distance, out over the water, but they looked far away.

His back was sore from a night on the carpet in the room. Max had offered him the bed, saying she'd be fine on the floor, but that didn't seem right at all, so he'd been the gentleman. He wished now that he hadn't been so chivalrous.

'How far do we have to walk?' He asked Macgregor after she'd finished chomping down a gobful of her mud sandwich.

She pored over the Ordnance Survey map that she'd partially unfolded on the table.

'We'll park the car around here somewhere.' She jabbed at the map with the handle of her knife. 'Then it looks like a about a three- or four-mile walk, looping round. Difficult to be exact, looks a bit of a winding path.'

'Why can't we just drive all the way?'

'Are you familiar, Ryan, with the term "covert"?'

'From *films*, Maxine, *yes*.'

'Don't be sarcastic. We can't just drive up and ask the first person we see "hi there, do you know who owns this land?" We want to be subtle, like we're two ramblers out for a stroll. Then, if we meet anyone we can just make casual chitchat. Geddit? Besides, I don't think the Agency car is designed for farm tracks and bridle paths. Greenwood would probably take it out of my salary if I damaged the suspension.'

'Whatever.'

'There you go, luv.' Mrs Richardson brought Macgregor her second helpings. 'You can certainly pack it away for a small girl, can't you?'

'Do a lot of running.' Macgregor grinned at her, then started spreading the fresh lava bread over more toast. 'Mrs Richardson?'

'Yes, luv?'

'Do you know this area, up here?' She pointed to the approximate site of the farm on the map.

'We go for a walk up through there a couple of times a year.' Mrs Richardson replied. 'In the summer, you know, when the weather's nicer.'

'Is there much up there? Farming wise? Agriculture, crops, that sort of thing?'

'I'm not sure, luv. It's pretty desolate in places, until you get to the National Park and the beaches, but they're much further up, to the north. Twenty miles maybe? You'll see some sheep around and about. Is that the sort of thing you're after? The farms with, you know, fields and crops and the like, are further inland. I can ask Mr Richardson to show you another route, if you like?'

'No, that's okay. We'll have a stroll along the coast. I just didn't want to wander into someone's field and get shot at or something!'

'Ha! No danger of that, luv. Stay on the path and I doubt you'll see another soul all day. Not this time of year! Now, may I just check, will you be requiring the room for a second night?'

'We're not sure whether…' Willis started to reply.

'Oh darling, we can stay, can't we?' Macgregor grinned at him. 'Thank you Mrs Richardson, we'd love to stay another night.'

'Wonderful, luv. I'll book a table for you at the pub in the village for this evening. They do a lovely cooked dinner.' She scuttled off.

'*Why*, Max? Why say that? She's going to think we're a couple or something.'

'We just shared a room for the night. She wouldn't think that already?'

'Yeah, well. I don't know, I just…'

'Stop babbling. As soon as I've finished this we

better get going. Don't like the look of those clouds.'

'It'll be okay, they look a long way out to sea and…'

'Hey! Why so offended anyway, by being thought of as my other half? You wouldn't go out with someone like me?'

'No. No. I mean yes. Oh, I don't know. Yes. Oh, that's not what I mean at all.' He blushed, stood up and left.

Macgregor allowed herself a little smile as she began polishing off the remainder of her breakfast.

22

He woke early.

Much earlier than usual for a normal workday. And he'd slept well, which slightly surprised him.

He made and ate some toast. Along with a mug of tea.

He kept glancing at the time, through force of seven years' habit, but nevertheless was still enjoying the feeling of not being on the Henleys clock today. He'd have to call in later to explain his absence, but he hadn't taken a 'sicky' in three years, so felt that one was long overdue. He'd tell them that he had an upset stomach. Something suitably non-specific.

Not exactly sure what to wear, he eventually went with a plain black suit, wanting to look professional. Decided to dispense with a tie though. Unnecessary. He also chose a slightly more casual and comfortable shirt than his normal *HenleyWear* item – it would be a long drive. He'd take his big coat though, it was probably colder way down west, he assumed – and the weather forecast was pretty grim.

Allowing himself plenty of time, he planned to set off before rush hour peaked on the M25. That would allow him a leisurely drive down to and along the M4. He'd been advised to observe speed limits so as not to attract unwanted attention, and he planned to arrive at the 'rendezvous' point a half hour or so ahead of schedule. That would give him sufficient time for a coffee and a freshen up before he called in for further instructions.

He'd also been advised that a car would be left for him in the car park at the Broadlands shopping centre. He glanced at his watch. The car should be there by now and it was better for him to get there early – no point in waiting around. He checked all the electric sockets and the gas hob rings were turned off and the back door locked. Then he let himself out of the front door.

One of his neighbours four houses down on the left-hand side was also exiting his front door. Ben could not recall ever seeing him before, but assumed he must have at some point in the past. His neighbour was carrying a briefcase to his blue BMW. It looked every inch the company fleet car. Ben stood in his front doorway and watched his neighbour. For some reason he found it compelling, fascinating viewing, almost like it was in slow motion. His neighbour dabbed his remote key fob and Ben faintly heard the Beemer unlocking in the semi-distance. He opened the front passenger side door and laid the briefcase on the seat, then closed the door, opened the back door and meticulously hung his jacket on a waiting hanger inside.

Every move was that of a man following a polished, well-crafted routine.

The neighbour then closed the rear door, walked around to the driver's side, waved, presumably at someone in the window unless he was waving goodbye to his house, and got in the car.

A few moments later he reversed off his drive,

turned in the road and pulled away. Ben watched the BMW until it turned out of sight at the end of the close, carrying the driver off to a breakfast *One to One* or on the start of a long drive to a sales conference someplace, maybe.

He turned his gaze to the empty street.

A line of virtually identical red-brick houses, on both sides of the cul-de-sac. In the years he'd lived here, he'd never spent anything like this long looking at the close. He barely knew any of the people that lived on it. Aside from his next-door neighbour, Bernie, he'd never said more than 'hello' to any of them. And it was a chore having to talk to Bernie so he went out of his way to avoid him.

Ben found himself looking at details that he'd never noticed before. The tidy front gardens with flowers. The scruffier lawns. The gravel gardens, like his own, that never needed any maintenance. The gardens with evidence of children's' activities – a tricycle, an old, semi-deflated football.

A drop of rain blew in under the porch and hit his coat. He forgot about the local scenery and pulled the door shut. He wanted to get to the car before this shower got too heavy.

23

'Damn it, Abi! Why lodge a formal complaint? Why?'

She sighed and turned around to face him.

One of her colleagues had asked her to cover their morning shift at the Hub and she'd just finished getting ready. By the look on the Retail Ops Director's face though, he wanted a thorough *One to One* to discuss her working pattern first. Maybe also her attitude.

'*Because*, Marc, there was no valid reason for my request to be declined.'

'Do *not* speak to me like that. *Nobody* speaks to me like that. Certainly not some fucking Level *Two*. *I* will decide whether there is a good reason to decline a request.'

'You're an Ops Director. I work in Premier Banking. It's nothing to do with you.'

'*What* did you just say? Nothing to do with me? Do you know the embarrassment that this could cause me? They'll all be whispering. "How can Marc Smyth manage a downsizing project effectively if he can't even control his fucking wife?"'

'What downsizing? What are you talking about? This is about my hours at the Hub, it's not about you.'

She saw no further merit in progressing with this line of discussion. So shook her head in frustration and started to turn away.

Out of the corner of her eye, she saw him lunge at her. She had no chance of getting out of his way.

The next thing she knew, he had her by the collar of her suit, pushing her backwards. She tried to hold her ground, but his bodyweight on the move carried too much momentum and she was slammed against the wall.

'Get your hands off me, Marc!'

He hit her just hard enough, with the back of his right hand catching her across the top of her head, to knock her off balance. She grabbed at a nearby table to break her fall, but he also kept his grip on her clothes, slowing her descent, so it ended up more of a slump, avoiding any significant impact with the ground.

She crouched, slightly relieved, on her knees, catching her breath and blinking her eyes, trying to clear her vision. Marc bent down and, for a moment, she thought he was about to apologise and help her to her feet.

The second impact was more aggressive. More angry. He caught her, with a sort of clumsy punch, just above her right eye. Although instantly painful, it had the opposite effect to what he'd probably intended, as her vision cleared and her disorientated confusion evaporated. She immediately covered her head with her arms, pushing with her legs to create space between her and him.

For a few seconds, she thought it had worked, but then her head was yanked backwards as he grabbed a fistful of her hair, pulling her sideways.

'You want to get hit again? Bitch.'

She didn't want to give him the satisfaction of

responding, so didn't.

'Didn't think so. You want to keep the Director happy, don't you? Skirt up. Slut.'

He relaxed his grip on her hair and the pain eased.

She decided to comply with his order.

He forced her into an uncomfortable, sort of all-fours position, before pushing it in. He wheezed and puffed his way through a half-minute of the most foul and unpleasant language she'd ever heard, then it was done.

Abi crawled forward away from him, then started to get to her feet.

Then he hit her again.

24

The car was a black Subaru estate.

After the knee-jerk reaction to last night's drunken wallowing in self-pity, Ben now found himself having to concentrate on the task he had found himself agreeing to undertake.

The Subaru was last year's model, if the registration plates were accurate. Ben had been told that this was a 'clone' of a car of similar make, model and colour. It had evidently been a while since it had seen any soap or wax though, which made it look every inch the bland, average family car, or maybe a sales rep vehicle. The keys were in the rear luggage area under the flooring panel in the spare wheel, as he'd been told they would be.

If he'd had looked closely, he may have spotted that the tyres were brand new, with unusual tread for a road car, or that the suspension had been adjusted, making the car look, very slightly, as if it was on tip-toes, like an off-roader.

But Ben was forcing himself to focus, totally, on the job.

And this was starting to *feel* like a workday. There was a job to do. A financial transfer, albeit in an unusual format. There was enough familiarity with routine for Ben to feel like he wasn't out of his depth here. Looking back on this later, Ben would probably concede that this was the time when he'd been closest to enjoying it all.

The instructions he'd been given were simple enough. Follow the M4 motorway all the way to its end at the Pont Abraham services in west Wales. There, he was to use the public telephones and call the number he'd been given. He would be given directions to a location for the meeting.

Ben started the Subaru and took a minute to have a look around the controls and instruments. Everything appeared straightforward, so he snicked the gearstick into first and guided the car out of the car park, changing through the gears as he wound his way out of the Broadlands estate and towards the M25. It was an easy car to drive and Ben wriggled himself around a bit in the seat to get as comfortable as possible – the only thing that was bothering him at this stage was the prospect of pretty much a full day's driving. He told himself that it couldn't be much different to sitting at a desk all day – and that took his mind off it.

The first exit from the roundabout ahead carried Ben onto the on ramp for the M25, but Ben had to hit the brakes as a little old Nissan, probably with a pensioner behind the wheel, suddenly veered across in front of him. Not wanting to get caught up behind the toodling supermini, Ben pulled out and changed down a gear, before pushing the accelerator down with his right foot. After a short pause, there was a sound like a small explosion from somewhere in front of him and the car suddenly lurched forward, commencing a savage burst of acceleration. Unprepared, for a moment Ben thought that he was going to lose control of the car, before the four-wheel-drive system straightened things out and Ben tore past the Nissan.

Then three other cars ahead of it.

By the time he arrived at the top of the slip road, Ben was doing ninety and he had to brake hard to merge safely into the heavy flow of traffic on the main carriageway.

Perspiration was pouring from his neck and back. Ben turned down the temperature on the air conditioning. There was clearly something fairly formidable under the bonnet of the Subaru and he decided it was unnecessary to explore it again for the duration of the journey. Blend with the traffic and observe speed limits, he had been told.

From now on, he'd do exactly that and…

25

…by the time he arrived at Pont Abraham services, the point where the M4 terminated at its western end, it was lunchtime.

Ben parked the Subaru in the middle of a sparsely occupied car park and headed inside.

He bought himself a cup of coffee and a sandwich.

The sandwich was fairly tasteless, as was the drink, but at least the coffee was hot and strong. Ben sat himself next to the windows overlooking the car park and the motorway, and watched the traffic drifting off the M4 onto the narrower A road, as the rain started to come down heavier.

He looked at his watch. He had half an hour or so until he had to call for further directions, so he took off his coat and made himself as comfortable as possible in the plastic seat. He was surprised by the lingering feeling of enjoyment. The novelty of roaming around the country while he should, contractually speaking, be sat at his desk in work, did not seem to be wearing thin. He thought of what he'd usually be doing at this time of day, the processing of payments, the signing off of hundreds of three-nine-three forms for his team. More payments.

He looked beyond the motorway, where the land

rose steeply up a tree-covered hillside. He'd driven for nearly four hours, longer than he could ever remember driving in one stint in his entire life. He'd covered more than two hundred and fifty miles, past Reading, Swindon, Bristol, across the Severn, past Cardiff and Swansea. He had an unusual feeling, of there being a world outside the premises of Henleys Bank. He felt a tinge of resentment, or frustration maybe, over the sheltered existence he'd adopted for the last seven years – before snapping himself out of the trance.

For christsake, Taylor, you've only pulled a sicky and gone for a drive. Get a grip.

He decided to consult the basic road atlas he'd brought with him.

Tommi had mentioned 'the coast'. That might mean a straight run further west, then 'up a bit' where the roads and towns were few and far between – to the north. If so, it looked to be about sixty, seventy miles. Given that the roads were likely to get narrower out there, he probably had another long drive ahead.

He looked again at his watch. Ten minutes.

Ben used the restrooms, washed his face to freshen up a bit, then stood and waited by the public phones, looking at his watch. There was nobody around to pay him any attention.

At the agreed time, he made the call. It was answered immediately. The connection was poor.

'Hi. It's Taylor again.' Ben wasn't sure whether to try and sound cheerful, or deadpan and professional. It came out as a weird hybrid of the two. What the hell, he thought, they know I'm a bank manager, not a villain. Why put on a front?

The voice on the other end of the connection

which, Ben couldn't be sure and he didn't want to ask, sounded like it could belong to Shorter One from Scotty's kitchen, was friendly – and slowly read through a list of detailed instructions and directions. Ben, with the receiver tucked under his chin, scrawled them down on a blank page in the back of the road atlas.

'See you in a couple of hours. Drive carefully, eh?' The voice said. Ben thought he even heard a friendly laugh, but assumed that was probably just due to the poor quality of the signal. Then the line went dead.

He bought himself another coffee and returned to the Subaru.

26

'Did you bring anything for lunch?'

'Max, are you serious? You ate the biggest breakfast I've ever seen.'

'What can I say? I have a fast metabolism. What did you bring?'

'Nothing! I'm not the one who's hungry. You should have brought something yourself.'

'Forgot.' Macgregor puffed her cheeks out and looked out over the cliffs to the Irish Sea. The dark storm clouds were a lot closer now. 'Nothing else for it, Ryan, you're going to have to forage something for me. Find a dead sheep or something.'

For a moment, just a split second, he looked horrified. Which made her smile.

Willis took the opportunity to flop down and have a sit on a nearby rock.

'Have you seen enough yet, we've been walking for hours?' He tried not to sound too downbeat, but his back pain was getting worse. 'We've walked right through the land acquired by Vladic. There's nothing here, except one stone hut. Nothing's gone on here for years. I bet he doesn't even own it anymore.'

'You're not enjoying the walk, though?' Macgregor was still sporting a broad smile. 'The scenery?'

'Bit bleak and desolate for my taste.' Willis was busy adjusting his laces and socks. Ignoring the views.

‘Do you mind if we just go another mile or so along the coast?’ She asked. ‘Then maybe inland a bit further? Just want to get a look at the surrounding area. Then we’ll head back, I promise.’

‘Yeah, sure.’ Willis stopped fiddling with his trainers and got to his feet. ‘No problem’.

27

By the time Ben left the narrow B road and turned onto the unsurfaced track, the heavens looked about ready to open. Dark thunderclouds had rolled in off the sea and were almost directly overhead. Ben hoped he could get this over and done with before they started emptying their contents on the land here – he didn't fancy the return trip if this track was subjected to heavy rain.

It had taken just under two hours from the Pont Abraham services to get here. He'd got lost once, just after leaving the main A road, but double-backed and soon found the right route again – the directions he'd been given had military precision, even incorporating references to landmarks and geographical features to ensure clarity.

After a couple of miles of rocking and bumping along between overgrown hedges and ancient stone walls, the track suddenly emerged onto open ground. The occasional gorse bush was the only feature above grass level, giving Ben a panoramic view of the sea, directly ahead. He brought the car to a stop and got out.

The wind, although not particularly strong, was bitingly cold, but other than a few drops of moisture being buffeted around in the moving air, the rain had not yet started falling with any serious intent. Ben re-read the last few directions that he'd jotted down in the back of the road atlas. At this point the track should bear to the right, which indeed it did, then run parallel to the clifftops, more or less due north. Ben followed the terrain with his eyes, until the track dropped out of sight in a dip before re-emerging further along, near what appeared to be, Ben peered through the misty air, a small stone hut maybe half a mile away. This was definitely the right place.

The only thing was, he was supposed to be met at that stone hut – and from here he could see that there was no-one there. No vehicle.

Ben assumed they must be heading up the same track as he had just driven. Or maybe they were coming in from the opposite side, down the track from the north, over that distant ridge. Ben decided that he felt more comfortable and less exposed staying here. He'd wait until someone else turned up before he drove the final part of the journey.

28

'A little further, you said! It's been two hours.' Willis trudged along, falling further behind a still enthusiastic Macgregor.

'I'm sorry. Needed to have good nose around though, didn't we? Seeing as we came all this way?'

'Yeah, I suppose. Sorry to moan. My back's killing me though!'

'You're definitely having the bed tonight.' She stopped on the crest of a ridge to let him catch up and have a breather. 'Look, won't be long now.' She pointed at something in the distance. 'We're nearly back at that stone hut.'

'Great.' He sounded relieved, but didn't bother looking for landmarks. Took her word for it.

'You honestly don't like it down here?' She asked as she allowed Willis to have a rest and stretch his back for a while.

'Well.' Willis reflected, in-between alternately touching his toes and then stretching skywards with his arms, hands clasped together above his head. It started easing the pain a little. 'I suppose it does have a certain, rugged charm? To be fair, it's probably not the best sort of day to see it on, is it? It's going to start chucking it down before long. It's probably awesome on a hot summer's…'

'Look out over the cliffs.' Macgregor grabbed his

arm and turned him to face the sea.

'Alright, take it easy! It's a nice view, I said. Probably looks fantastic on a…'

'There's somebody watching us, idiot. Point at something.'

'What?'

'Oh for fu…anything, pretend we're drinking in the pissing view.'

Macgregor swept her arm along the line of the horizon and Willis, taking her lead, pointed at some imaginary ships.

'What's going on Max?'

'I think there's someone on the track, way past the other side of the hut. I can see the roofline of a car and someone next to it. It's like they're just standing there. You have good eyesight?'

'Err…yeah. I think so.'

'Look right over the roof of the hut, then up, then ten, fifteen degrees to the right, you can see the end of a hedgerow, or trees or something, and what looks like gorse bushes.'

Macgregor did a bit more random pointing and Willis turned his head slightly, so as to look over her arm in the direction she'd described. It took a moment to follow the path with his eyes, *over the top of the hut…up…right…treetops…*

'Oh yeah! There is someone. Just standing there. Can't see a car though.'

'Can you make out any details, old guy, young guy?' Willis squinted hard.

'No, it's too far. Could be anything. A pensioner or a kid. Short or tall. Sorry.'

'No worries. Give me a hug.'

Willis just did as he was told. She wrapped her arms around him and turned him slightly, so he now had his back to the hut and the figure beyond. She tilted her head to look around his shoulder. She focussed on the figure for maybe thirty seconds, trying to let any features or detail drift into focus.

'Not sure whether that is a car. There's definitely someone up there though.' Come on, take my arm and walk me back the other way. Don't look round.

Willis complied and they retraced their steps northwards, away from the hut and down the slope away from the crest of the ridge. After maybe fifty paces, Macgregor glanced behind them and made sure they had descended far enough to be out of sight. When she was sure that they were, she stopped.

'Okay. Listening?'

'Can I have my arm back now?'

'Are you listening?' She kept hold of him.

'Yes.'

'We're going to go over there…' She inclined her head to indicate the direction of some scrubby bushes, maybe fifty yards inland, away from the cliff edge. '…crawl back up to the top of the ridge, then take another look, okay?'

Willis nodded to confirm his understanding.

'Now.' She continued. 'What will be important to remember?'

'Not to …err…poke my head up too high? To stay out of sight?'

'Good boy.' She kept hold of his arm and lead him in the direction she wanted to go.

They walked across to the gorse, then ducked through the bushes, walking slowly up the rise. After twenty paces or so, Macgregor released Willis' arm and dropped down to a prone position on the ground, so Willis copied her. They wriggled and crawled the remaining distance back to the top of the ridge.

The view was slightly different from here, you could see more of the small inlet, below them to their right and because they were now viewing from a different angle, it took a minute to find the figure on the distant slope.

'There.' They said in unison.

'He's not moved at all.' Macgregor whispered. Then realised that there was no point in whispering. 'Can you see the car?'

'No. But he's moving now, walking back.'

Macgregor squinted into the distance but saw nothing.

'Do you think he saw us?' She asked.

'What if he did? He's probably just some bloke out for a walk.'

'Didn't *feel* like that though, did it?'

'Not sure what you mean by that. All I'm feeling is cold. I *am* actually getting quite hungry now. Maybe we could…' He stopped and looked out towards the inlet. 'Can you hear that?'

'What?'

'Listen.' Willis tilted his head. 'Like an engine. Or a motor. Yeah, a motor.'

'Look.' She gestured back at the spot where the figure had been standing. A dark coloured, or black, car was emerging into view, turning a sharp right to follow the track as it veered parallel to the coastline on their right, the driver's left. From this angle, the car was now pointing straight at them, bumping and lurching its way towards the stone hut which stood about halfway between them and the car.

Willis pulled on her coat sleeve to attract her attention, then pointed at something entering their view, down in the inlet below them.

'An engine *and* a motor.' He suggested, as the shape of a small dinghy with an outboard motor bobbed its way between the cliffs, passing out of view as it, presumably, pulled up on the rocks or sand or whatever was down in there. 'What do you reckon is going on?' He sounded less fatigued now. Excited, almost.

Macgregor just made a face. 'Don't know. Might be nothing. I suppose we'd better stay and watch though, eh? Keep your head down!'

Willis lowered his head until his chin rested on the cold, wet ground.

The rain was starting to come down hard.

29

Ben guided the Subaru down the track and started the gradual descent into the dip where the hut stood.

He'd heard the motor of the boat and assumed that it was being piloted by the person or people he was meeting. If it turned out that it wasn't them, he decided he'd just sit in the car down by the hut instead.

The two hikers, or ramblers, whatever those types called themselves, had made him nervous, but after taking in the view of the sea from the opposite ridge, they'd wandered away.

As he drew the car up near the hut, he saw two familiar-looking characters climbing up the last few yards of the footpath from the inlet below.

Ben got out, pulled his collar up in a fairly futile attempt to shield himself from the now driving rain, and walked over to them.

30

'Shit.'

'What?' Willis whispered. They were both whispering now, even though they were at least two hundred yards from the stone hut.

'The two coming up the footpath are carrying shotguns.'

'What! They are fucking *armed*!?' Willis somehow managed to shout whilst still whispering.

'Stop making a fuss and keep your head down. They can't see us here. Look at the size of that big guy! He looks about seven foot.'

'Huh. Maybe the other two are just really small?'

Macgregor smiled. At least Willis wasn't panicking too much yet. She felt bad, a bit, for having dragged him along, but thought it was unlikely that they would be spotted all the way back here.

'Just keep your head down.' She reminded her colleague.

'It is down.'

'Good.'

31

'Nice to see you again.'

Shorter One transferred his shotgun into his left hand and shook Ben's hand with his right. He was much friendlier this time round. A warm smile on his face. Even his freaky-big colleague seemed to be less cold, in his general demeanour, than before.

'Yeah, you too.' Ben replied.

'Good drive down?'

'Err…yeah…no bother.'

'Good. Good stuff. Cam will get the cases for us now. Cam?' He gestured to the big man, who moved over to the door of the hut and withdrew an amusingly huge fob of keys from inside his coat.

Ben watched 'Cam' go through a sequence of locks, each requiring a different key, set into what appeared to be a modern steel door daubed in rough-looking paint. From a distance it looked like rusting iron. After completing the sequence, Cam dipped his shoulder against the door and started driving hard with his legs. Despite his huge bulk and, presumably, his considerable power, the door opened very slowly.

'This is actually a sealed, steel box.' Shorter One picked up on Ben's expression of curiosity. 'Top, sides and floor. The stone walls and tiled roof have been built around it to make it loo …you know…'

'Like it belongs here?'

'Exactly. But it's essentially a vault. You'd know

all about them, I suppose, ha?'

Ben smiled at his quip.

Cam emerged from the hut/vault with a big metal cash case in each hand. Like larger versions of those used by the security companies when delivering and collecting. He was concentrating hard on not losing his footing on the dampening ground.

Ben moved around to the back of the car, opened the rear door and retracted the parcel shelf as far as it would go. He stood back as Cam reached the Subaru, but rather than lift them in, the big man placed them gently on the ground, before returning into the hut.

Obviously that was as much assistance as Cam was prepared to offer.

Shorter One shook his head and laughed, then lifted one of the cases as Ben took the other. It was heavy, maybe twenty kilos, Ben estimated, comparing it to weights in the *HenleyGym*. Shorter One let Ben slide his case in first, before lifting his in too, with a little more ease than Ben had managed. They fit very snugly into the back, which Ben assumed was not merely by chance.

As Ben closed the boot, a big squall of rain began sweeping in, reducing visibility to just a few yards.

'Here, let's go inside.' Shorter One ushered Ben into the hut. 'Can't have you driving off the edge of the cliff because of the weather!'

Cam stepped aside to let them in, before resuming his position standing inside the doorway, looking out to sea, preventing most of the light from entering the 'room'.

Ben was aware of the metal surface beneath his feet and the boxes and other items in close proximity.

'This'll blow over shortly. The storm's not due to hit for another hour.' Shorter One reassured him.

32

'Can you see anything?'

'Not much, not in this.'

The rain was driving, more or less directly, straight into their faces.

'They loaded something into the car. Then I think they went inside that hut.' Macgregor ducked down below the highpoint of the ridge, shielding herself from the rain, as visibility was poor now anyway. Willis did likewise.

'Did you get a good look at them?

'Not really. Might recognise a couple of them if I saw them again, I suppose. That big one, definitely.'

'What do you think they were doing?'

'No idea. Looked a bit odd though, didn't it? I don't think any of those three were farmers.'

'They're not going to hang around here for long. We'll wait it out and then…'

'Come on.' Macgregor dragged him to his feet. 'Let's get to the Volvo. Maybe we can pick that Subaru up on the main roads somewhere.'

'What? The car's miles away, and I don't want to walk past them.'

'You chicken! Besides, we're not going that way, we're cutting across.' She started striding out inland. 'I reckon the car is due…over there!' She thrust her arm straight out in a vaguely south-east direction. 'Can't be more than a couple of miles. We only went the coastal path route on the way up to get a good look at Vladic's land. This way'll be much shorter.'

'Are you sure the car is over in that direction?' Willis was already lagging behind.

'Not a hundred percent certain, no…' She waited for him, shaking her head. 'But come on, we'll jog it! Keep warm.'

Willis made a huge effort to stop his facial expression belying his feelings of dread at the prospect of a two mile run across fields.

33

Ben looked around as his eyes adjusted to being 'indoors'. There were three or four large, wooden boxes on the floor, one of which was now being used as a seat by Shorter One.

It looked a pretty unpleasant space, and had a stale, acrid feel to the air. Which maybe was why Cam was standing in the doorway.

Absolutely everything was covered in dust and dirt, except for a sturdy, steel table in the corner, which looked brand new and/or polished – and three heavy duty, state-of-the-art cash-counting machines on the tabletop. They were the kind of kit that Henleys Cash Managers could only dream about having at their disposal, given their restricted budgets.

'Did you find out what happened to your mate, Steve Scott?' Shorter One asked Ben, at the same time offering him a hipflask that he took from inside his bulky jacket.

Ben waved his hand to decline the drink.

'No, actually. Looks like you were right though. His real name wasn't "Steve Scott".'

'Didn't think so. Tommi wasn't best pleased about the whole business. Made him look bad in front of the Old Man.'

'Old Man?' Ben queried.

'Business associate of Tommi's.' Shorter One appeared, for a moment, as if he was going to offer a more detailed answer, but then stopped. Ben decided against pushing the point further – and changed the subject.

'So, how do you know Tommi?'

Shorter One looked momentarily confused, as if he was being asked something that he knew Ben already knew, but then answered anyway.

'We go way back. Ten, eleven years. Back around the time when *we* met?

'When who met?' Ben was slightly confused.

'You and me.' Shorter One took a sip from his flask and replaced it in his inside pocket. 'Have I changed that much?'

'I'm sorry, I…I've never been good with faces!' Ben tried his best to look apologetic.

'No worries, I've put on a ton of weight over the years. I thought it was weird when you didn't say anything at Scott's house the other day. We met when I was fresh out of the army. I was pretty skinny back then.'

Ben looked hard at the Shorter One, but there wasn't even the slightest flicker of recognition. Which Shorter One evidently noticed.

'It was in the City? At a bar? Near the Henleys building on Lombard Street? Ninety metres to the south, on a side street, think it was called "Pinstripes" or some shit like that? I'd just done my first job for Tommi and he introduced us. You'd just joined his team at the bank. We talked about rugby – you'd been signed by a premiership club after captaining the British Universities team.'

'Yeah, now I remember! You'd had a few games in the forces league, didn't know if you should stay playing back row or move into the centres if you transferred to a civilian club?'

'Yeah, you got it! That was me!'

They grinned at each other as recognition finally dawned on Ben.

'Sorry I didn't recognise you. I mean, the face is the same, but you've bulked up a bit since then. In a good way, I mean!' Ben thought to add.

'That's all from the last five years. Every day in the gym with that big unit.' He jerked a thumb in the direction of Cam, who remained stoic in the doorway, his back to them, looking out over the cliffs. 'So, what happened to the rugby, Ben?'

Ben shrugged. After all these years, still getting asked this question. He gave his stock answer;

'Had a couple of injuries. Rugby wages weren't much back then, not like nowadays. City salaries were better and there wasn't time to do the both.'

'Fair enough.'

'How did you start working for Tommi?' Ben was curious.

'Put in touch by a friend of a friend. Tommi Vladic knows *a lot* of people. He had a bit of an unpleasant situation that he needed specialist help with, so to speak.'

Ben nodded, not thinking that there would be any further explanation. Shorter One, he still couldn't remember his name, however, carried on talking.

'This is pretty much common knowledge these days anyway – so no big secret. Tommi's missus went back home to visit family. The political situation in their country was still pretty unstable back then, and there turned out to be a problem with her travel papers, visa or whatever and she couldn't get back out. Tommi's brother was some sort of local MP or whatever the equivalent is over there, and he tried to get it sorted, but as the political situation turned violent, an opposition MP got wind of it and it went bad very quickly. Word was that Tommi's wife's life was in danger.'

'Serious? I never heard any of this.'

Shorter One shrugged, like he was describing a routine job.

'Anyway, you've seen his missus right? It wasn't a nice thought – her being captured by some local militia or whatever. Fuck knows what would have happened to her before they finished it.' He retrieved his flask from his pocket and took another little sip. 'So' he continued 'we went in and got her.'

'You "went in and got her"?'

'I had a lot of experience in the area. So did a couple of my former team. One spoke the language. We knew our way around. No big deal, really.'

Ben found himself thinking about the hullaballoo and fanfare that Henleys Business Managers would create when they, say, advanced a new commercial mortgage for a nursing home or restaurant. Name splashed all over the *HenleyNews*. Self-nomination for the monthly *Diamond Awards*.

This guy went in to other countries and rescued peoples' wives. From death.

And then described it as *no big deal, really.*

Ben glanced over Cam's enormous left shoulder. The rain was easing, but only slightly. He looked back at Shorter One, who was sitting very still, eyes focussed on some indistinct point on the floor. He looked very relaxed, like he was just killing time, waiting for the weather to improve.

'Can I ask you something?' Ben enquired.

'Sure.' Shorter One looked up and blinked his eyes a few times, as if he'd been on the point of nodding off to sleep.

'Why don't you and Cam just take the cash to the bank yourselves? I mean, for the money they're paying, ten percent, you could…'

'It's illegal.'

'Pardon?'

'What Steve Scott was doing. What *you're* about to do. It's illegal.'

He'd confused Ben again. 'Sorry, no offence, but I didn't think you'd be too bothered by that sort of…'

'I've never broken a law in my life!' The steady gaze convinced Ben that he was being deadly serious. 'At least,' he conceded 'not a UK law at any rate.'

Despite his sincerity, Ben saw an immediate flaw in his claim.

'Breaking and entering? Scotty's house?'

'Afraid not.' Shorter One shook his head. Tommi arranged the necessary authority, in writing, to go in there – from Henleys' Corporate Lets department.'

Ben sat down on the box opposite Shorter One. He suddenly felt out of his depth, like he was having a conversation about a subject that he didn't understand. Actually, having a conversation where he didn't know what the subject of the conversation really was.

'Look, Ben, I don't judge people. I don't care why you're doing this. Maybe you're a greedy bastard, your judgement affected by the temptation of some quick cash. Maybe, as I'd quite like to hope is the case, Tommi called in a favour and you felt obliged. I don't know and in reality, I don't care. But what *I* do, my consulting work, is totally straight. It's a legitimate business. I have an accountant and everything.'

He could obviously see the bewilderment on Ben's face – and watched Ben's eyes being drawn to the shotgun.

'See, we've done a lot of different things over the years, for hundreds of clients, but it mostly comes down to glorified security work. Except we're one of the very best, so we can charge high rates. But it's all totally legal. In the last couple of years, we've been based here a lot, because it's gotten so ridiculously busy and we're pretty much full-time for Tommi, but we're not his *employees*. He contracts our company as, I suppose now I'm thinking about it, groundsmen – or maybe gamekeepers is a better description.

'We keep an eye on the place, make sure ramblers stick to the paths, campers stay off the land, that kind of thing, but the main part of it is making sure that the people coming here on business are left alone, no unwanted onlookers. That they find this hut safely and meet up with whoever they're meeting up with. I have no idea what goes on in here most of the time. And the things I do know about, nobody can prove I know about, 'cos I is just the gamekeeper, see, yezzzirrr I am. Sez so in my contract. Understand me now?'

'And the guns?' Ben's voice wavered. He felt a bit light-headed. With the realisation that some people were so much smarter than he was. He knew he was totally out of his depth.

'These? Just standard Berettas. All licensed and

completely legal for work on agricultural land. How's it looking out there?' Shorter One peered low, around Cam's legs. 'Good. Clearing now. We'll be underway before long. Keep an eye out for the storm later, though, the M4 can be treacherous when it unloads down here.'

Ben was really struggling to process the information he'd been presented with. He felt the need to try and clarify a couple of things before he had to leave.

'Who…who are all the people that have meetings all the way down here?'

Shorter One gave him a funny look. Like '*are you winding me up?'* mixed with '*how fucking stupid are you, boy?'*

'I don't know and I don't want to know. None of my business. We just get told when to come and open the place up. People bring stuff in by boat, others meet up with them, cash changes hands in here, I assume, then we lock up again. Often it happens the other way, stuff gets taken away. You should see some of the people that pass through – scare the shit out of me. Even Cam's wary of a couple of 'em.'

'But…' Ben was finally getting his head around what this little enterprise was all about, but Vladic's involvement in this kind of thing didn't ring true.

'…why is Tommi involved in this kind of thing? I appreciate your role in this, you've been shrewd enough to spot a legal gap in the market, for your services. But what Tommi's doing, it's so risky. He's so wealthy, why is he…'

'This is nothing to do with Tommi.' Shorter One was looking at Ben with such a look of contempt that

Ben could barely retain eye contact, but then his face relaxed and he gave a little, friendly, smile. 'Ben, you fuck this up and you're looking at what? Fourteen years in prison? Yet you have done no research *whatsoever* into what you're getting involved with?'

'Well. I sort of took Tommi's word for it and…'

'The land here is Tommi's, but he lets it out. The Old Man I mentioned? He's the one that sets up all the deals. He's the tenant. Takes a big cut of everything that goes on here, pays rent back to Tommi. A fairly generous rent, I assume.'

Ben's confusion came back. Tenfold. He wasn't sure who he was even working for now – Vladic or the 'Old Man'. It wasn't a particularly nice feeling. He started wishing that this whole business could be over and done with, *asap*, as they liked to say in work.

'And the Old Man?' he asked.

'Only met him a few times – and never here, always in London, with Tommi. Posh hotels, all that stuff. Big guy, real nasty-looking old fucker. I think he's some kind of government minister in Tommi's country, some shit like that. Get the impression that Tommi doesn't exactly like him much, but he's the only person I've ever seen Tommi sucking up to, so, I don't know, must be some Eastern European shit going on between them.' He leant forward again, peering outside. 'Good, it's stopping. Let's go big fella!'

Ben stood up too, but as he did so, Cam suddenly turned around and stepped towards him. Ben didn't like the look of this at all. Ben stood still.

Then Cam smiled, reached out a giant palm of a hand, which grabbed Ben's hand in a sort of upside down handshake, then he gently bumped his right shoulder into Ben's, with surprising delicacy of touch. Still gripping Ben's hand in a friendly shake, he looked down and spoke.

'You *th*eem like a ni*th*e guy.' He had the quietest voice, with a soft lisp. 'You drive carefully, okay, get the cash there *th*afe *and th*ound. Good luck, buddy.' With that he spun around and headed outside.

'Christ, that's a first.' Shorter One muttered, at no one in particular.

Ben followed them out. The fresh air was welcome after the dank interior of the hut/vault.

Cam relocked the door then, without looking at or speaking to either Shorter One or Ben, headed back down the path towards their boat.

'All the best, then!' Shorter One offered a handshake. Which Ben ignored for the moment.

'You said you didn't care why I was doing this?' Ben said.

'That's right.'

'I'm not greedy. I agreed to it because I wanted the satisfaction of getting one over on Henleys management, or something like that. For what they've done to the bank, for how they treat people and...'

'I don't care.'

'I'm probably not even going to keep my ten per...'

'Ben. I wasn't saying it to make you feel better. I *genuinely* don't give a shit. I want to get back to the cottage for my dinner before the storm hits, okay? I'm doing a risotto.'

'Sorry. It's just. It's just that you knew me before I was...before I became...I just liked myself better back then, so…'

'I get it.' Shorter One smiled and grabbed Ben's hand to shake it. 'I'm not giving you a hug though, so fuck off. Like Cam said, just get it there *thafe and thound.* You can sort out your fucked up life later!'

With that, he bounded down the footpath and a few seconds later was out of sight.

34

'I think I'm having an asthma attack.' Willis collapsed against the side of the Volvo.

Despite the onshore wind and the fact that for most of the run there had been cooling rain, the inside of his clothes were drenched with perspiration.

'Seriously?' Macgregor leapt around to where he was slumped on the bonnet.

'Well, no' he admitted, 'but it was touch and go for the last quarter of a mile.'

'Don't joke about things like that. Hurry up and get in. Take that wet jacket off first.' She ran back around to the driver's side, unlocked the doors, threw her coat into the back, then jumped in and started the engine. Willis was still moving slowly but she decided to give him a bit of a break as he'd busted a gut on the run back to the car.

Eventually, he'd removed his coat, heaved it onto the back seat and sat in the car. She spun the wheels and managed to turn in the road in one movement, then floored it.

'The heating and climate control is really good in this car.' She reassured Willis. 'We'll dry out in no time.'

'How do we know he's going to head south?' Willis managed to wheeze in response.

'We don't. But he came in from the south, so I reckon it's better than fifty-fifty. There's nothing east of here and he can't go any further west without a boat, so…'

'Do you reckon we'll catch him up?'

'All depends how long he stayed in that hut. That shower was pretty heavy. I wouldn't have fancied driving back along the track in that rain, next to the cliffs. Maybe he sat it out.'

'We're guessing a lot of this, aren't we?'

'*We* aren't, *I* am! But yeah, we're going to need a bit of luck to find him. I'm wondering whether we just go flat out until, say, Swansea, park up on a bridge and see if we can spot him passing underneath. That will only work if we manage to get back to the motorway ahead of him, of course.'

She was gunning the engine hard, but Willis felt much safer than he thought he would have. She was very calm, just gazing ahead, eyes on the road, so to speak, making very economical movements with her hands on the wheel. They were covering the ground rapidly.

'Can you grab the road map, out of the glovebox? Make sure we're going shortest route back to the M4?' She asked him.

'Yeah, no problem.' A minute or so later he'd pinpointed where they were on the map – and held his finger over it. He'd check all the road signs and villages they passed through against the page, he told himself. 'You always drive like this?' He asked.

'Did a stint in Traffic. Went through all the courses.'

'We can take a left a little further along this road, it cuts a corner off the route – rather than having to go through the next town.'

'Nice one, cheers.' A few moments later she made the turn without lifting off the accelerator. The road widened out a touch and was less winding for a stretch ahead. She shifted in her seat and relaxed slightly.

As she settled into a rapid cruising pace, Willis turned to her.

'What do you reckon was going on back there?'

'Was thinking about that on the run back to the car.'

'Yeah?'

'Yep. Looked so strange didn't it? Guy waiting on the hill for two others to turn up in their little boat, then they all load something into the car. The way it happened though, it was like they weren't working together? Like the one guy was just meeting the other two?'

'Like a customer?

'Exactly. Or they were *his* customers. Those cases looked too big for cash, unless it was an absolute ton of it. I reckon he was collecting something.'

'Yeah!? Like what!?'

'Could be anything couldn't it? Use your imagination, Ryan!' She glanced across at him and smiled. 'See, what if we take a hypothetical scenario, as you banker types like to say. What if Vladic saw an opportunity, all them years ago, for money-laundering opportunities at Henleys Bank, 'cos their systems are ancient, they have no controls and checks and they pay their cashiers a pittance? But he's a smart guy? He realises that sooner or later all the drones will be running around doing little deals, taking all the risks by carrying the cash themselves. Vladic doesn't think like other people, he's an "outside the box kinda guy" right?'

'Yeah, so?'

'What if he does what he's best at? He's got loads of contacts, he's like some sort of champion networker. Handsome European, insanely glamorous wife, they probably throw amazing parties, meet all the right people?'

'He sounds that type of guy.'

'I bet those types also meet all the *wrong* people too? What have all the money-laundering markets got in common, whether it's narcotics, arms…people?'

'Err…products have to be imported or exported?'

'Very good – have a gold star, Ryan. So what if Vladic one day, during his brief tenure as a Debt Recovery Director, sees some repossessed land coming up for sale? It's a desolate bit of real estate, out on the arse end of Wales, sticking out into the Irish Sea, no use for farming any longer, so he signs off on it being sold at a rock bottom price, just enough to cover the bank's exposure, then arranges himself a loan to acquire it?'

'A cheap piece of land, no use to anyone except, possibly, someone who knows people who would appreciate a quiet way in and out of the country?'

'Exactly. You *are* a bright boy. There's no customs, no controls, no borders between here and London, Birmingham, Manchester, Glasgow, the biggest population centres in the country. With the contacts list that Vladic has, he knows he's sitting on a potential gold mine, if he manages the situation effectively. Not by direct involvement, he's way too clever for that, but by renting out land to people who need a sneaky, safe place to import and export. He could charge by the day, the month, annually, who knows? But I bet it would be a healthy sum – maybe this even explains his disproportionate wealth?'

'Hang on though.' Willis pondered over her theory. 'This is all just conjecture. For all you know, Vladic sold this place years ago, those three are nothing to do with him whatsoever and we've just witnessed someone buying two cases of…fertilizer or something.'

'*Yes*, Ryan, I am aware of the potential holes in my theory. But it all fits, doesn't it? Explains a lot of what we actually *do* know about Vladic. We suspect he's involved somehow in money-laundering activity, we find a record of land he acquired just prior to leaving Henleys Bank, we pay a visit to that land and we witness, what you must admit was, a very odd looking transaction.

'Besides, what would you be doing on an ordinary day at Henleys? Ticking back a list of entries on a computer printout?'

Willis looked down at the map and kept quiet. Aside from the cross-country running, and the shotguns, he was quite enjoying himself.

'How much petrol do we have?'

'Half a tank,' she replied, glancing down at the gauge, 'let's get to the motorway? We'll fill up there.'

35

The track had been turned treacherous by the rain and Ben had to pick his way very carefully back to the main road.

He still felt self-conscious. Embarrassed almost. He had got a little carried away with his own self-importance today. 'Expertly' arranging a sick day, driving a big powerful car across the country, doing a deal for Tommi Vladic, no less. Every inch the main man. Benny Taylor out in the big world.

When he'd met Shorter One and Cam in Scotty's kitchen, he'd been slightly intimidated, of course, but was of the general opinion that they were low-rent villains whilst he, himself, was a professional man. Someone who'd achieved something in life.

Now, it was clear that it was really the other way round. *They* pitied *him*, for being a greedy money launderer. They ran a successful, legal business. Not only that, but they did real work in a real world. Protecting people and property.

Ben recalled a time when a plumber had come round to his house to repair a leak under the sink. The guy had worked really fast, been polite, chatty and tidied up meticulously when he'd finished. Ben had given him a generous cash tip because he'd felt a bit sorry for him, having to work on pipes and drains all day. Later, he found out that the plumber was actually the owner of his own firm, employed six, and made pretty much double what Ben did in a year.

Today felt much worse. He'd made an arse of himself.

The fun was over. He wanted to get the cash back safe, pay it in first thing in the morning and be done with this whole business.

When he got to the A road heading east, he sped up as much as he dared. The rain was getting heavy again and the sky to the south was black with storm clouds. He'd have to stop for fuel at Pont Abraham and, allowing for rush hour traffic between Swansea and Bristol, he might just get home at a reasonable hour.

He tried to get as comfortable as possible, turned the heating up and settled in for the long haul back to Broadlands.

36

Sam sat, exhausted, at her kitchen table, sipping a well earned mug of tea.

The boys' flu was clearing a little but they'd been a handful all day and she was delighted when they'd both collapsed into a reasonably contented sleep on the sofa in front of the TV after an early supper. She covered them with their duvets and hoped they'd get a good couple of hours' sleep, at least.

Her tea didn't taste quite right, so she went back to the refrigerator to get an extra splash of milk.

Closing the fridge door after adding a more acceptable amount of semi-skimmed, she noticed an old photograph, poking out from under the kids' crappy drawings, dental appointment notes and other assorted junk. She put down her tea, adjusted some of the fridge magnets, then carefully, so as to not send everything crashing onto the floor tiles in a heap, eased the photo out.

She took it back to the kitchen table and sat down, sipping some more tea.

The photograph was taken two summers ago, when the boys had been very young. Her and her ex-husband had booked a trip to Disneyland for them. As it turned out though, in-between booking it and going on it, he'd decided to leave her for, and move in with, his PA, Amy Airhead. Amazingly, he'd also managed to convince the travel agent to refund the cost of *his* portion of the holiday. 'You'll be okay taking them on your own, surely!' He had rationalised.

She hadn't wanted to disappoint the boys, so decided to go ahead with the trip, but when Ben realised what was going on, he offered to pay for his own ticket to go with them and help out.

It had been the best holiday ever. And this had been probably her favourite ever photo. She couldn't believe she'd forgotten about it for so long. It was taken the day before they flew back. A photographer had taken a few shots of them and the kids, but when they picked up the prints later in the day, she saw he'd also taken one of just the two of them. He probably assumed they were a couple, which was, of course, entirely understandable.

They were sitting together on a low wall, or bench of some kind. The kids must have been just out of shot. Shame.

Her hair was longer back then. She thought that it made her look a lot younger. She had on her white vest, lime shorts and her nice sandals. Her legs were tanned and, crossed in front of her, they looked really slim. She had her arm in Ben's. He was sitting leaning forward, with his elbows on his knees, resting his thick, tanned arms on his legs. He had his old smile on. It was still her favourite photo, she decided. It was perfect.

She was going to talk to him properly when she went back to work. Probably next week now, given that the kids were unlikely to recover super-quick. She'd have to take holidays rather than *compassionate leave*, but what the hell, she deserved a break. But next week she'd talk to him. Apologise for the way she'd been acting. Tell him how she felt, all that sort of thing.

Probably not the full-length edit, actually. Not the version that went:

Been in love with you since the day we met at university, can't believe you're so stupid that you never noticed, only agreed to marry Scumbag 'cos you were getting really serious with Natasha and I thought I'd lost you. Didn't say anything after the divorce because I didn't want you to think you were second choice.

You were always first.

That might disconcert anyone. All in one hit, as it were. Bit too much of an *Information Dump*. Didn't want him to think she was some lunatic stalker.

She'd tell him though. Tell him that she thought they should, at least, *try* a relationship? Although she'd probably use different words. Better ones.

She'd think of some.

If all went well, then the rest of it, her undying love, her regret at marrying the wrong man, et cetera – that could *cascade* out, over time. As and when she decided he was ready for it. She picked up the photo again.

It had been a wonderful holiday.

37

Ben queued up to pay for his petrol. He'd filled the tank – which should be more than enough to get him home – and also decided to buy a bottle of water. He wasn't thirsty, but thought that he might be at some point over the next four or five hours – and didn't fancy stopping again.

The shop was busy, as was the forecourt. The roads had been getting busier for the last twenty minutes or so, as the rush hour traffic began streaming its way out of the towns and business parks along the route, heading for the M4.

He paid for his petrol and the water, then walked back out to the Subaru, unlocking the doors as he approached the driver's side door. The rain was now torrential beyond the canopy of the forecourt and Ben debated whether to go and take a longer break up at the cafe, where he'd 'enjoyed' a coffee and sandwich earlier in the day.

He started the car, pulled around the Vauxhall at the next pump in front of him and headed for the exit onto the roundabout.

As he manoeuvred around the Vauxhall, he heard a chorus of car horns going off behind him and he glanced in the mirrors. A dark blue Volvo was cutting out of the queue line and driving half up on the grass verge to get around the queue and cars waiting at the pumps.

People filling up were gesturing angrily at the driver.

‘Huh!’ thought Ben. ‘Driver must be too impatient to wait in line – going elsewhere for his fuel.’

He brought his attention back to driving – the roundabout was very busy and he needed to time it right to find a slot.

38

'What the hell's going on, Max?'

Willis had been studying the map while they waited for an available pump. It was shaken out of his hand as Macgregor suddenly accelerated and bumped the car up over the kerb, two wheels on the grass, so that she could drive around the pumps and out from the forecourt.

'Look!' She slammed the brakes on as she pulled up behind a car waiting to join the roundabout.

It was a black Subaru estate car.

'Shit! Is that *him*?'

Willis left the map on the floor and peered through the rain at the car in front as it found a gap in the traffic and filed in.

His heart rate soared as he heard Macgregor revving the nuts off the engine and start dropping the clutch. There was nowhere near enough time to pull out safely.

'No!' Willis screamed, closing his eyes as Macgregor went for it regardless. A white van was forced to take evasive action, its driver hitting the brakes and skidding inches in front of the Volvo's bonnet. Macgregor tried to pull around to the left, disregarding oncoming traffic behind her, but there wasn't enough room and she was forced to stop, budged up tight to the rear of the, now slightly sideways, van.

Which wasn't moving.

A few moments later Willis could see why. The driver was now out and inspecting the back of his vehicle, presumably to see whether there'd been any contact, which there hadn't. After glancing over the rear end of the van, he started to approach them, maybe to give Macgregor a piece of his mind.

Traffic was cannoning past Willis' left shoulder, the occasional car horn blaring. Headlights were flashing everywhere.

The van driver approached the car. Macgregor cracked down the window an inch or two.

'What the fuck you trying to do, luv? You fucking blind or…'

Macgregor retrieved her Met ID from her pocket and pressed it up against the glass, facing outwards. The van driver squinted at it as she spoke to him, quietly and precisely.

'Move your van. Now.'

'Fair enough, luv.' He broke into a broad, pleasant smile. 'Sorry to keep you waiting, like!'

He trotted back to his van and a few seconds later they were underway again.

Willis breathed the largest sigh of relief of his life.

'Max, we could have been killed. On a roundabout. In Wales. Do you think you could calm it down a bit? We don't even know if that's him yet.'

'It's him. Did you see the way that Subaru pulled away? Like a fucking Lotus or something.'

'So? It's a fast car.'

'It didn't *look* right though, did it? I think he spotted us.'

'What? The driver wasn't just trying to get onto a

busy roundabout? How would he even know our car? You're not wanting this so bad that you're seeing things that aren't there? Are you?'

'Bullshit.' Macgregor joined the motorway and cut straight across to the outside lane. A driver in a car behind hit the horn and flashed his main beams. She ignored it and accelerated as quickly as the car would allow to over ninety.

Willis didn't like this now. Whereas her driving from the coast to the service station had been very professional, very precise – she was now taking chances. It felt reckless, unsafe. Her face, previously composed, was now taut with tension.

'Max. Cool it down? We're going to catch up with that car any second. Slow down!'

'What if he went the other way, back west?'

'Well, then, it wasn't the same car. Okay?'

She didn't slow down. Forward visibility at this speed, in this heavy rain, was patchy at best, the wipers unable to clear the raindrops as fast as they were landing.

'Max!'

She glanced across at him, but didn't slow down. He kept his mouth shut and said a silent prayer.

After a couple of minutes of tearing up behind cars in the outside lane, flashing the lights and forcing her way past, Macgregor finally lifted her foot off the accelerator.

'There he is!' She eased her way back into the middle lane, slowing to just under seventy.

The deceleration was so pronounced that to Willis it felt almost like you could open the door and get out.

'You sure?' Willis decided to leave any further feedback on Max's driving until later.

'Looks like exactly the same car. Wish I'd got a better look at the registration plate at the farm, but it looks the same. Last year's model. Driver, no passengers.'

'Can't you just pull him over? Show him your ID? Ask him to show you the contents of his boot?'

'Unfortunately not, Ryan. I don't have blue lights on this car, and I'm not a uniformed traffic officer. So…err…n …'

'Alright! Only a suggestion. So what do we do, then, just follow him?'

'For the time being, yes.'

'Until when?'

'Until I think of something.'

'How much fuel do you have left?'

'Just under the quarter now.'

Willis thought, in silence, for a minute.

'You know what you should do, don't you?'

Macgregor allowed herself a smile. At least he was remaining enthused.

'I can't do anything, Ryan. I am a Financial Crime Agency official. I have to comply with rules and regulations. For the safety of myself and the public.'

'No. I mean, what you should do is – phone the police.'

'What?'

'Phone the police. Tell them who you are, say you're off duty, been away for a night with your boyfriend, or whatever, and you just got carved up on the Pont Abraham roundabout by some maniac in a tuned-up Subaru. Nearly caused an accident. Driver's being very reckless and you're worried about public safety.'

'But. But that's not true!'

'This doesn't feel a lot like the girl guides, Max! What does it matter? You just need someone to look in the boot of that car, don't you? Get it done, whatever it takes. Phone them!'

Macgregor drove in silence for a minute or so.

'You're a devious little bugger aren't you? That way, though, I wouldn't be breaking any rules, would I?' She paused for another short while. 'Tell you what, get my phone out of my coat for me?'

Willis reached into the back and retrieved Macgregor's phone.

'There should be a number in there for "Police Comms"?'

'Yeah, got it.'

Macgregor fumbled around and pulled some earphones from the pocket in her door.

'Can you plug those in for me, then dial Comms? Hold the phone up so I can speak into it?'

Willis followed her instructions and she put one of the earplugs in. The phone line connected.

'Hi, this is DI Macgregor of the Met. I'm seconded to the FCA and am presently off duty. Can I speak to someone about a traffic situation on the M4 in south Wales, please?'

There was a pause of a few seconds, then Macgregor repeated what she'd just said, along with her police ID number. Then Willis heard her start talking to someone:

Off duty...noticed a suspicious vehicle...driving recklessly...western end of the M4...heading east...black Subaru estate...we're in a blue Volvo...

Willis watched as she appeared to be listening to some instruction.

'Okay, understood, thanks. Oh, just one other thing. There is a possibility that the driver could be in possession of a firearm.'

39

The vehicle that had been tearing up the fast lane behind him had suddenly dropped in to the middle lane and slowed down. He couldn't see exactly where it was, his mirrors were ablaze with headlights and the fast car had blended in.

It was odd, perhaps, but nothing to be concerned about. Ben looked at the speedometer. He'd been travelling at less than seventy since he joined the M4.

Something kept nagging at him though. Carrying the volume of cash that he was, he told himself that these were natural concerns – nothing to panic about – this was just unfamiliar work, he was bound to be a bit jumpy.

But. That car at the petrol pumps, mounting the kerb, and now this one looking, almost, like it was trying to catch up with him.

Then he thought, *same car*?

He slowed slightly and moved across into the inside lane, into a line of traffic. His speed dropped to sixty. A set of headlights loomed up in his wing mirror, before slowing.

Still, could be nothing, he told himself. The motorway was busy. Plenty of vehicles would be travelling at a similar speed.

Nevertheless. His mouth felt very dry all of a sudden.

He was glad he'd bought the water.

40

'Shit. I think he's spotted us.'

Macgregor slowed for a few seconds, then decided against it and accelerated again. Willis saw the Subaru in the inside lane as they overtook. The rain was too heavy and it was too dark now to get any meaningful sort of look at the driver.

'What do we do now?'

'Just stay ahead of him. Hope he doesn't turn off. Wait for Traffic to find us.'

'When will that be?'

She just shrugged. Her eyes remained on the road. 'Just have to keep an eye out for them. Shouldn't be too long.'

'What will they do?'

'Put the blue lights on. Invite him to pull over onto the hard shoulder.'

'Max?'

'Yeah?'

'What if that isn't him?'

She pondered the question for a long time. They'd covered at least a mile before she answered.

'If it isn't him, I'm going to look like an idiot. We'll probably just drive off, okay? Wait for the call to Greenwood's office in the morning, eh?' She laughed, but Willis noticed a real tension in her voice that hadn't been there before.

'I'm sure it is the same bloke, Max.' It sounded so

lame when Willis said it that it didn't convince either of them.

41

Ben was relieved when the Volvo drove past, but he remained uneasy. It was too much of a coincidence to see the same type of car, jumping the petrol queue at Pont Abraham and now hovering around him on the motorway.

If they *were* shadowing him, he had no idea who they could be. The police would just pull him over, wouldn't they? Were they working for someone involved in the deal, which seemed plausible, keeping an eye on things, or the authorities, which was more concerning, or neither?

He moved out and overtook a slow moving lorry, then accelerated until he saw the rear of the blue Volvo ahead.

Whether or not it was anything to do with him, it made him feel more comfortable keeping it in view.

42

'Well. I think we've established that he's the guy.' Macgregor nodded at the mirror. Willis turned in his seat to look through the back window, which was being cleared every few seconds by the rear wiper. 'He's following *us* now.'

'That's him?'

'Yeah, watch this.' Macgregor accelerated gently to seventy. The car behind seemed to be keeping pace with them.

When Macgregor then let the Volvo drift down to fifty-five – and the car behind stayed the same distance back, Willis was convinced.

'What's happening here, Max?'

'Honestly, Ryan? I have no idea. Not comfortable with this.'

'*You're* not comfortable, Bloody hell, Max, what if…'

Her phone rang, startling the pair of them.

'Answer it, answer it…' she instructed, fumbling to put the earpiece back in. 'Hold it up again so I can talk. Hi this is DI Macgreg…ANSWER IT!'

'Shit, sorry Max. There it goes.'

'Hi this is DI Macgregor. Yes, we're just ahead of it, approaching junction…forty-two. Okay… yes…understood…' She removed the earpiece.

'Well?' Willis asked.

'They're coming up behind us.'

Willis looked back over his shoulder and saw flashing blue lights in the distance. Then he looked over at Macgregor, who glanced at him with a somewhat nervous smile.

'Check your seatbelt is securely fastened, Ryan.'

43

He surprised himself by how decisive he was.

As soon as he glimpsed the blue lights, flashing some distance behind him, he pushed the accelerator to the carpet and pulled across into the middle lane. He knew what to expect, but when the rev counter hit four thousand rpm and the power was poured on, it was still disturbingly violent. The car seemed to squat down slightly, the tyres finding grip despite the standing water, then launched itself at the traffic ahead. Ben gripped the wheel as tight as he could, despite being fully aware that this probably made no difference whatsoever.

He managed to get the car up to over a hundred in a matter of a few short seconds, before having to slow for traffic ahead. Rather than wait for them to move over though, he held his breath and started weaving between cars. It was a terrifying and exhilarating thing to do Ben discovered, though it required intense concentration to avoid what would presumably be a serious impact if he misjudged the gaps and spaces. For a few minutes he progressed with this zigzag tactic, but when he looked in the mirrors again the blue lights appeared a lot closer. Presumably drivers were getting out of the way for them, facilitating a relatively rapid pursuit.

Ben eased off the power.

This wouldn't last more than another few minutes before they were right behind him. Totally unsure of whether or not it would work, he guided the Subaru to the inside, slow lane and accelerated again. Traffic here was lighter – the rush-hour commuters were all glued to the outer two lanes. It allowed Ben to blast the car along for reasonably long stretches. The downside was that when he did start bearing down on a vehicle in front, it was one that was travelling *very* slowly. Lorries mostly, with occasional slow cars, maybe with pensioners behind the steering wheels.

Ben decided that it was futile to keep trying to overtake at this speed. Sooner rather than later probably he was going to hit something. Hard.

So, he started undertaking. On the hard shoulder. It felt right, as it was immediately effective. He could maintain high levels of speed, well over a hundred, for long periods on the relatively quiet inside lane, then ease off slightly to drift around lorries, pensioners or whatever, on the inside. It became a fourth lane for him.

He looked in the mirrors again. The blue lights were still back there, but not closing at anything like the rate they had been previously. Encouraged, he started to think through his options. Staying on the motorway, with this weaving/hard shoulder strategy, was not attractive. The traffic would, most likely, stay busy all the way to Cardiff, another twenty miles. If he left the motorway, given the power of this car, he thought he may have chance of losing them, but he was very aware that he had no experience of evasive driving and it may test his abilities to beyond their very finite limits.

He swept past a small convoy of articulated lorries on the inside. They blasted their horns. The rain was still heavy though, thankfully, not getting any worse. By concentrating hard, sort of focussing his eyes into the far distance, Ben could get a reasonable view of the hard shoulder and inside lane ahead, as the wipers fought a constant battle with the water striking the windscreen. It was pretty intense going though, hard on the eyes.

Ben was coming to the conclusion that at some point, fairly soon, he may have to abandon the car.

There was no way he was going to outrun them long enough to slip away somewhere. If he left the motorway and went for A roads, he wouldn't know the route and their driving abilities would give them a massive advantage, despite the power of the Subaru. Abandoning the car and then finding alternative means of getting home was, regrettably, going to be the most likely means of success.

It was just a question of where.

Then it occurred to him.

HenleyWest was near the M4.

It was on a business park, north of Cardiff. He'd been there a couple of times, although he'd gone by train rather than by road.

If he could keep enough distance between himself and the police, he could abandon the car – maybe try and hide it in a car park or something, then grab the cases and try and make it to the Hub on foot. His *HenleyPass* would get him in. The Hubs were quietest in the evenings. He could stay in there until he figured out what to do. Maybe get a taxi to the train station. Although the cash cases were very obvious. They'd attract all sorts of unwanted attention. Public transport was not a particularly attractive option with this amount of cash in his possession.

Anyway, just get to the Hub. Worry about other things afterwards.

It wasn't much, but it had some components of a plan.

As he drafted back into the inside lane, the motorway crested a hill and there was suddenly an uninterrupted view across a wide valley.

The motorway fell away for maybe a mile or so, then swept up the other side, red tail lights and white headlights forming a long, snaking line into the distance. Ben remembered this section of motorway from his drive down this morning; the steepness of the valley sides made it very different to the motorways he was familiar with from around London and the South East. It also afforded him, as he started the descent towards the valley floor, a perfect, almost birds-eye view of the traffic that lay ahead. He could pick a line of least likely resistance. Pointless wasting time pondering, he thought, and swept the car to the outside lane, pushing the accelerator pedal all the way down. Gravity-assisted, the Subaru's speedometer needle was soon nudging a hundred and thirty. He passed the first cluster of traffic, then resumed his now perfected move of cannoning down the hard shoulder as the road flattened out at the bottom of the hill.

The blue lights were still there, behind him, but looked slightly further back now, up near the top of the valley.

Ben cleared the slower moving stuff then moved

back to the middle and outside lanes, needing nothing more than 'normal' overtaking to climb his way up the other side of the valley. The engine sounded like it was working a lot harder here, but he maintained a speed of just over a hundred and ten.

He looked in the mirrors. The blue lights were just starting to climb the hill. If they were still gaining on him, it wasn't very quickly.

A sense of satisfaction crept up on him. He'd been, quite clearly, out of his depth earlier today, and Shorter One had picked up on it, much to Ben's embarrassment. Now, he was in an equally unfamiliar, equally dangerous situation and he was coping. Thinking things through, working out his options, devising ways of getting through traffic quickly, formulating a plan. It was more intense and more satisfying than even the most demanding of *Henleys Workplace Aptitude and Problem-Solving Tests*.

Once out of the valley, the road levelled off for a few miles and Ben made solid progress. Then he passed a motorway junction and, in the blink of an eye, completely lost his nerve.

More police.

On the hard shoulder of the slip road, on Ben's left-hand side, blue lights flashing. They were already accelerating hard as Ben blasted past – and slotted in directly behind him, some distance back by the time they matched Ben's speed, but still much closer than the others.

There was no way he could get away from this one. It was matching his pace with apparent ease.

Ben started planning again, but the ideas didn't

find their way into his thoughts as smoothly as they had done earlier. Every few seconds his eyes were drawn to the blue lights in the mirrors.

He gradually slowed the Subaru to seventy and the police car following him, tucked in behind.

Within half a minute there was a mass of blue lights behind him as the others caught up.

The thought that Ben kept clinging to was that with other traffic still busy and all around them, they wouldn't try and force him off the road – but he wasn't sure how valid this assumption was.

They kept their distance for the time being, with one of the police cars on the right-hand side of him, in the outside lane, the others remaining behind. They were probably communicating with each other, Ben thought, planning this according to whatever rulebook they worked to.

The situation rolled along like this for some time. Much longer than Ben had anticipated. He started to get very apprehensive, uncertain of what they intended to do. The motorway was getting even more congested. Drivers, seeing the blue lights, were pulling in and slowing down, so the two inside lanes were getting crowded, the flow slowing to sixty.

The police car in the outside lane, behind and to Ben's right, started to accelerate and pull alongside.

Ben pushed his right foot down.

The outside lane was virtually empty as people had cleared a path, seeing the blue lights behind them. Ben was able to pull out and pick up his pace again, open a big gap, using the abundant power at his disposal, between him and the police cars, and keep his foot on the power for a long stretch.

Abandoning the car was definitely the best plan. The fact that he appeared to be able to accelerate much quicker than the police cars was to his advantage. It was probably his only one.

Ben kept the Subaru in the outside lane, although eventually he found himself catching up to traffic ahead and having to slow. He kept checking the mirror. The police cars started looming again.

This time, they didn't spend any time lining up behind. One car found a gap and went straight down the inside of him, then decelerated to match his speed, while another moved up to within inches of his rear window. If they managed to get a car around and in front of him, as seemed to be the strategy, then this wouldn't last much longer, Ben realised.

He accelerated, sending the Subaru surging clear of the police cars again, but he couldn't hold the power on for long before he started catching up to more cars, their drivers slow to react to what was happening immediately behind them.

His lack of driving ability started to frustrate him. He felt sure that, with a car as powerful as this, someone who knew what they were doing behind the wheel could get away.

The police were being much more aggressive, sticking much closer despite Ben's power advantage and closing the gap back down as soon as Ben had to lift off the accelerator pedal.

Out of the corner of his left eye, he saw more flashing lights. He glanced across and saw one of the police cars apparently taking a leaf out of his book and driving down the hard shoulder. A few moments later the car was threading its way through moving traffic, jockeying to find a position ahead of him. One police car was sitting behind him. Only an old Toyota 4x4 on his inside, its driver having nowhere to go, was, at the moment, preventing them from closing him in on three sides, the central reservation barrier doing the job on the fourth side.

He was, pretty much, out of ideas. As soon as a space opened up inside him, in the middle lane, they would close around him.

After another maybe half a minute, the Toyota pulled into the inside lane, its driver evidently finally realising that this police activity all around was directed at the black car alongside him.

A police BMW instantly filled the gap.

Ben dabbed the throttle, just to disrupt how easy their routine was becoming, but he didn't really have much space ahead and the police soon closed the gap again. If the third car got in tight ahead of him, then it was over, they would surely force him against the barrier and just grind this rolling block to a halt.

Something started playing in Ben's head. Over and over, like a brief sound sample, or whatever they're called, in a music track. Shorter One in the stone hut saying the words *'fourteen years in prison, fourteen years in prison'*. Over and over.

He decided that he was going to accelerate as hard as he could for as long as he could. He'd get some distance between him and the police cars, then hit the brakes, but stay against the central barrier. They might just not be expecting him to do that. Then he'd open the window, climb out, jump the barrier and run alongside it, back the opposite way, until there was a gap in the traffic. Then he'd cross over and head into the fields, or whatever was over there, beyond the motorway to the south. He'd have to leave the cases behind, of course, but at least he'd be giving himself half a chance of getting away.

He'd find a way into Cardiff, even if he had to walk it, and get a room for the night somewhere.

Then, if all this actually worked, he could worry about what the hell he was going to tell Vladic – or maybe he'd do a 'Scotty' and disappear. He could worry about that later.

He accelerated again, the Subaru's grip and power pulling him clear of the two BMWs, then aimed the car at…

It wasn't going to work. They'd anticipated this – the BMW that had gone along the hard shoulder was already sweeping across to block him. In a few moments the other two would catch up and they'd be surrounding him. He'd have to be out of the car and over the barrier seriously fast. He unbuckled his seat belt and opened the window, ready to climb out and run for it. The only comforting crumb of thought that he had left was that the police probably had health and safety guidelines precluding them from running down the fast lanes of motorways. He clung to this thought as he prepared to slam the brakes.

Then he saw it.

No time to think, he pulled the steering wheel hard left, managing to get just ahead of the accelerating BMW inside him, which, apparently caught unawares, moved in behind him, then shifted to the outside lane, as if to overtake. So, now, both BMWs were to his right, overtaking. The third, the one that had got ahead of him, was also in the outside lane, but some way ahead, maybe fifty yards. Another set of headlights was full on in his mirrors, although Ben didn't notice any flashing blue back there. Must be an unmarked car.

He didn't have time to analyse it in detail, he had to keep going left. Hands fighting with the wheel now, Ben finally found the limits of the Subaru's grip; as the back end started sliding out, Ben could feel the steering going light and the car no longer travelling in exactly the same direction as the wheels. His natural instinct was to brake, but something in him made him push the throttle. The car's slide didn't get any worse, although it wasn't straightening out at a rate that Ben thought would make this move successful. It was going to be very, very touch and go whether he'd make this turn.

Drivers behind had evidently, finally, identified the intended target of the police activity and were easing off their speed in lanes one and two, as Ben cut across in front of them. Some filtered through, in the centre lane, overtaking Ben as he slid into lane one, blocking his view of the police cars which appeared to still be travelling fast in lane three, a long way ahead now.

The car straightened out. But not in time to make it onto the off ramp at the Cardiff Gate junction without the rear offside wheel thudding, with sickening impact, into the barrier.

There was a deathly silence as the car rolled a few feet further, the engine stalling, then stopped. Ben looked out of his window. The blue lights of the three police cars were disappearing into the distance, either unaware of what he'd done or, Ben supposed more likely, heading to the next junction so they could come back along the other carriageway. He briefly pondered how long that would take them. Then he saw a set of brake lights illuminated on the hard shoulder, two or three hundred yards ahead. Presumably the unmarked car, as it had no blue lights on the roof.

Then he saw its reversing lights come on.

He turned the ignition key and restarted the Subaru. Got going again, ignoring the car horns and skidding sounds from behind as he forced his way along the off ramp. The rear end of the car was making some alarming clanking sounds and the ride felt all wrong. He limped the car up to the roundabout at the top of the slip road and allowed himself time for a quick inspection of the side of the car by opening the door and hanging himself as far out as he could. It didn't take a lot of inspection to establish that the problem was with the rear wheel – a quick glance confirmed that there wasn't a lot of it left.

He had to find somewhere to ditch the Subaru. Before that unmarked car caught up with him.

Despite the damage, the four-wheel drive, or rather three-wheel drive as it now was, gave Ben enough grip to pull away reasonably rapidly, if noisily, on to the roundabout, drive around and take the third exit of five, before the unmarked car, the Volvo that had first seen him at the petrol station in Pont Abraham in fact, arrived to see which way he'd gone.

44

‘Thank you Miss Fern, is there anything else I can help you with this evening?…Okay, thank you for calling Henleys Premier Banking. Goodbye.’

She couldn’t get into the swing of things at all, although she’d managed to avoid turning her phone off for extended breaks as she thought she may have to.

The calls were, thankfully, few and far between tonight. She wasn’t in the right frame of mind to listen to a stream of Premier customers pronouncing their ill-informed views on the Commercial Bank of China takeover, or regurgitating the advice that their ‘brokers’ were giving them, or how much bonus they’d made this month or any of the other nonsense that people with a little bit of wealth seemed to spout.

Once or twice a shift she’d get a call from one of the *seriously* wealthy customers – the millionaires. The sort of customer that this Premier, bend-over-backwards, *call-a-local-office-not-an-overseas-call-centre-twenty-four-hours-a-day* service was designed for. Almost without exception, they were the most down-to-earth, unassumingly polite people. They had no need or desire to create a fake image of importance.

It was the *area sales managers* and the like that you had to be careful with, getting impatient if you couldn’t tell them within five seconds, off the top of your head, if this month's commission had been credited to their account by *BlahdeBlah Selling Limited.*

Her head still felt numb. Not hurting exactly, just numb and sort of cold down the side where he'd struck her. Her eye was more of a concern, although the swelling had more or less subsided now, she noticed, checking it with her compact mirror. She'd applied a bit more make-up than usual and was fairly sure that no-one would notice. There were only half a dozen people on shift this evening, scattered around a department that in the daytime sometimes held fifty. There was no-one within thirty feet of her.

She looked at the 'goals and targets' whiteboard on the wall. Today's '*Quick Blitz'* product was home and contents cover. The sales tip underneath,scrawled in blue marker was '*ask every customer who they is using for H & C insurence.*'

Not tonight, Abi thought, I'm one of the top performers on cross-sales – one night just going through the motions is not going to bother anyone.

Melanie, one of her colleagues in the distance, was reading a book and Will looked like he was taking a quick nap. None of the phones were ringing.

Retrieving her budget planner from her top drawer, she did some financial tweaking, based on the assumption that she could get some support from the union and increase her hours, by just a few. If she saved hard – cut out every last bit of discretionary spending, she may be able to scrape the deposit to qualify for her own staff mortgage within a year. It *had* to be a staff mortgage – regular customer rate would make the monthly repayments unaffordable on a part time wage. And to get the staff rate you needed a qualifying deposit – it was a non-negotiable rule.

She was, though, basing the mortgage amount on the price of the most modest properties being constructed on the new development adjacent to *HenleyWest.* She hadn't factored in what would happen if prices went up over the next twelve months, or if they all sold out and she had to look elsewhere, nearer the city. Then she'd have fuel costs to allow for and…

…she dropped her pen down on the desk and rested her head in her hands, gently massaging her eyes. She'd give it five minutes then recalculate it again. There *had* to be some more savings she could make.

Abi thought again about her father. She'd been thinking about him, on and off, for most of the afternoon. Thinking about him always made her feel better.

She imagined what he would have done to Marc if he suspected that Marc had so much as even thought about hitting her. Her darling dad bending Marc's arm around behind his back, making him apologise for contemplating hurting his *Number One Girl*. Or bouncing his head off his desk, making him cry and…

'Good evening, welcome to Henleys Premier Banking. Abigail Smith speaking, how may I help you?'

45

'Which way?'

'What!?'

'Which way do you think he went?'

Macgregor commenced her second lap of the roundabout, debating which exit looked the most likely option.

'Which way do you think?' She repeated.

'To be honest, Max, I couldn't care less. I hope he's long gone.'

'Huh?' She slowed slightly, but kept her eyes on the exits that were flying past outside.

'What you just did, reversing down the hard shoulder like that? That was just idiotic.'

'Leave it out, will you?'

'Max, I'm asking you to calm down and pull over. You need to wait for the traffic officers to get here.'

'Don't be such a…'

'Max, I'm serious. There's no way we should have been so closely involved in that pursuit, and definitely no way you should have reversed down a motorway. You're probably in a lot of trouble as it is. Now, just cool it and park the car. The traffic officers will be here any minute.'

'They won't know I reversed. I'll tell them I just made the turn, like that Subaru did.'

'If you don't stop the car now then I will tell them myself. You're not thinking straight, you're letting things affect your judgment.'

She glared across at him for a moment, then lifted off the accelerator and let the Volvo slow. She pulled in on the side of the roundabout, out of the way of passing cars, and put her hazard warning lights on.

'Happy now?' Her tone suggested that *she* wasn't. She sat there, in silence, her body visibly trembling with pent up adrenalin and frustration.

Willis decided against further comment for the time being. At least she'd pulled over. He thought he was going to soil himself when she'd started reversing along the M4.

Her phone, still in his lap, started to ring and she snatched it from him, ripping the earpiece out before answering it.

'Macgregor…yeah, on the roundabout over the motorway…' she turned in her seat and looked out of Willis' side window. 'Yeah, I can see you. Okay…what? No, no, I didn't reverse, I made the turn.'

A minute or so later the police BMWs were pulling in, one behind them and two in front. Macgregor leapt from the Volvo and ran to the lead car, bending to speak to the driver through the window.

By the time she returned, she appeared to be slightly happier. More composed, anyway.

'Sergeant Jones, in the first car, is going to accompany us onto the business park.'

'What about the other two?'

'He said something about one going into the city. Think the other one's staying here in case he doubles back. Jones is going to speak to Traffic in Gwent too, in case he's back on the motorway and heading for the Severn Bridge.'

They followed the BMW onto the business park, exploring narrow roads between modern, brick and glass buildings. Every so often Macgregor would leave the lead car and they'd explore a side road on their own, where she'd start short, precise conversations with Willis. *'Where would you go if you were him?' 'Does that look like a good place to hide?'*

They looped around for a few laps, but it was clear that this site was big enough in the dark and in these weather conditions to hide an entire fleet of buses if you really wanted to.

After ten minutes, the BMW pulled over and Macgregor parked behind it, before jumping out and running over to have another word with Sergeant Jones. This time when she returned she wasn't stressed, happy, angry or visibly frustrated. She was just blank.

'They're calling it off.'

Willis tried to think of something supportive to say, but couldn't.

'Can't spare any more time.' She continued. 'Jones said they've already put out the call, and they'll keep an eye out, but there's been incidents all along the M4, because of the weather, so they've got to head back.'

'You want to do another few laps?' Willis suggested, in the absence of anything else to say.

'Do you mind?' She perked up slightly.

'Not at all.' Willis replied.

They moved off and Macgregor resumed picking her way, slower this time, through the business park.

'I was *so* sure we had him. If it hadn't been for the weather and that fucking thing he was driving! So frustrating. If the weather wasn't so bad we could have had air support too.'

'Have we been over there?' Willis pointed out another side road.

'Don't think so.' Macgregor turned left as suggested.

'Do you think he swapped cars or something? That he was always intending to leave the motorway here?' Willis was, after the unpleasantness of the motorway, starting to enjoy this whole process again.

'Who knows? Maybe.'

The road levelled out onto a plateau at the southern end of the business park. There was a view down to the city. The lights were just visible through the rain. Macgregor pulled to a stop alongside the kerb.

There was a silence and calm in the car now, that both of them welcomed.

'What do you reckon that is?' Macgregor pointed, semi-interested, at a large, sprawling building lit up in the dip, between them and the outskirts of the city.

'Probably *HenleyWest*, judging by the size of it.'

'Pardon?'

'*HenleyWest* is around here somewhere. That's probably it. I've been there a couple of times with audit work.'

'And you didn't think to mention this until now.'

'Why would I? I've been sort of distracted. What was I supposed to say in the middle of a car chase? "Oooh, you'll never guess, I think I did some work around here once."' He laughed at his own joke.

'Not that you once worked here, fool! That there's

a Henleys nearby. Henleys? The money launderers' favourite bank? Do you not think that's maybe where our friend in the Subaru has been heading? To drop off his cash?'

'You said you didn't think it was cash, you said he was probably carrying…'

'I've changed my mind.'

46

Ben finished wiping the last of the mud from his shoes with paper towels.

He'd managed to avoid getting too much on his trousers and coat, but gave them a wipe down too. Henleys Hubs were pretty generous with their toiletry budgets, so Ben treated himself to a thorough freshen up, even removing his shirt and doing as complete a job as possible of washing, using hot water in the washbasin. There was a hair gel dispenser too; they didn't have that particular luxury at *HenleyEast*, for whatever reason, so Ben also took advantage of that.

If the next part of his hastily conceived 'plan' was going to work, he had to blend in as an average Henleys employee, which of course he was, complete with photo ID around his neck. He couldn't give the appearance of someone who had just carried two heavy cases for half a mile in a rainstorm, hidden them in thick undergrowth before jumping over a fence into the car park. Which he also was.

He'd been to *HenleyWest* a couple of times for *HenleyWorkshop* courses. It had taken him a while to get his bearings, being on foot rather than having taken a taxi from the station, but after abandoning the Subaru he'd decided to head south, towards the lights of the city. Within half an hour he'd found some buildings that he recognised and managed to guide himself towards the Hub.

He was reasonably confident that the car was well hidden. He'd found an unlit road on the edge of the business park and jammed it in behind a completed but untenanted new unit, so as to be completely out of sight of the road. He'd also left all the doors and windows open, to allow as much rain as possible in, as well as wiping down the steering wheel, gear lever, controls, petrol cap etc. Whether his efforts would stand up to scrutiny by a forensic team he had no idea, but if he managed to make it through to the morning he was sure Vladic would have the car picked up anyway.

He was less confident about the cash cases. They were very close to the Henleys fence – they'd been way too heavy to be thrown over. It was highly unlikely that anyone would be wandering through some rough overgrown bushes on a business park of an evening in heavy rain, but nevertheless, leaving that amount of cash unattended, even for a short while, was disconcerting.

Ben wanted to get this part over and done with as soon as possible.

He checked his handiwork in the mirror. He didn't look *completely* squeaky clean, there was a hint of the dishevelled about his appearance, but it was passable. Evening shift was always pretty quiet. Days and nights (nights because of the enhanced pay for IT workers) were the busiest, so there shouldn't be too many people here.

He needed at least a few staff to be around though, or his plan wasn't going to work.

47

Macgregor waited while Willis spoke to the guard in his little hut at the barriers to the car park.

It didn't 'sit well' with her, relying on him like this, but she knew that his *HenleyID* could get them in much quicker than her police and/or FCA identification.

After a couple of minutes, he came back and jumped into the passenger seat. Moments later the barrier was raised.

'He says nothing has been in or out in the last hour.' Willis explained. 'He's also certain that he hasn't seen a black Subaru going by, only a few cars have been past all evening. He says we can have a look around anyway, though.'

Macgregor drove slowly around the car park, although it looked unlikely that it would achieve anything – it was a very peaceful, very quiet scene. After one lap of the grounds she started heading back to the exit.

'You want to go inside?' Willis asked. 'Freshen up and get a coffee?'

'Can we?' She slowed the car.

'Sure.' *HenleyID* cards will swipe you into any of the Hubs, apart from cash areas, obviously.

'Yeah, great. I'd love a cup of coffee.' She smiled at him.

48

Abi switched off her phone and stretched her back. It was time for her break.

She wandered down through the mostly deserted department to the first floor staffroom/employee lounge near the stairwell. She couldn't be bothered to go all the way down to the branded 'coffee shop' franchise on the ground floor. Besides, during evening shift, they only put on one member of staff, the rather soap-shy Olga, who struggled to produce a drinkable black coffee, let alone anything more adventurous like lattes or mochas. The coffee from the machine up here was a much safer bet.

There was someone standing by the machine, but he stepped aside as she walked over.

'Can't decide what to have,' he said. 'Please, after you.'

'Thanks.' Abi replied. He had a pleasant face, she found herself noticing. 'Are you new here?'

'Started here this week.' He held up his ID. She didn't pay it any attention. Staff drifted in and out of Hubs all the time. There were always new faces around.

She did notice something though. 'Have you been out in the rain?' She glanced him over. 'You look rather…damp.'

'Err…yeah…only went out for a quick cigarette, got caught in a downpour. Been *ages* drying off at the hand-dryer in the gents, haha.' He pointed at the coffee she'd chosen. 'Is that any good?'

'It's okay.' She motioned as if about to hand him the appropriate sachet but then, semi-consciously, started making it for him. 'So, what do you do here?'

'Me?'

'No, the other soggy chap standing behind you.'

He, almost, looked around.

'Ha. I'm training the Payments and Processing team on the new *Venture* system. I'm working late tonight, putting together tomorrow's sessions.'

'Oh. I've heard about that. Interesting.' She replied.

'Not really. It's insanely boring.'

She smiled.

'Boring, but all Hub staff have to learn it and sit an assessment before the end of the quarter.' He continued. 'Compulsory.'

'I know. I have to go on a *workshop* in a couple of weeks.' She sipped her coffee and handed him his.

'Thanks. You work in Premier?'

'Good guess.'

'Not really. It's on your ID.'

'Oh.' She felt herself blush. 'Yes, I do. I'm a Customer Service Adviser, a "*CSA*". At least that's my job title this week. Premier like to change them regularly, as you probably know.'

She glanced up at him. It felt good, bizarrely, to talk about work. Took her mind off things. As did his smile, she found herself thinking, rather to her own surprise.

'Look.' He said. 'Shouldn't do this obviously, but if you want I can go through some of the *Venture*

Assessment questions with you?'

'Why?' She eyed him with a degree of suspicion.

'Hey, you made me this delightful cup of coffee. It's the least I could do in return.'

This all felt a little odd to her, *but* if it made her assessment easier, then so what? Also, talking to this chap for a few minutes longer wasn't the most unappealing prospect. It would even count as work time, so she'd have another few minutes without having to answer the phones.

She led him back through the silent department to her desk.

'This is it, the nerve centre of Premier's entire worldwide operation – my desk.'

'You enjoy Premier Banking work?' He asked her, pulling up a chair.

She couldn't remember the last time anyone had shown an interest in what she did, as opposed to what her husband did, and she couldn't immediately think of an answer.

They looked at each other for a while, as she pondered her response. She found herself liking his face again, which slightly irritated her – she was never usually so easily distracted.

She also realised she needed to visit the ladies room.

'I'll be back in a minute, just off to powder my nose. Make yourself at home!'

Powder my nose! Make yourself at home!!! Honestly. *Pull yourself together,* she told herself as she used the toilet and then washed and freshened up. *You've been through a bit of emotional turmoil today and just because some nice looking man is chatting to you, there's no need to get all girly, for crying out loud. Any other day and you wouldn't be acting like this, so sort yourself out!*

She decided it would be acceptable, however, to let him run through the *Venture Assessment* answers before she sent him on his way.

Except when she got back to her desk he wasn't there.

Must have popped to the gents, she thought.

Then she noticed her chair had been pushed back and her top drawer was slightly open.

And her coat was on the wrong arm of the coat stand. She went straight to it, putting her hand into the inside pocket.

Her keys had gone.

49

'This coffee is *horrendous*.' Macgregor pushed her cup away from her.

'Mine too.' Willis concurred. He'd had his suspicions about the woman behind the counter in the coffee shop as soon as he saw the state of her uniform. Her coffee-making skills had proved to be as bad as her personal hygiene. 'I'll go and find a machine.'

'It's okay. Leave it. It's just nice to be taking a break from driving!' Macgregor yawned, stretched and rubbed her eyes.

'I'll drive the rest of the way back. If you like?' Willis offered.

'Thank you, Ryan.' Macgregor gave him a smile. 'That would be most kind of you.' She thought for a moment, then decided to continue. 'I'm sorry, by the way – for the way I was back there. I should never have put you in any danger like that. Very unprofessional of me.'

Willis shrugged. 'It's okay. The reversing thing was a bit wild. And I didn't like the near miss at the roundabout. The chase was terrifying and as for the cross-country run! Apart from that it's been a…'

'Ryan, I don't apologise very often. Don't make me regret it, okay?' She smiled again.

Willis was about to prolong the banter, enjoying her company, when her phone rang. They both had the same thought at the same time – that Traffic had found the Subaru.

'Macgregor speaking…oh …hi…' The excitement immediately evaporated from her voice 'I'm fine, how are you?'

Her tone suggested to Willis that this was a personal call. He gestured to her that he'd get some coffees and she smiled and nodded.

He wandered off to find a machine, eventually discovering one halfway along a side corridor, outside a conference room. As he placed the first sachet in its slot, he found himself wondering who was calling Macgregor at this time of the evening. She'd not mentioned a boyfriend. There'd been a tenderness and familiarity in her voice though. Maybe Greenwood? Checking up on her? He was a rugged sort of bloke, good at his job. Perhaps he and Max had a thing going?

He was surprised by how interested he found himself becoming in her personal circumstances. Forget about things like that, he told himself – she's an absolute nightmare.

'Who was that? Greenwood?' He asked her as soon as he brought the coffees back to the cafe.

'No. My mum.'

'Oh.' Willis felt a sense of relief. Which bothered him.

'She worries if I've stayed out all night. Doesn't think I'll eat properly.'

Willis nearly choked on a mouthful of powdery latte.

'You still live at home?' He spluttered.

'So?' She suddenly sounded defensive. 'You know

what property prices are like. We're not all on *HenleyAudit* salaries, you know.'

'Sorry, I just…you don't seem the type that…and you were teasing me about the same thing, so…'

'Careful, boy. I'll kick your arse! Thanks for the coffee, by the way.'

'So, what's mummy doing for dinner tonight? She going to put something aside for you for a late supper?' He was chuckling so hard he could hardly get his words out.

'Casserole, if you must know.' She smiled.

'Mmmm. I love casserole. Can I come over too?' Willis was not going to let this drop.

'If you like.'

'But I *love* casser…can I? *Really?'*

'If you like. Mum won't mind. I have men staying over all the time.'

'Oh. I…' He suddenly looked taken aback.

'Joking!' Blimey, she thought. *Shouldn't banter with the best if you're so sensitive, my boy!*

'Oh!' Willis saw the funny side.

'It's going to be past midnight by the time we get back though. I might leave the casserole until tomorrow. Unless, you know, you fancied something else?'

'Tomorrow?'

'Yes.'

'Sure. Whatever's she's making would be great.'

'We don't have to stay in, Ryan.'

'So, you mean, get something to eat. Out?'

'Yes, Ryan, I am asking if you want to *go…out …to…dinner.'*

'Yes – definitely. That would be lovely.'

She laughed and shook her head.

'Thanks for today, by the way.' She leaned across the table and kissed him, firmly but gently. Then stood up and grabbed her coat. 'Now, you offered to drive me home?'

50

'What's going on?'

He looked up from the second case that he was about to lift into the back of her Audi estate. She was standing at the side of the car, maybe ten feet away, near the driver's side door. In a position where he'd have to push her aside if he wanted to get in. He didn't know whether or not that was deliberate on her part.

She was shielding herself from the rain with a giant *HenleyGolf* umbrella – standard corporate promotional issue. She had a look on her face that wasn't quite upset or angry. She looked sad more than anything. It made him stop what he was doing.

'Just need to borrow this for a while.' He explained. He remained under the open rear door of the car. It was doing a reasonable job of keeping the rain off.

'I don't think so.' She shook her head. 'I'm calling security. And the police.'

'This is a *HenleysFleet Car*, according to this.' He pointed to the sticker on the open rear screen, above his head. 'I'm a Henleys manager. Not sure a Henleys manager borrowing a Henleys car is something security would be particularly interested in. The police definitely wouldn't.'

'We'll just have to see about that. Won't we?' She sounded confident – but didn't make a move back to the building.

'Look. I'll have it back here tomorrow. You've seen my ID, you know who I am. I'm asking, please, can I just borrow the car until tomorrow?'

She watched him for a few moments in silence.

'Your ID is probably fake.'

'You can check it if you like. ID me properly via the system. It's genuine, I swear. I am a Henleys Manager. I'm just not based here. I work in *HenleyEast*.'

There was another silence as they watched each other. Neither sure what the other was going to do, or say, next.

She looked at the case on the ground. Then up at him again.

'*HenleyEast*? I suppose I can guess what's in the cases, then. Bit of a reputation, your Hub has, if rumours are to be believed?'

Ben didn't want to lie to her. She looked very much like the sort of person you'd rather be nice to than lie to. So he stayed quiet.

'Look, I want no part of this, either way.' She said. 'Unload the car and give me the keys. I won't say anything about this to anyone. I don't need any hassle.'

Ben considered the alternatives. This was probably a very fair offer.

He lifted the one case back out of the car and clunked it back down on the ground, closed the rear door and walked over to hand her the keys.

'Well, it was nice meeting you.' He said.

She didn't take the keys from him immediately.

'What are you going to do?' She asked.

'No idea yet, actually. My initial thought is to go back in and try and do a better job of stealing someone else's keys.'

She almost smiled.

'You see.' He continued. 'This is all very new to me. I'm pretty much making it up as I go along.'

She watched him for a long time. Ben couldn't think of anything else to say, so just kept quiet, the keys still in his hand.

'Put those cases, or whatever they are, back in the car.' She eventually instructed him. 'Then come with me.'

Her voice carried such natural authority that Ben just complied – and was following her back into *HenleyWest* before he started worrying about where they were headed. Her relaxed demeanour, and the fact that she'd offered to leave him go, gave him some comfort, but still, this all felt a bit odd. He decided to clarify things.

'Where are we going?' He tried to make it sound like a light and cheerful enquiry.

'I'm going to my workstation.'

'Okay.' He couldn't immediately work through the implications of this.

On arrival back at her desk, she pulled across a chair for him to sit on, then logged on to her terminal.

'Full name?' Her fingers were poised over the keyboard.

He told her.

She then went on to ask him his date of birth, mother's maiden name, first school that he attended and several other ID questions, confirming each in turn against the Henleys database.

After a few minutes, she seemed satisfied, logged off and powered her terminal down, then grabbed her coat and bag.

'Come with me.'

They descended the stairs again, but instead of heading for the exit, she turned left and started down a wide corridor. At the end, she told him to wait where he was before disappearing through some double doors.

Ben was alone in the empty corridor.

He wondered if she was going to return with someone from security. He remained relatively unconcerned though. Henleys security officers tended to fall into two categories – the over-sixties and the over sixteen-stones. If she did, which seemed a little unlikely given her demeanour and the fact that she hadn't asked for her car keys back, he would head straight for the fire exit opposite, across the grass and car park and be out through the security barriers in her company Audi.

Maybe she'd left through another exit and was on her way home? That was plausible. She could easily have another set of keys in her bag or desk. It would be odd that she'd bothered to ID him first, but then this was a slightly unusual set of circumstances, and maybe she'd changed her mind as to whatever it was she had been planning.

He was just about to pop his head through the double doors when they were flung open and he saw her backing her way through, carrying something bulky in each hand.

'A little help would be nice?' She was clearly struggling.

'Sorry!' Ben held the door open and took one of the items, now revealed to be a baby-carrier, complete with small child inside it.

'Can you manage this one too?' She handed him an identical object, with a seemingly identical child.

Although an awkward shape, they felt a lot lighter than the cases he'd been lugging around earlier, so it wasn't too much of a burden.

She adjusted her coat and ran her fingers through her hair a little, then flashed him a very quick smile.

'Ready?'

Ben shrugged. He'd given up trying to figure out what the plan was, assuming that at some point in the near future she would update him accordingly.

They walked outside, back to the Audi and Ben helped her to buckle the baby-carriers into position in the back. They were obviously designer-fit for this car and snapped in very precisely, securely and quietly. The small children remained asleep. It looked a very pleasant place to take a nap, in amongst the leather and wood and sumptuous seats.

She got in the passenger side so Ben clambered into the luxurious driver's seat.

'Okay.' She said, once they'd both got themselves comfortable. 'I've been thinking. How far is *HenleyEast* from here? Two and a half, three hours?'

Ben nodded. 'About that, I'd say.'

'Are you going directly there, or to wherever it is you reside?'

'My house. But I live very close to it.

'Good. Now, I have a proposal for you.'

'Yes?'

'I've just seen your account. Your salary is a lot more generous than mine, and I assume that you're making a reasonable amount from this little venture that you now so obviously need my help with. So, if you pay me Henleys night rate, per hour, and cover the cost of fuel – then I'll take you there.'

'Right, okay, that's interesting' Ben pondered, 'although, wouldn't it just be easier to let me borrow the car? I'll pay you the same.'

'What if something happened to it?' She shook her head. 'What if you had an accident? The paperwork would be a *nightmare*. How would I explain it to the bank's insurers? Besides, it could look like I was involved in some way, providing you with a car. Fourteen years in prison for assisting money-laundering activity, you know?'

'Yeah, I know.'

'This way, if anything untoward does happen, I can say that a *HenleyEast* manager told me he'd missed his train and asked for a lift. It still sounds weird, but at least giving someone a lift isn't illegal. I can deny all knowledge of what's in the back. I'll say you must have bundled the cases in when I was struggling with the twins.'

Ben thought he saw some logic in this.

'Thought this through, haven't you?'

'Not just a pretty face, eh?' She laughed. 'Well, do we have a deal, Benjamin?'

'It's Ben.'

'That's not what your ID and staff file says.' She laughed again. 'Abigail Smith, pleased to meet you.' She held out her hand.

'It appears, Ms Smith, that in the absence of any

better alternatives, I should accept your kind offer.'

He shook her hand.

51

Macgregor and Willis approached the Severn Bridge, heading east.

They were enjoying spending time together, talking about anything and everything other than *HenleyAudit* and FCA work: films, TV, music, places they fancied going for dinner.

Macgregor was appreciating having someone else doing the driving; she was sprawled out in the passenger seat, boots off and feet up on the dashboard. It was very comfortable.

She was enjoying the drive so much that she wasn't even bothered when they had to slow down for a queue of traffic on the approach to the bridge.

'Must be for the tolls.' She suggested, leaning her head back and resting her eyes.

'Tolls are the other side. Might be a crash or something.'

'No matter. No rush.'

Willis smiled at this new and improved, relaxed version of the person he'd spent the last few days with.

They trundled along for a few minutes, not making much progress, regularly stopping as the queue inched its way onto the bridge.

Macgregor was nodding off to sleep.

'Hey. I bet that Subaru driver won't like it if he gets caught in this, eh?' Willis chuckled.

‘Huh?’ Macgregor stirred in her seat.

‘I bet that Subaru driver will get a bit frustrated if he’s caught in this, after belting all the way from west Wale…’

‘Go down the hard shoulder!’ She was wide awake again, sitting up, putting her boots back on.

‘What?’

‘You heard me. Down the hard shoulder, go! He could be in this traffic jam, ahead of us. Come on Willis, GO!’

‘But…’

He gave in. He was tired, hungry and had nothing left to argue with. So he gave in.

He forced his way across the hard shoulder, put his main beam headlights and his hazard warning lights on, before absolutely flooring it down the empty lane.

‘Fast enough?’ He asked her. His voice monotone as he hit seventy.

‘Yeah, just slow down a tad, though, eh? No need to be reckless.’

Halfway across the bridge they saw the problem. An articulated lorry was at a sideways angle, on its side, across two and a half lanes of the carriageway. Willis slowed the car to a stop, headlights and hazards still on.

There were several Traffic cars in attendance, and a fire engine. Two Traffic officers, in yellow fluorescent tabards, were guiding cars through on the hard shoulder, single file, around the obstacle. On seeing the Volvo parked there, apparently trying to jump the queue, one of the officers started striding over.

‘Max?’ Willis prompted her.

She reached into her pocket, opened the door and got out, waving her ID at the approaching officer.

'Can I have a quick word?' She shouted.

A minute later, Willis was parking the Volvo between the police cars on the far side of the lorry, next to the fire engine.

'He's okay with me standing with them as the cars pass through.' She pulled a borrowed fluorescent bib over her head and slipped her arms through. If I see the Subaru, they'll stop it. You stay here. Do not under *any circumstances* get out of this car, do you understand? It isn't safe. I'd be in a lot of trouble if anything happened to you.'

With that she was gone. Willis watched her run over and take up a position next to the two uniformed officers.

52

'Will they be alright?' Ben glanced into the back seat.

'Should be.' She nodded. 'They generally sleep right through the nights – and always sleep anytime they're in the car. I changed them before we left too, so they should be quite happy back there.'

'Well. There's plenty of services along the M4, so give us a shout if you need to stop and, you know, check stuff?'

'Check stuff?' She laughed. 'Good with children, are we?'

'Expert.'

The Audi was extremely luxurious, the front seats reminiscent of expensive armchairs. It was a world away from the car he'd been driving all day. It still had plenty of power, although without the savage, uncivilised delivery of the Subaru, and was much more pleasurable to drive, thanks in part to the semi-automatic transmission – you could just leave it in '*D*' and the car would do everything for you except stop and steer.

Abigail Smith had apparently made herself comfortable in the equally sumptuous passenger seat, her long legs curled up, sort of underneath herself, almost side-saddle style, half facing Ben.

'Can I ask you something?' Ben asked.

'Sure.' She was playing with a lock of her hair, looking out at the motorway ahead.

'You said you were a customer service advisor in Premier?'

'That's right. One of the very best!'

'I'm sure you are, but, and please take no offence at this, Henleys don't normally provide executive Audis to *anyone* in the Hubs. My boss at *HenleyEast* only gets a basic Beemer.'

'It's not mine.' She carried on playing with her hair, looking out at the traffic and the rain.

'No? Who's car are we actually borrowing here?'

'My husband's. He's the Director of Retail Ops, or Retail Operations Director, whatever it's called.'

Ben thought for a moment or two. Or five.

'Marc Smyth? You're Marc Smyth's wife?'

'Oh?' She stared straight ahead. 'You know him?' She asked, seemingly without much interest in whatever the answer would be.

'My boss's boss. Never met him.'

'You haven't missed much.' She mumbled, not really as a reply. Ben didn't quite catch it.

'Sorry?'

'Nothing.'

'I didn't pick up on the connection, I'm afraid. Your ID suggests you haven't adopted the revised spelling of your surname, with the "Y"?' Ben tried to make it sound like a joke, but then regretted it.

'No.' She didn't appear to take any offence.

'And the kids? Will they be using the "Y"?

'Absolutely NOT.'

He decided to leave it there.

'So, just to confirm, he's not going to be expecting you back any time soon then?'

'He's away. Preparing for the *Tomorrow's Bank*

Roadshows.'

Ben drove on in silence for a while. This sort of explained things. She *looked* like she could be a rich, career-man's wife. Maybe Smyth was a bit of an arsehole, played around, neglected her, whatever, that's why she was working evenings, dumping the kids off in the nursery, maybe spending her wages on booze and pills. That's why she'd jumped at the chance to earn some cash by taking him back home.

Whatever, it wasn't his problem – and she seemed calm enough at the moment. If it got him through the rest of tonight and enabled him to pay the money in tomorrow, then god bless the arsehole Smyth and his trophy, somehow strangely familiar-looking wife.

'Shall I put the radio on?' Ben nudged a couple of the buttons on the sound system, keen to relieve the silence.

She reached over and interrupted his fumbling – pressing the pre-set button that brought up Dragon FM, the local radio station.

'Thanks.' He said. 'We'll be crossing the Severn shortly, look.' He pointed at the bridge, illuminated in the distance. 'Be back at *HenleyEast* in no time.'

She didn't reply.

Ben gave up trying to make conversation. They'd be over the bridge soon, maybe she'd fall asleep.

Traffic was getting busier ahead. This was odd, as he thought that the motorway would be getting quieter at this time of the evening. Maybe it just always got busy at the bridge.

The Dragon FM broadcaster said the words '*a reminder to all those heading east on the M4 that they should use the old Severn crossing due to a serious accident on the second bridge'* at the exact moment that Ben drove the Audi past the turn off for the alternative M48 route.

'Sorry, too late!' He apologised to Abi, who remained silent in the adjacent seat. 'We may have a bit of a hold-up by the look of it.'

The queue ahead looked pretty slow-moving. It covered three lanes and was nose to tail, stretching into the distance. Ben couldn't see from here how long the tailback stretched. It looked like it covered at least half the bridge.

They joined the back of the queue and started inching their way forward with the rest of the traffic.

After ten minutes or so of ponderous progress, Ben found the silence starting to become oppressive.

'You still okay with this?' He asked her. 'If you're not comfortable with it then…'

'Are you still going to pay me?'

'Of course.'

'Then I'm comfortable with it.'

Another ten minutes of silence followed, during which Ben noticed something and debated whether or not to ask her about it. As the minutes crept by, he was unable to take his mind away from it. It became like an itch. He didn't want to scratch it but in the end, almost couldn't help himself.

'So, how often does the Retail Ops Director hit you?' He regretted asking it before the sentence had fully left his mouth, suddenly very aware of the fact that this was none of his business.

Her gaze snapped away from the road as if her head was mounted on a spring release.

'What *are* you talking about?'

Although Ben noticed that her eyes had briefly flashed with that look that indicates a woman is about to go ballistic, her response had been very calm and measured. She sounded, or was trying to sound, bored, rather than angry. As if his question was insignificant to her. Ben now agonised over whether to let this drop. In the end, he felt that he owed her an explanation as to why it was so obvious.

'You have fresh bruises on your arm and your wrist.'

She pulled her coat up around her, covering her arms that were exposed by her short-sleeved *HenleyBlouse*.

'And your eye is swollen.' He continued. 'Just a little. Maybe you should have used even more make-up.'

She instinctively put her hand up to her eye, although she was immediately aware that there was little point now that he'd seen it.

'I don't need a lot of make-up, *thank you*. What are you, anyway, a doctor? Thought you worked at *HenleyEast*?' She sounded as if she was trying to lay the sarcasm on thick.

'Used to play rugby. Saw a lot of bruises caused by knuckles. You look like you played a game today. Of course, I'd be really embarrassed if you tell me now that you're captain of the Cardiff Ladies Team.'

She allowed herself a little smile.

'I'm sorry.' He continued. 'This situation is just a bit weird for me. I was trying to make conversation. I'll shut up now. Why don't you take a nap? I'll wake you up when we get there.'

She looked across at him. Still with a blank sort of

expression on her face. Then she looked back at the road.

'I wasn't meaning to be rude. This isn't exactly a normal situation for me either and it's been a long day. I was tired and confused a bit, that's all. I wasn't expecting to be asked about the bruises. Didn't think they were that noticeable. He's never done anything like that before and if he ever tries it again I'll go to the police immediately. I'm not a "victim" and I don't need any *advice* or *support*. Not a lot more to add, okay? Now, tell me about *HenleyEast*. Is it the den of thieves and launderers that everyone says it is, Benjamin?'

He was glad she was talkative again. He started telling her about his job and the various 'characters' in the departments.

They were both surprised by how different *HenleyEast* and *HenleyWest* had become over the last few years. They were supposed to be clones of each other, as with *HenleyMid* and *HenleyNorth*, but the different Hub Managers had obviously tried to make their own mark on the centres that they managed, which sort of defeated the whole object of the system.

They both found it rather amusing, Henleys' middle management trying to carve their own niches in a completely regimented environment.

'Maybe something good will emerge from your husband's plan though?'

She stopped laughing. 'What plan?'

'The new information cascade – the plans for the Hubs. Recommendation to the Board and all that.'

'Marc doesn't tell me anything. Never discusses work at all. I don't know anything about any cascades,

I'm afraid.'

'Oh, well, sorry to be the one to break it to you, but this one's a real gem. They're proposing to…oh no! Oh no, please. Not now!'

'What? What's the matter?'

He was staring straight ahead.

At the police officers, in fluorescent bibs, that were controlling and guiding traffic into single file along the hard shoulder – around an overturned lorry.

More specifically, at the smallest one of the three who was walking down through the lines of cars and had already started to turn and wave at her colleagues to attract their attention.

Waving and pointing.

Pointing at the Audi.

Pointing at Ben.

53

She'd been on the point of giving up. She'd started walking down the lines of stationary traffic – the officers hadn't said she wasn't allowed to – in an effort to speed the process up, but there was no sign of any Subarus at all, let alone the big, black estate.

Then she'd started to think about what Willis had said about the driver swapping cars. If he was experienced at this kind of work, maybe it would be a sensible precaution. If you *were* going to drive from the South East, say, down to the far end of Wales and wanted to avoid being followed, then maybe you *would* use two cars. Take one about half way then swap over, and do the same on the way back. Maybe it was just coincidence that they'd caught up with him just as he needed to turn off. After all, if you were going to change cars somewhere, then a densely populated area was the place to do it – and he'd turned off at one of the Cardiff junctions.

So she started to walk back along the line of cars, not seeing much at first, but when she got back to the other two traffic officers, and after one of them had issued her with a bit of a bollocking for wandering off, she started paying more attention to the drivers than the cars. She focussed on the drivers of bigger vehicles, assuming that if there had been a swap, it would be for something of similar type and size to the Subaru.

A few minutes later, she saw the Audi.

She walked forward a few paces, peering through the rain. On one arc of the wipers she got a reasonably good look at him.

It was definitely a possibility.

She went closer and got herself a better view, then waved at the traffic officers, trying to attract their attention, so they would stop the flow and he would be held in line.

She was convinced that this was him. Same looks, same colouring, wearing a collar and coat. She wanted to speak to him.

Eventually after much waving and gesturing, one of the two officers at the overturned lorry stopped the cars from going through. It held the queue, preventing the Audi from going anywhere. There was no way he could barge past an overturned lorry – and the three lanes behind him were filled with cars.

She turned and started striding back to the Audi.

54

It was all over.

Even if he'd been on his own, he would have conceded defeat now. It was one thing to have a wild blast along a motorway, weaving in and out of traffic, but a step too far to try and force a way through police officers attending a serious accident.

And Abigail Smith/Smyth was with him, along with her sleeping kids. He should never have agreed to her accompanying him, he should have walked away from this at *HenleyWest* car park. What if she got into trouble for helping him? Even if she didn't, what would that arsehole of a husband do to her if he found out she'd been driving around with some bloke from another Hub? What if he hit her again? Really hurt her badly the next time?

It had all, suddenly, gone way too far.

He lowered the window as the small police officer approached the car. It was a woman, Ben could see, accounting for her lack of stature.

She held up her ID as she strode up to the car.

'Get out of the car and open the back.' She instructed.

'Of course, look, I can…'

'Just get out of the car please, sir.'

'Yes. I am. Just…'

'Will this take long, officer? The children are tired and we really need to get home.' Abi leaned across him and spoke to the policewoman.

Ben froze.

His hand remained on the door release lever but he didn’t open it.

The police woman also froze, her ID still held up in mid air.

55

Macgregor realised that she had no idea what to do next.

After a few seconds, she noticed that her ID was still in her outstretched hand, flapping uselessly as if attached to a paralysed limb.

What the *hell* was this *woman* doing here?

She'd been convinced that this was the guy. Okay, she hadn't got a great look at him from the ridge on the abandoned farm, when he was at the stone hut, but she would have *sworn* this was him.

She couldn't account for the appearance of the woman, though. The attractive woman that was resting her hand on his leg as she leaned across him. Obviously very comfortable in his company. This wasn't someone he'd just carjacked along the way.

And what had she just said about getting home to the children?

Macgregor was very aware of the gaze of the two traffic officers boring into the side of her head as she stood here in silence. Trying to evaluate the situation, ID waving about in the rain, getting nowhere.

'Officer?' The woman repeated, slightly impatiently. 'The children are exhausted. Will this take long? I want to get them home to their beds.'

The children are exhausted.

She wasn't talking about getting home *to* children, she was referring to children that were *here*?

Macgregor stepped across to the rear windows and peered in. At two bundles in their car-seat cots. She saw the face of the nearest one through the window. Looked deep in sleep. She saw its body rising and falling as it breathed in and out.

She felt the hairs on the back of her neck prickle and the blood rushing to her face. All she was suddenly concerned with was the traffic cops not noticing this and, more importantly, Willis not knowing about it.

He'd been so right it was embarrassing. The whole situation had got to her and she'd let it affect her judgement.

'Sorry.' She went back to the front window and spoke to the couple in the car. 'I'm sorry. Just a routine check. Apologies for the delay.'

She gestured to the traffic officers that they could start the line moving again.

Macgregor walked away from the line of cars towards the overturned lorry and leaned on the central barrier, ignoring the rain. She felt like crying. Maybe she'd been in the FCA too long. You couldn't get wound up over cases like this, to the point where you started interrogating families in estate cars, mistaking them for potential criminals.

Willis wasn't like this – he stayed calm and professional. That's what audit and FCA-type work required.

She didn't want to be the loose cannon in Greenwood's team any more.

She decided she'd take a few days off when she got back. Think about what she wanted to do, work-wise. Whether it was best to return to the Met or embrace a more composed, methodical method of working – to fit in with the FCA.

She'd talk it over with her new friend. He'd promised to take her to dinner. It would be something to talk about over pizza and beers.

Max took a deep breath and headed back around, relieved to see that the Audi had already passed through. She thanked the two police officers for their cooperation and was glad to see they either hadn't realised the significance of her discussion with the occupants of the estate car, or were too polite to mention it.

Then she returned to Willis in the Volvo.

'Anything?' He asked as she threw her drenched coat onto the back seat.

'Nothing.' She replied.

56

‘Oh, my god! Did you see what I did!’

She was bouncing in her seat, clapping her hands together in an excited frenzy.

She turned to look through the back window at the scene of her performance.

‘She was going to make you open the back! I asked if we could move it along because of the twins! She thought we were a family, Ben! She moved us on. I tricked her! Ben!’ She gripped his left arm in her two hands. So tightly that it hurt.

He couldn’t speak. He could hardly *see*. He’d been seconds away from giving himself up and then she’d just calmly talked her way through the situation. The proximity of what might now be happening if she hadn’t been with him was hard to rationalise in his head. It wasn’t a pleasant feeling.

Not *at all* pleasant.

He pulled over to the hard shoulder, stopped the car, found the hazard lights switch and put them on, got out and ran around the front, leaped over the barrier, trying to put some distance between him and the car, a few feet at least, so there was less chance she would see him as he vomited the contents of his stomach onto the grass.

It was five minutes before he felt well enough to return to the car. And he still felt rough when he pulled the Audi back onto the carriageway.

She appeared to be still wound so tight that he felt sure she'd barely noticed that he'd gone anywhere.

'Wow! That was *fantastic.* I haven't felt a rush like that since…well…ever.'

She picked up the conversation from where she'd left it.

'A *rush*?'

'Yes, you know, a rush, a buzz.'

'Yeah, it was a real *buzz*.'

She continued babbling about how much fun it had been for several minutes, slowly coming down off the high as the adrenalin subsided. She's going to be very tired shortly, hoped Ben. Maybe fall asleep.

She didn't though. She sort of just, gradually, regained a composed calm. Eventually, after looking in the back to check the twins were comfortable, she resumed her side-saddle position, playing with a lock of her hair and watching the road.

'Being sick in the bushes like that?' She had a contented look on her face. Very relaxed now. 'Do I assume that you were travel sick? Or that you are not exactly experienced in this money-laundering, err, profession? Is that the right word?'

'That obvious?'

'The throwing up did rather give it away. Also…' she peered across at him, '…you don't look the *type*. You just made a big mistake then, did you? Getting involved in this?'

Ben shook his head. 'I knew exactly what I was doing.'

The car was silent for a while.

'So…?' She eventually asked.

'What?'

'Are you going to tell me about it?'

'Why?'

'Well. It's either that, or a game of "I spy"? I suppose we *could* do some icebreakers, like on a *HenleyWorkshop* course? Career history? Hobbies? Something that nobody knows about you? Claims to fame, your dream holiday, your dream job, your favourite…?'

'Okay!'

She smiled again. Not just content, enjoying herself.

Ben told her, without mentioning any names, about Tommi Vladic. He told her about the Subaru that was provided and the long drive he'd been on, without being specific about the location.

Abi stayed quiet for a while.

'So, you're just a courier?'

'And, I suppose, a cashier. Paying the cash in. Placement of the funds, so to speak.'

'Why drive it all the way back to *HenleyEast*? Why not use a branch, or *HenleyWest* if you were going there anyway?'

'It's too much for a branch. They'd complete a report. And I only thought of going to *HenleyWest* five minutes before I made the turn off the motorway.'

'We could just go back and pay it through the cash centre?'

'Look a bit odd wouldn't it? *HenleyEast* manager's and a Premier Banker's staff numbers on a cash deposit in *HenleyWest*? Even *HenleyAudit*, understaffed as they are, may stumble across that one on an audit print. Besides your, and more importantly, my, staff numbers would have been all over it.'

'Didn't think of that. So, how *are* you doing it then?'

Ben thought for a moment, before deciding that there was no reason not to divulge at least some of the plan. It would keep the conversation going.

'Through a customer account.'

'Ah!' Abi sounded like she was figuring this out. 'You're one of a team. You have other people involved!'

'No and yes. Not part of a team. Other people *will* be involved. They just won't know about it. Hopefully.'

'Intriguing! So, if you…'

'Much of it going on at your Hub?'

'Pardon?'

'At *HenleyWest*? Have many staff been involved?'

'Oh, I…I mean you hear the rumours and…but we're a smaller Hub than yours, hasn't got the same reputation. Every so often, someone leaves without giving any notice and, you know, someone will see them a few days later in a new sports car – that sort of thing. There was one girl, fat, perma-tanned, suddenly seemed to be spending a lot more than usual, car, holidays, buying her parents extravagant gifts, then she left – without giving any notice. And *none* of it was going through her accounts so…'

'How do you know?'

'Had a look at them.'

'*Data Protection Act*, Abigail?'

Abi shrugged. Wrinkled her nose. Then continued.

'She claimed that she had some new wealthy boyfriend, supposed to have had his own business, nursing homes or something. But no one ever saw any evidence of him. Want to know my theory?'

'Okay.' He did, actually.

'She was sending money overseas for someone. Offshore accounts and the like.'

'That easy to do? In Premier?'

'Ridiculously easy. We're so short-staffed we have virtually no controls and checks on anything deemed to be *within acceptable risk-weighted parameters*.'

'Who decides what's acceptable?'

'Anyone's guess. Whoever it is, they've never worked in a Hub, so they've decided that we can send anything up to a million, under sole discretion, offshore.'

'*One* authorising official?'

'Exactly. I could do it myself. No second official required. To be fair, really huge amounts would be a bit risky – they could be spotted. But three or four hundred thousand? Cash or transfer, wouldn't matter. I could lose it, like that!' She clicked her fingers to emphasise the point. 'Undetectable.'

'Easy as?'

She nodded. 'Of course, I wouldn't, because *I'm* not going through a mid-career crisis and I don't owe any favours to wealthy former mentors from *back in the day*.' She said it with an upper class accent, making no attempt to hide the fact that she was teasing him.

‘Hey! Mid-career crisis? I’m barely into my thirties!’ Ben couldn’t successfully fake total indignation as her posh voice had made him laugh. ‘That accent suits you though.’ He said.

‘We all talked like this at Boarding School, donchya know?’

‘Boarding School?’

‘I lost my parents when I was young. I was passed around a few relatives’ houses before they decided that what little inheritance I had was best spent on my education.’

‘That must have been tough.’ It was all Ben could think to say.

She didn’t answer immediately.

‘It was at first. Then…I…You said you used to play rugby?’

‘What? Oh, yeah. Years ago, though.’

‘My dad used to play at college, I remember him telling me. He was a…blindman anchor?’

‘Blindside flanker?’

‘That’s it.’

‘Hard-man position.’

‘He was a pretty tough guy, from what I recall of things my mum told me. Were you any good, when you played?’

Ben had a think. The question was usually ‘*who did you play for?*’ or ‘*why did you give up?*’

‘I was okay, I suppose. I played for England Schools, the Universities team, got offered a professional contract.’

‘So why did you give up?’

Yep. There it was.

He had his stock answer ready.

'No money in the game back then, not like nowa…' It felt all wrong. He'd known Abi for an hour, yet he didn't want to give her stock answers. Didn't want to tell her things he told to others to fob them off and change the subject. This wasn't a performance management review meeting. 'Actually that's not it…'

There was a lengthy silence. After a long time, Abi asked him what he was going to say.

'I gave up because I started to get scared all the time.'

'Scared? Rugby player?' She laughed for a moment.

'Well, exactly.' Ben laughed too. 'That's why I couldn't go on. I enjoyed the games, liked the camaraderie. Absolutely *loved* the training and the tactics. Then, during a game at The Stoop, I got trapped underneath a pile-up of players and someone started stamping on me. I couldn't move and I couldn't free my hands to cover my head. From that point on, it was never the same. I couldn't handle being thrown and knocked around by blokes bigger than me. It started to become terrifying. Couldn't get over the helplessness you feel if you're pinned at the bottom of a ruck and someone's size fourteen is about to crash into your ribs, or somewhere worse. By the end I was having nightmares. Knew that I couldn't handle the professional leagues, so I quit. Money was good at Henleys in the City back then, so it wasn't too hard a decision.'

'No regrets then?'

'I regret that I wasn't tougher. I don't like having

to admit that…actually…I've never admitted that to anyone before, not even my dad.'

Ben waited for the wave of epiphanic joy to wash over him. The weight of ten years of denial suddenly lifted from his shoulders. But it didn't come – and he started to regret telling her. It felt indulgent, like a *self-help* thing. She'd just, calmly, saved him from an almost certain prison sentence, and now he was dumping personal issues on her. He'd known her for an hour. He wasn't even sure why he'd wanted to tell her – he could have made any old nonsense up – like he always did.

He resolved to keep his mouth shut on such matters for the remaining duration of this trip.

Ben concentrated on driving for a while, noticing the distance to the next services on the road sign and starting to calculate how long it would take to get home. If they turned off at Swindon and went through Oxford, rather than going round the M25 then it might be slightly shorter than if they…

'My husband raped me this morning.'

57

There was no emotion. No visible signs of stress, anger or loss of temper.

Her statement was just left hanging in the space between the two front seats of the Audi.

For what, to Ben, seemed like hours, but could have only been about a minute, because a mile or so further east on the M4, she started talking again.

'After I left school, I wanted to try working for a year or two, before I decided if university was for me. I took loads of jobs, usually two at a time, over the first year. Clothes shops, occasional customer service positions in the day – then I'd waitress or do bar work in the evenings. I used to save really hard, thinking I may be able to rent a place, then stay part-time if I went to college. After another year or so, I came across a scheme with Henleys Bank where you could work in their Hub centres and they'd include a corporate flat in the deal. It was supposed to be for graduates but they accepted me because I had good A-levels and a lot of experience of dealing with the public. The only condition was that I moved down to *HenleyWest* and continued my studies, but I wasn't bothered by that so I moved.

Anyway, after about six months, this new guy was transferred down to run our team. Some high flyer from London, so we were told. When he got there, all the girls liked him. All the divorcees, all the married ones too. He was nice looking, funny and really easy-going for an older chap. Then he got promoted to Centre Manager and he asked me out. He told me that he'd only taken the promotion because he didn't want to ask me out when he was my Team Leader. Which, at the time, I thought was a really cool thing to say.

'Not long after, I moved in with him and within a year we were married. It was the happiest time. He had to work longer hours, but I used to work overtime and wait for him, so I was really flush with cash too! Then after work we'd usually go out. Talk for hours then crash back at the house for a few hours sleep. On weekends we'd just have lie-ins and then go into town in the afternoons.'

She paused and looked out of the side window, into the darkness. Ben was very aware of the silence. He left it for a long time, but didn't want her to think that he felt awkward about this conversation. He'd offloaded his, rather trivial in comparison, issues onto her. He wanted her to know that it was okay for her to talk as much as she wanted.

'How long before he got promoted again?' He asked.

She slowly turned her head to look out through the windscreen again. She didn't look across at Ben, but resumed talking.

'Eighteen months, two years, something like that. He got an Associate Director job, covering the South West, branches and the like. They allowed him to base himself at *HenleyWest*, so it wasn't too bad in terms of travelling, and if anything I saw more of him because he didn't do any long hours. But he wasn't the same anymore. It was like, when he was a

'Manager' he was normal, but when he got the word 'Director' in his job title, he became a different person. I sometimes get embarrassed even thinking this, because it sounds so weird, but I'm not making it up.'

'I don't think you're making it up.'

'Then he got promoted to full Director and started spelling his name differently.'

'That's when you knew for sure?' Ben tried to make it sound light-hearted.

'Well, honestly!' She allowed herself a smile. 'And now he's had another promotion, to Level Ten or whatever the hell it is. I don't know him anymore. He doesn't even *look* the same, he's stuffing his face at corporate lunches, dinners at the golf club, freemason charity events. The sort of lifestyle the two of us used to make fun of.'

'Easy trap to fall into. If you crave that sort of life.'

'Re-spelling your name! Is that any easy trap to fall into?'

'Well, no. My opinion? No offence. That's just insane.'

'What were you saying earlier, about a *cascade* that he was involved with? With your boss?'

'Pardon?'

'When we were on the Bridge, before the roadblock. You said something about a cascade?'

'Oh, yeah. Forgot about that, in all the excitement. Your husband, and my boss, have put a *Phasedown* proposal to the Board. They want to close the Hubs within the next year.'

'What?'

‘Close the Hubs within a year. *HenleyWest* within six months.’

‘What…what about all the jobs?’

‘Well, if it works, which is not at all guaranteed - the work will get absorbed into other sites. Apart from cash handling which will be outsourced.’

‘Why propose this now? Because of the Chinese bank thing?’

‘That, and other factors. You’ll do your head in trying to figure out why middle management submit some proposals up the line. In this instance, they’re probably trying to get the money laundering investigations postponed, because that isn’t going to look good on anyone, and they don’t want to be victims of the clean-up that the Chinese and the Bank of England are calling for.

Also they, and we’re talking about your husband and my boss here, think they may just get themselves a seat at a higher table after the government broker this takeover deal.

Something else to factor in, of course, is the possibility that my boss tossed a coin and your husband decided to go along for the hell of it. Such is the modern banking world, Abigail.’

‘This isn’t fair.’

‘I know. Thousands of people worrying about job security on top of…’

‘I meant it isn’t fair on *me*.’

‘Oh.’

‘He’s going to want to move back to London. The South East at least. I don’t want to go there with *him*. What am I supposed to do? I can’t get my own place yet. I can’t afford it. If *HenleyWest* closes I’ll lose my job. I've been saving for so long, I…'

'It'll work out, I'm sure. Maybe you…'

She suddenly slammed her fists down on the dash. So hard that it startled Ben and the steering wheel wobbled in his hands.

She remained bent over, her head in her hands, for a couple of miles. Ben thought it was best to let her have a cry uninterrupted.

After another couple of minutes he spoke, quietly.

'Abi, there's a service station coming up. Do you want to stop for a drink, or something?'

She slowly lifted her head up and sat upright in her seat. She looked very tired now, and still quite angry, but she hadn't been crying, Ben was somewhat relieved to notice.

'Yes. That would be really nice actually.' Her voice was also calm. Composed and quiet.

Ben pulled into the services. There was a space in the car park near the entrance, protected a little from the rain by a line of trees overhanging the tarmac.

'What would you like?'

'Just a black coffee, please.' She gave him a nice smile.

Ben walked across to the main building. It felt good to stretch his legs. He bought two black coffees from the shop and took them back.

Abi was waiting for him, leaning back against the front wing of the Audi, her coat wrapped tightly around her. She obviously fancied some fresh air too, thought Ben.

He handed her cup to her and leaned next to her against the wing, taking a sip of his coffee.

The trees provided reasonable cover from the weather. It was still cold and breezy, but only the occasional drops of rain were dripping through the branches onto them. It was just nice to be out of the car for a while. Ben had been driving, almost uninterrupted, for more than half a day.

'Ben?'

'Yes?'

'Don't think I'm being too cheeky or anything, but would there be any chance we could stay at your place tonight? I'm going to be too tired to drive back. It won't be safe. And the twins need to be set down properly somewhere.'

'No problem.'

She shifted across slightly and rested her head on his shoulder.

A few minutes later she passed her coffee cup from her right to her left hand and took his hand in hers, letting their fingers slip together.

They stayed there, like that, for a long time. Neither bothered saying anything.

Eventually the rain started to get heavier and the wind picked up, so they got back in the Audi and drove off.

Abigail fell asleep in the passenger seat.

58

'Ben. Wake up.'

His eyes opened but his head remained pressed against the cushion on his sofa. He was as tired as he could ever remember.

'Wake up.' She whispered again.

He looked up at her. She was sitting on the coffee table, watching him. She had her *HenleyWear* trousers on but had evidently explored his airing cupboard and was wearing an old, short-sleeved jersey, with the collar turned up. Even three sizes too baggy, it looked a lot better on her than it ever had on him, he thought. Her long, slender arms were resting across her legs. She made no attempt to hide the bruises now.

Ben sat up. She didn't move to make any room, so he had to place his legs, one either side of her knees, to accommodate the two of them in the space between sofa and table. He was glad he'd remembered to leave his underwear on. But she was too polite, or too uninterested, to glance down. She kept her eyes on his.

He was about to reach out and hold her hands, when she gently took his in hers. She smiled a little. Their faces were quite close. She smelled lovely. He dreaded to think how rough his breath was, not having brushed his teeth yet, so committed to keeping his mouth closed.

He wasn't sure if she was closing the gap between

them, or whether he was, or both. Neither were trying to stop it though.

Eventually, they were at the point where there was virtually no space left between his face and hers. He felt her soft breath on his face. He closed his eyes. He could feel his chest rising and falling in time with his breathing, which was quickening slightly. He made sure he only breathed through his nose. Quietly. Their hands were still linked together and she was stroking her fingers back and forth through his, with tiny movements. His legs gently squeezed inwards against hers, and she didn't resist, just gripped his hands ever so slightly tighter.

When, later, he thought back on this, he thought that he recalled his lips grazing hers for the briefest moment. But he wouldn't have sworn to it that it had actually happened.

'I have to go.' She whispered, after a long, long time. 'And so do you.'

There was, suddenly, a space between them again, although he held on to her hands. Knowing that this wasn't going to last much longer and trying to preserve the moment, even for a short time.

'Abi?'

'Yes, Ben?'

'You can stay here if you want.' He hadn't thought this through, at all, but wanted to say it anyway. 'You know, as friends, until you can sort out things at home. I don't want him to hit you again.'

She looked back at him with no discernible expression on her face.

'I can't. It would be so complicated. If I try and divorce him, then how would it look if I'd already moved in with a member of staff from another office? Just isn't practical.'

'One of the corporate lets, then? I know an empty one. You could transfer to *HenleyEast* and…' he tailed off, hearing the rather unpleasant desperation that had crept into his voice.

She didn't seem to mind though. She looked like she was thinking things through.

'Maybe. I don't know. I can't make a decision like this now. I had a plan, Ben, I had my heart set on one of the new-build houses near *HenleyWest*. It might still work. We don't know that the Hubs will definitely be closing yet. There's too much going on. I need some time to think about this.'

Ben smiled and gave her hands a gentle squeeze. There was nothing more he could add.

Their fingers separated. She stood and turned to start packing her bag.

'I'll get your cash.' He said.

'Don't you dare, I'm not taking any money off you, that was the best night out I've had in years!' She laughed. It made Ben smile.

'If you don't take it, I'll just credit it to your account, so…'

'Okay – I'll buy the twins something with it, if you're insisting, you fusspot!'

Ben helped her carry the twins out to the Audi in his garage. He'd parked his Volkswagen out on the road. He removed the cases from the back and pulled the car out onto the drive for her.

After she'd double-checked that she'd collected all her, and the twins', stuff, she came back out to the car. Ben held the door for her. Before she got in, she reached her arms over the top of the door for him to hold her hands – which he did, upside-down-style, fingers pointing to the sky.

'I'll phone you at work?' He asked.

She smiled and shook her head.

'I don't think that's a great idea. Not for the time being, if that's okay? I…I have so much to sort out and you're…I've never met anyone that I…and I don't know if it's real or because of the present circumstances…I've only known you a few hours…I might get tempted to take you up on that offer to move in here, and that would mess a lot of things up, for both of us. Understand me? I'll call you when things are sorted out?' She smiled in a way that convinced Ben to let the matter drop.

He nodded. She slipped her fingers from his.

'For what it's worth, whatever happens over the next few months, I'll be thinking about you.'

With that, she got in, closed the door and drove off.

Ben watched her go. He knew he didn't have much time to hang around, but he also found himself not particularly caring about what happened to the cash now.

He felt like taking the cases directly to Vladic and telling him to sort it out himself.

After returning to the house, having a shower and thinking it through, he realised the simplest, most straightforward thing would be to finish the job. Put this whole thing behind him.

He had a couple of people that he needed to speak to, and he needed some time at his desk.

By the end of the day, all being well, it would be over and done.

59

Macgregor gave him a smile, which he returned.

'What's this all about?' She asked him.

'Word is, there's a proposal been put to the Board to close the Hubs.'

'What's that got to do with us?'

'It means we're off the case. Well, off *this* case anyway, *Audit* will find something else for me to check.'

Macgregor gave him an excited, cheesy grin.

'That means no more helping *you* with ticking back audit lists!?' She was obviously less than distraught by this prospect. 'Maybe Greenwood will let me have a few days just focussing on Vladic before I have to go and start something new!' She seemed unable, or unwilling, to stop smiling.

They followed the bloke that had introduced himself as Greg Lamb (*you can call me 'Lamby'*) from the foyer of the *HenleyEast* centre, up some stairs and along a corridor, to Conference Suite '*Guinevere*', where there were already a dozen or so suited individuals sitting around a table. They saw Marc Smyth, the Ops Director they'd met in the City, at the far end, chomping down on a bacon sandwich while holding court with a couple of those sitting nearby. Macgregor vaguely recognised a couple of other people from the FCA; they nodded at each other as she walked past. They must be her colleagues that had been assigned to the other Hubs.

Willis and Macgregor took two of the remaining empty seats, about three-quarters of the way along. As they sat down she held his hand under the table, which made him laugh, so he pushed it away. He looked across and she poked her tongue at him, which started him laughing again, so he pretended to be having a coughing fit. *Oh, god, if she's going to be like this for the entire meeting*, he thought.

Just ignore her, he told himself, and kept his eyes focussed on the front of the room.

After a long few minutes, during which the Henleys people tried to look energised and the FCA people looked bored senseless, Marc Smyth stood and addressed the room.

'Thank you ladies and gentlemen, and Greg Lamb, haha, for taking the time out of your busy schedules to meet here today. I have some important information to cascade regarding the anti-money-laundering audit that is currently taking place.

Jon Greenwood sends his apologies – he has a meeting at the Bank of England this morning. I believe, for those of you here from the FCA, that Jon will be meeting with you tomorrow to cascade further information specific to your roles.

I believe we're also missing a couple of people from your team, Greg…what?…on the sick? Ben and Sam is it? Okay, no problem…we'll speak to them…or sack them for not turning up, haha, later.'

Willis started tuning in and out, rather than listen to the whole thing, which appeared to be a tedious mix of technical information and the announcement that the Hub investigations at *HenleyEast,*

HenleyWest, etc were being postponed while a *Phasedown* proposal was being reviewed by the Board. Smyth wasn't explicit with the detail, but Willis assumed that most people around the table would guess, if they cared, that it was some sort of closure plan.

Smyth advised them that he hadn't been told where the FCA analysts would be reassigned to, but that Greenwood would brief them on that tomorrow. *HenleyAudit* staff would also have a separate briefing, from their line management, about their new assignments.

Willis hoped that he and Max would get lucky, and get assigned, together, to a nice quiet group of branches somewhere, where they could take long pub lunches and go for relaxed drinks after work.

He surprised himself by this lack of ambition and a craving for a quiet life for a while.

After the presentation, he turned back to Max, who gave him another beaming smile.

'You gonna request we get assigned together?' she asked.

'I was, maybe, thinking the same thing.'

'I'm not so sure.' She shook her head. 'It's been fun, but I fancy a change and…'

'Funny.'

'Ryan?'

'What?'

'Any chance you could get me some printouts of the Vladic accounts and those other property entries?'

'You haven't asked Greenwood yet.'

'He'll be okay with it. Besides, I'm keeping it in

perspective from now on – priority caseload comes first. I'm going to be the consummate FCA professional! I've decided I'd like to stay with the Agency, rather than go back to the Met, so I need to keep Greenwood happy, stop being the naughty one. The Vladic thing is just a sideline from now on, in my own time. A hobby, if you will.'

'Wow. A whole new you!' Willis was impressed. 'Come on then, we'll find a nice quiet office somewhere and…'

'Mmm! Nice quiet office eh? Do the doors lock?'

'Max, you said you were going to be the consummate prof…'

'If they do, then I'm going to show you what hot-desking really means, my boy!'

'Maxine, really!' He protested. Enjoying it.

60

Ben sat at his desk, thinking things through for the third time.

It *could* be pretty straightforward. The weakness of it was that each stage of the process relied entirely on the preceding phase. If one didn't work, then the whole thing, the whole plan, would unravel.

And he'd have two point five million, in cash, still jammed between his company car and the back wall of his garage, so tight that the cases had buckled slightly, with no realistic means of getting rid of it.

And Vladic, or the 'Old Man' or whoever it turned out he was working for, wouldn't have completed their deal on time. Ben didn't want to think about the consequences of that. Maybe he'd have to follow Steve Scott's example and leave the country.

Worse-Case Scenario, as Henleys liked to say, was that he started the process and then, midway through, it faltered. That would leave him exposed to even the most rudimentary audit check. His name, or rather his staff number, but it amounted to the same thing, would jump out from every page of the audit print if he couldn't also work it that the account closed the same day.

Even with a completely successful plan, his staff number would still be on the final transaction. But he'd known that would be the case all along. There was nothing he could do about that – it was a risk he'd always known he'd have to take, relying on the shortcomings of an overstretched *HenleyAudit* team to ensure his payment instruction remained undiscovered amongst the hundreds of thousands that the *HenleyHubs* would process across the country today.

Five stages. Five steps to putting this all behind him and resuming a quiet life.

He'd run through it one more time, just to…

He changed his mind. He could run through it a hundred times and still have doubts. Time to just roll your sleeves up and get stuck in Benny, he told himself.

He picked up the handset on his desk phone and dialled.

61

She was at her desk in Milton Keynes branch, looking at the solitary appointment in her electronic diary for today, when her phone rang.

She was in two minds whether to answer it. Glen, the branch retail manager, had been pestering her for a couple of weeks, wanting to see her more often, getting a bit serious about their '*relationship*' as he called it. She was starting to feel a bit guilty, him having a wife and kids and that, and was in two minds whether to call the whole thing off.

She looked again at her diary. It was getting harder and harder to find new business. Maybe this, just maybe, was a new customer. Better answer it. If it was Glen she'd make some excuse and hang up.

'Good morning, Henleys Business Banking. Grace Millar speaking, how may I help you?'

It wasn't Glen, thank god, although it was only marginally better in that it was Ben Taylor from the Hub. She'd enjoyed the other night, Taylor used the *HenleyGym* a lot and still had his '*rugger muscles'* as one of her friends called them, but he wasn't much of a talker and, well, she wasn't in the mood for another casual fling right now. She'd let him down gently, though.

'Ya, hi Ben…ya, enjoyed it too…look, I was meaning to call…no, silly, I was…anyway…I'd love to meet up again but I've been seeing someone and

…pardon?…customer?…a new one?…deposit…ya, I can do that for your friend…need all the deposits I can get, haha…***HOW MUCH*?**'

Her hand was trembling as she picked up a pen to take some details. If Taylor wasn't bullshitting, and he wasn't that type, then this would wipe out her deposit-target shortfall in one go. It would mean an extra…she tried to do the mental arithmetic but then resorted to grabbing a calculator, Taylor could wait for a minute, an extra, oh my god, *five grand* on her quarterly bonus!

'Okay, Ben…Ben!…ya I have a pen…okay…ya that's fine, you can fax me the ID later, let's get the account open first so it shows on my figures for today …no I'll sign it off here and send you a fax with my signature and my staff number…you're sorting out the credit are you?…just don't mess it up eh!…ya, thanks Ben…hey, Ben, how about I bring a bottle of wine over to yours later to cele…oh, okay, another time, ya, no worries…'

She put the phone down.

Some corporate contact of Taylor's, a property company, had sold some land for development, or something. She wasn't interested in, and didn't understand, property stuff. Taylor had managed to persuade them to open an account with Henleys, and if they did a good job on this they would bring their main banking over to Henleys Bank too. 'Switchers' got big points towards her targets, so if they sorted this out she might get a big hit towards next quarter's figures.

Taylor said they were going to pay in via bank

transfer and a cash bonus, which seemed reasonable enough (she hadn't a clue really, but assumed that most property deals were done via bank transfer). So Taylor had asked her to sign off her account opening forms '*bank transfer OR cash*' – that would cover any scenario and not cause any hold ups.

That would be okay – Taylor was a smart bloke and knew how to do things properly.

He said he'd get the ID over to her later, but she wasn't actually that bothered. Henleys systems were so shit, she reminded herself, that it would count towards her target even if the account rejected.

Might even be easier that way, less paperwork to do later.

Five grand extra on her bonus! She felt a little retail therapy session would be appropriate.

She was glad, now, that she'd given Taylor the works.

62

She sat in her small security office, in *HenleyEast* Cash Centre. She was processing deposit entry information, a routine job but one which she enjoyed as she was a fast worker, keeping up with the flow without getting stressed, and she could listen to the radio all day long, which you couldn't do in any of the departments upstairs.

She was on her sixth or seventh entry of the morning, singing along to an old Take That song, when her phone rang.

'Good morning, *HenleyEast*. Helen Heplow speaking, how may I help you?'

'Helen,' it was Little Dave, on the front security desk. 'Ben Taylor is here from Payments and Processing, says he has an appointment to see you?'

'Sure Dave, send him down.'

Helen quickly checked her hair and make-up in her mirror, then put her packet of chocolate chip muffins away in her bottom drawer and turned the radio down.

She felt terrible that she hadn't taken Ben for a coffee, as she'd promised. But Jason and her had made up and were discussing whether he should move out after all. Jason was a bit of a drinker and lacked ambition, he'd probably be stuck on nights here in the Cash Centre for years, but he was pleasant enough and it was nice having someone there for the kids, since her husband, a Henleys Financial Advisor, had left her for some tart in his branch.

She cringed at the thought, but admitted to herself that probably the only reason that she'd ended up taking Ben home a couple of times was that he was one of those that was always in the *HenleyGym*, keeping himself firm and trim, and she and Jason hadn't done it for more than three months. Oh my god – embarra*ssing*!!! Still, Ben was a lovely boy. She'd let him down gently.

'Hi Ben!' She gave him a quick hug after releasing the security doors to let him through. 'Can I get you a drink, I have tea, coffee, hot chocolate?'

'Coffee would be lovely, thanks Helen.'

'I am so sorry that I didn't come up to see you. It's been so incredibly busy down here the last few days.' She explained as she brought the kettle back to the boil. 'We're twenty percent busier than this time last year, which is strange considering the Bank of England stats on cash usage in the economy as a whole.'

'Yeah?'

'I am *really* sorry though. About, you know, everything. I've really enjoyed spending some time with you and I really value our friendship.' She handed him his coffee. 'It's just that Jason may not be moving out as soon as we'd thought. We're…you know…'

'Trying to work things out?'

'Exactly.'

'I'm delighted for you. Really. I mean, I'm a bit gutted, obviously, but, it's for the best. For you and the kids and everything.'

'Ben, you are such a nice guy!' She reached over

and squeezed his thigh. 'Thanks for being so understanding.'

She watched him take a sip of his drink.

'While I'm here, can I ask a favour?' He asked.

'Of course, anything.'

'Well, it's not really for me, you know I wouldn't want to put anyone out.'

'Of course.'

'But I gave a new business lead to Grace Millar in Business Banking a while back, for an old contact of mine from the city. Well, Grace is not the sharpest tool in Henleys' box, as you've probably heard, and she's made a bit of a hash of it – forgot to open the account.'

'No! Silly cow.'

'I know! Anyway, the customer is going ballistic, threatening to go to Head Office, the Bank of England, the ombudsman, the whole works, and my name is going to get dragged into it. Don't need that kind of aggravation, Helen! And it's a bit unfair on Grace as, well, she can't help being a bit dim.'

'How can I help?'

'They need to pay in cash today, or they're going to kick up a hell of a stink. Grace can get the account opening confirmation to us by fax and will sign off a transaction confirmation.'

'No problem, Ben. How much is it?'

'Two point five. Company sold a property to some African footballer that's just landed in the country, or something.'

'No problem. I will definitely need Grace Millar's signature on it though, as it's over a million. Can't cut corners on things like that these days, Ben!'

‘Of course, I’ll bring it down as soon as I get it.’

‘How are they bringing it in?’

‘Personally delivered. Cash boxes. I was going to meet them out front and bring them around to the drop-off zone, if that’s okay?’

‘No prob. I’ll put your name in the system, that you’ll be calling at the security gates. What time?’

‘Err…probably next couple of hours?’

‘Fine. I’ll just specify a morning delivery. Show your ID to Big Dave on the outside gate, and drop the cases with Kev in Secure Bay Two. You know the way, don’t you?’

‘Yeah, I’ve been down there a few times.’

‘Okay, make sure the cases are closed but unlocked – and stick one of these…’ she retrieved two large, barcoded and reference-numbered, sticky labels from a roll on her desk, ‘…on each one. Do NOT forget to include a paying in slip with this,’ she handed him a cash deposit form, ‘or there’s a chance it could go astray and they take *days* to trace back.’

‘Understood.’ Ben stood up and placed his half-empty coffee cup on her desk. ‘Thanks Helen, I really appreciate this and…’

Helen glanced around then grabbed Ben and gave him a long, deep kiss.

‘I’m sorry Ben.’ She whispered. ‘I really wish things could have been different.’

He smiled, looked a bit sad, then left.

Poor Ben. She didn’t really wish things could have been different, but she felt so guilty for using him for physical contact that he deserved one last kiss. Just to make it a little easier on him.

He was such a nice guy.

63

Ben stuffed the stickers and forms into his inside pocket and headed back out past Little Dave on security.

After leaving the secure Cash Centre area, he turned left, back towards the corridor that ran to the main part of the Hub, then headed along it until he reached the central atrium.

From here it was up a flight of stairs and across to Payments and Processing. As he entered he bumped into Janet, the lady who was covering for Sam.

'There's a fax here for you, from Grace Millar.' Janet held it out for him.

'Thanks.' He took it from her.

'And Lamby's been around.' She advised him. 'Someone told him you were back in work and he came round looking for you. He said that, if you were in, you should have been in a cascade meeting this morning?'

'Oh? If you see him again, can you tell him I've had to pop home, I won't be long, just forgot my…prescription.'

'Okay. Don't think we'll see him again though, he's supposed to be spending the day with that Marc Smyth guy. They're *hot-desking* around the Hub for the day. Getting "out with the teams", or some nonsense.'

Ben smiled, then headed back to his desk, made sure his terminal was logged off, then grabbed his coat and keys.

He went back down to the atrium, out of the main doors, and broke into a run across the car park to the main gates.

64

Willis was printing out the Vladic information as they talked through the possibilities of where they could be reassigned.

They were still enjoying each others' company, laughing at the same things and even sharing some of their personal career 'aspirations'.

Macgregor got up from her seat in the small meeting room that Willis had arranged for them and wandered over to the coffee machine next to the window.

She absent-mindedly stared out as the coffee machine did its thing.

'Ryan?'

'Latte, please.'

'Ryan?'

'Just a latte.'

'RYAN!'

'What!?'

'I didn't tell you this earlier, but I stopped a car last night on the Severn Bridge. The driver looked like the guy from the farm. But he had his wife and kids with him, so I just let them go.'

'So?'

'So. Would you think it slightly odd if I told you that the same guy had just run across the car park?'

65

Ben opened his garage, went in, closed the door down behind him and then moved the car forward a couple of feet, unpinning the cases.

He retrieved them from the behind the car, made sure, somewhat nervously, that the cash was still in them, then closed the latches but left them unlocked. He completed the stickers and the credit slip as Helen had instructed. Stuck the stickers on the cases and attached the form.

They were too wide to both fit in the boot of the car. He had to put one along the backseat, which wasn't the most professional-looking arrangement, but he had no choice. He doubted that Kev at the Cash Centre, even if he did notice, would be too bothered.

The run up from the Hub, whilst quite exhilarating, had left him a bit dehydrated. It was probably sensible to use the toilet, freshen up and have a drink of water before he headed back to the Hub. There was still a lot to do.

After visiting his bathroom, he walked back down the stairs and down the hall into his kitchen at the front of the house. He ran some water from the tap, until it was cold, then filled a glass. This was sensible – he congratulated himself on his coolness and peace of mind. Take your time, make sure you're thinking everything through, be composed and professional. It's just like a normal workday, it's just payment processing, in a different format. A relatively modest amount, just cash rather than electronic transfer.

He sipped the water and looked out of his kitchen window at the close. He was getting quite used to enjoying the street during the day, when it was deserted. His thoughts started drifting to the salesmen and managers and team leaders that lived all around Broadlands.

Then he stopped daydreaming.

And stopped sipping the water.

There was a woman in a suit and a man in *HenleyWear* walking down his close, slowly, directly towards his house, looking around them, as if they weren't quite sure where they were.

Odd.

He took another sip of water and watched them, opening his kitchen blinds slightly to get a better look. Perhaps they had just been transferred to the Hub. Had gone for a walk to check out places to live, maybe? He felt sorry for them. If Smyth's plan came off they'd be moving out again before long.

He took another sip and watched them looking at all the houses as they gradually came closer to his.

It was strange, Ben thought, it was as if they weren't looking at the houses as such, but more at the cars *outside* the houses and almost peering *in* through windows, as if trying to see if anyone was home.

Pretty elaborate scam for would-be burglars, Ben thought, to dress like office workers out for a morning stroll. Wouldn't be surprised by anything these days, though.

He drank some more water and watched the woman, small and lean, turn herself through three hundred and sixty degrees in the middle of the street as she walked along, almost like she was making sure nothing was happening behind her.

It all looked very peculiar – she moved almost like you see trained people, army and police and whatever, on the TV, checking out an unfamiliar location. Except she wasn't wearing camouflage gear and carrying a gun. Maybe more police than army…police …

As she completed her turn, Ben saw her face.

He dropped the glass into the sink, shattering it, the remaining water splashing up over the sink and worktop.

He dropped himself to the floor.

Hopefully, in time to get out of sight.

66

'Are you sure he came this way?'

'No. You asked me what I *thought*, not what I was sure of.'

'Shit, this entire fucking estate looks exactly the same! What sort of people live in a place like this?'

'Half of the *HenleyEast* staff. They probably refer to it as a development. Rather than an *estate*.'

'Depressing.'

'What are you going to do now, eh? Start knocking on doors?' Willis was wheezing badly after the sprint up the hill.

'Maybe I will, *AsthmaBoy*! Just to embarrass *you*.' She gave him her best smile. This was fun. 'Can you believe it though? What are the fucking odds?'

'You sure it was the same guy?'

'Definitely. And now I'm certain it was him at the farm too. He moved the same, like…like…'

'Like what?'

'Can't explain it. You know when you watch sport on TV? Footballers or athletes or something? Even when they are just walking, they look balanced, strong, like it would be difficult to knock them down?'

'What?'

'Yeah. He looked like that. It was him. I'd swear.'

'We're looking for a sportsman who's difficult to knock down? This makes no sense. Besides, how are we going to arrest him, if he makes a run for it, if you can't knock him down?'

'I've warned you before about your sarcasm!' She laughed. 'I just want to talk to him, that's all. See what the hell's going on here.'

'Yeah, well, there's nothing down here, it's a dead end.'

'Shite. Oh well, if he's Hub staff, I suppose he'll have to come back at some point. We'll just have to keep an eye out for him.'

She turned around outside the gravel garden of the last house and started walking back. She raised her arm, inviting Willis to take it, so he did, and they walked arm in arm back down the close.

'We could get a house on a development like this one day, Ryan?' She suggested, pointing around, estate agent-style, with her free hand.

'No way that you'd leave Mummy and Daddy!' He replied, pleased with himself at the speed of his response. She blushed, visibly, which pleased him more. He may be well behind on the scoreboard, but at least he was competing now.

67

Ben took a peek.

Over his sink, over the window sill and between the blinds.

They were walking away arm in arm, slowly, laughing and joking by the look of it, down the close.

It made no sense.

Was that really the same woman as from the Severn Bridge? Why would a policewoman from a hundred and fifty miles away be wandering around Broadlands, in a business suit? If that was the guy that he thought he'd recognised from *HenleyAudit*, why didn't they just knock on his door, if it was him that they were looking for?

Was he imagining the professional, movie-style search that he'd sworn he'd noticed a few moments earlier? Were they just two members of staff, house hunting?

Whatever it was, his nerves couldn't take much more of this. He wanted to get back to the Hub and finish this as soon as possible.

He'd watch them leave the close, leave it ten minutes in case there was actually more to this than met the eye, then drive the long way round back to *HenleyEast*.

Even if they had been looking for him, they hadn't seen what type of car he had. It was still in the garage.

He started to clear up the glass from the sink, but

then decided to leave it. That wasn't really a priority at the moment. He used the bathroom again, and washed his face in an attempt to clear his head.

By the time he returned to the garage, he was feeling a bit more composed.

He raised the garage door slowly, crouching to look out as it lifted up.

Then he pulled the car out, went back to close the garage door, then eased the car out off the drive onto the close.

It was only a few minutes to the Hub, even going the long way around, so he took his time.

There was no sign of the Traffic Cop/Audit/Nothing To Do With Him couple as he drove around the northern side of Broadlands – as he'd anticipated. They would have taken the shortest route back, down the hill.

After passing the Best Western motel and the Prince of Wales pub, the one nobody ever went to, he saw *HenleyEast* at the bottom of the slope. This was the view from the 'other' side, so the first part of the complex that he arrived at was the Cash Centre's secure entrance.

'Hi, Dave.' He smiled at the security guard, through his open driver's side window. 'Helen Heplow's booked me an appointment.'

Big Dave just stared at him, then, apparently somewhat reluctantly, started checking through information displayed on his computer screen. Security staff and clerical/managerial staff never really saw eye to eye. On anything.

'Says on here that you're bringing in customers?' Big Dave said it in a tone that suggested, unless Ben went and found a couple of passengers from somewhere, he wouldn't be coming in.

'Just met with them at the Best Western for coffee. Believe me Dave, they weren't the type of people you'd want in a Henleys Cash Centre. Thought it best that I leave them there.'

'Christ!' Big Dave chortled. 'A Henleys manager that's security conscious! I've seen it all now.'

Then he raised the barriers.

For just the briefest moment, Ben thought he saw a glimpse of an expression on Big Dave's face that hinted he knew exactly what was going on here – but for minimum wage he couldn't be arsed to get involved.

Ben drove down through the Cash Centre area, found the lane that took you into Cash Bay Two, and followed it in.

Kev was having a cigarette next to the enormous steel cage that was his personal managerial responsibility. Seeing that it was most likely a Henleys car, and then noticing it was Ben Taylor driving it, he didn't bother stubbing out the cigarette. He pushed some buttons and the front gate of the cage rolled up, allowing Ben to drive in.

After the gate had closed behind him, Kev let himself in through a smaller, door-sized gate at the side.

'Awright, Ben?' He took a long drag of his cigarette. Ben got out of the car and started unloading the cashboxes from the car. Kev didn't help him.

'Not bad, son. Haven't seen you down the Lion in a while?'

'Nah.' Kev snorted some phlegm out of his nose

and spat it onto the concrete floor. 'We mostly go up the Prince now after work. Red Lion's full of tossers these days.' He took another drag of his cigarette.

'You're not wrong.' Ben placed the first cash box on the floor, then walked around to the boot.

'Word is you're bangin' the Hippo?' Kev grinned.

'Sorry to disappoint, Kev. *Helen* and I are just friends.' Ben started levering the second cash box out of the boot. His glance across at Kev for some help went unnoticed.

'Shame. I was well jealous. Fit as fuck she is. Some of the boys don't see it, but I like a curvy woman. Big thighs and arse and that.'

Ben stopped struggling with the cash box for a moment, pinched the top of his nose and then wiped his brow.

'Maybe I could put in a word for you, Kev?'

'Yeah?' He spat another gobful of phlegm on the ground and dragged the last millimetres of life out of his cigarette. Then started lighting another. 'Tell you what, she deserves better than that Jason she's living with. Lazy fucker he is. Don't appreciate her at all.'

Ben managed to get the second cash box out and rested it alongside the other on the ground.

'Check the stickers and forms for me will you, Kev? Don't need any errors on this one.'

Kev's demeanour changed.

He placed his fresh cigarette, carefully, on a handrail, took the forms from Ben and started running his gaze across them, in a bizarrely demonstrative manner, as if he was mimicking a robot or something. For a moment, Ben thought he was taking the piss, but then he tuned in to Kev's quiet murmuring;

'...six one twos complete...top boxes fine...second column fine...second portion complete' He glanced down at the stickers on the cashboxes *'...matching barcodes ...whoa, Ben!'*

'What? What's up Kev?'

'Missed out the sort code box here mate! You managers are shit at detail!' He chuckled, handed the form back to Ben, then retrieved his cigarette.

Ben let out a deep breath and completed the missing details in the box, before handing the forms back to Kev.

They each took a case, Kevin proving to be surprisingly strong for a bloke who must have been nine stones in weight when soaking wet, and passed them through a narrow, keypad-protected flap into which Kev input a code. It was almost like a baggage carousel at an airport that took the cases on a moving belt, to the next stage, to the secure, underground Counting House.

'Thanks, Kev.' Ben was about to turn and get back in the car when he thought of something. 'Kev?'

'What?'

'You know, you could apply for a job in Payments and Processing. Here or some other bank. Attention to detail and all that, you'd move up the grades, get better pay?'

'Fuckin' hell! Positive feedback? And to think, I nearly took a sicky today!'

'Just saying, Kev.'

'Nah. Appreciate it Ben, but, to be honest, can't stand the "strategic" wankers upstairs. *Cascade this ...get a flavour for that...running things up flagpoles into the blue sky...* rather be down here in, or near anyway, the fresh air, no fucker telling me what to do.'

'Don't blame you.' Ben smiled. 'I'll buy you a drink up at the Prince one night.'

'Yeah?' Kev smiled back. 'That'd be nice.' He coughed up another greeny and spat it onto the floor. Then took another drag of his cigarette.

68

'Listen!' Greg Lamb was losing patience. 'I don't understand what you're telling me and I don't understand what you want me to do about it, okay?'

'What we're telling you, is that one of your staff members is possibly involved in money-laundering activity.' Macgregor replied, trying, unsuccessfully, to keep her voice calm.

'That's hardly news though, is it? The whole reason you were here was because there are probably dozens of staff at it.'

'What Max is explaining,' Willis interjected, before Macgregor completely lost it, 'is that this isn't a case of taking a backhander to send a few electronic transfers or pay in some cash. This individual was at a possible money-laundering meeting yesterday in Wales.'

'Wales!?'

'Yes, Wales.' Willis, too, found himself getting frustrated by this guy now. 'Appears to be the same chap that we also saw on the Severn Bridge…'

'Severn Bri…?'

'Yes! And he has turned up, here, today.'

'This is fantasy. Aren't you two *not* supposed to even be here anymore? I thought you were being reassigned elsewhere.'

'Not until tomorrow.'

'Well, may I suggest that you take the rest of the

day off and go home. This is such far-fetched nonsense. Marc and I are trying to run a business here! Isn't that right, Marc?'

Marc Smyth sat in the corner of the conference room. He'd been listening with a fair degree of interest, smoothing his tie and taking it all in. He was in no particular rush to get back to the *hot-desking* route that Lamby had set up for the two of them. Lamby seemed to be sitting them next to all the old, ugly birds.

'What are you proposing to do?' He eventually asked.

'We need access to all departments, including cash, and we need to look at the staff files through the photo IDs.' Willis replied.

'I think we can accommodate that, don't you Lamby?'

Lamby looked a bit irritated, but said nothing.

'We'll arrange for the staff files to be sent down to the office that you are using.' Marc Smyth gave Macgregor his most accommodating smile.

Willis and Macgregor turned and left the room.

'Oh, just wondering!' Smyth called after them. They, somewhat reluctantly, returned. 'What does this chap look like?'

'Average.' Macgregor replied. 'I'll know him when I see him though.'

'Moves like someone with balance, who exercises.' Willis added, then smiled. 'Like a *sportsman*, apparently!'

Macgregor bundled him back out and they were gone.

'Why bother, Marc?' Lamby asked. 'That was the

biggest load of nonsense I've heard in ages. They're just a couple of stupid kids getting carried away with being given some scraps of responsibility.'

'So?' Marc smiled. 'No skin off our nose. If they waste a day pissing about chasing their tails then so what? However, if they *do* manage come up with something, then we can claim the credit for letting them investigate it.'

Lamby didn't buy it, but was prepared to let it drop.

'And,' Smyth continued, 'whatever else those two are – they certainly aren't stupid.'

'Not so sure.' Muttered Lamby. '*Someone who was in Wales yesterday?* How would they have managed that? Taken a sick day? Ha. Moves like a sportsman? What the hell does that even mean? It's bollocks.'

'Come on.' Smyth raised himself out of his seat. 'We have some high profile *hot-desking* to complete. See if you can find me a cute little temp to sit next to and…Lamby? What's wrong?'

Lamby was just staring straight ahead, ignoring him. His face had turned ashen.

'Lamby!'

Lamby's eyes slowly moved around towards Marc, but it was like he was just staring straight through him.

'Greg!'

'Not here yesterday? *Moves like a sportsman*?' He mumbled, then stared into space again.

'Greg! What the hell is wrong with you? Greg!' 'I just need to go and have a quick word with Willis and Macgregor.'

69

Ben dropped the car back at his house. He left it on the drive. There was no reason to bother with putting it back in the garage.

He went back in to the house and had another glass of water.

He was pleased with his morning's work. But it had been the easy part, in many respects. This afternoon he was going to put his staff number/name to something that, if the auditors stumbled across the sequence of apparently unrelated transactions that had led up to it, could result in him going to prison for fourteen years.

Ben needed a toilet break.

Heading back across the upstairs landing after freshening up, he heard a car heading fast up the close. Curious, he went into the front spare room and looked out of the window, before ducking back, quickly, out of sight.

The woman and the auditor were back, getting out of a car. Walking towards his house.

He descended his stairs, trying to move as quietly as possible, and slipped his shoes back on as someone knocked hard on the front door.

Ben went through the kitchen to the back door.

The woman, or the auditor, banged at the front door again.

Ben turned the key, slowly, in the back-door lock, eased the handle down, opened the door and slipped through, closing the door behind him. He debated for a moment whether to lock the door, but then decided against it, they might come round the back any second.

He sprinted to the end of his garden, then jumped up on the wooden fence between his and the garden of the house behind. He was pretty sure he'd never seen or heard any evidence of a dog back here, but couldn't be completely sure. He balanced on the top of the wooden boards, gauging the height of the drop on the other side and quickly running through in his head what he would say to anyone if he saw them. He'd claim some sort of domestic emergency, a water leak, and he was running to his friend's house to call a plumber. Awful, but he didn't have time to think of anything better so…

…his foot slipped on the wet fence, sliding from under him. He tried to grab the fence with his left hand, but didn't get it right, cutting his hand on the rough wood. He lurched forward, his right knee hitting the top of the fence. Then he fell.

His head was the first part of him to hit the ground.

70

'I've got some serious doubts over this, Max. You said he was in an Audi estate.' Willis pointed at the Volkswagen hatchback on the drive.

Macgregor shrugged and knocked the door for a third time.

'This Taylor guy is probably in bed with flu, that's why he isn't in work. You're getting a sick man out of his bed!' Willis continued. 'Just because Greg Lamb says he used to play professional rugby, years ago, doesn't mean that…'

'*That* car wasn't *there* earlier.' Macgregor gave up on knocking the door and turned to Willis.

'So?' He looked confused.

'That car wasn't there, when we were here earlier.'

'We were *here*?'

'We walked up this street, when we followed him from the Hub. I joked we could get a place together, remember?'

'You sure that was *here*? All these streets and houses look the same to me.'

'Definitely. There's a red Mini Cooper on the corner drive at the other end, a house halfway along has a Neighbourhood Watch sticker in the window and next door has oil stains on their driveway.'

'Fair enough. But this isn't an Audi.'

'That's not the point. It wasn't *there* earlier.'

'And?'

‘So, if he’s home, on the sick, why’s he driving around?’

‘To get a prescription?’

‘Then, where is he, now his car is back here?’

‘Well, maybe he…’ He tailed off. He couldn’t think of an answer to that one.

‘I’m going round the back.’ She announced.

Willis had come to the conclusion that it was too much hard work to debate this sort of thing with her. He followed her round through the side gate.

She walked around the side of the house, turned the corner, then walked up to the back door and banged on it.

Before Willis could object, she’d tried the handle, discovered it open, and went in.

‘Max!’ Too late.

‘Ben? Ben Taylor! Are you here?’ She was calling.

‘Max, what are you doing?’ Willis stayed in the doorway.

‘Seeing if he’s here, what does it look like I’m doing? Ben!’

‘Well it doesn’t look like he is. Come on, let’s get out of here.’

‘I’m just going to check.’ Macgregor slipped her shoes off and walked through the kitchen into the house.

Willis stayed by the back door, his heart thumping and his throat feeling as if someone had their hands around it. He started running through things to tell Taylor if he suddenly appeared.

*Very sorry, the staff at the Hub were worried about you…part of HenleyAudit’s new brief and…*oh, god – he hoped Taylor wasn’t here.

Willis puffed his cheeks out and emitted a sigh of relief when Macgregor reappeared in the kitchen doorway.

'Nobody here.' She walked across and put her shoes back on.

'Good. Can we go now? Please.' Willis beckoned her to move faster.

She appeared to be more subdued, in a 'reflective' mood maybe, thought Willis.

He waited until they were off Taylor's property, safely back in the car, before resuming the conversation.

'You okay?'

Macgregor rested her hands on the steering wheel, stretching her arms, looking straight ahead.

'Can you make any sense of this?' She asked him.

'No. But I'm confident *you* will at some point.'

'I'm starting to think you were right all along.' She took her hands off the wheel and started massaging the temples of her head. 'I'm seeing things that aren't there. Just because some things seem slightly odd, am I putting them together to *make* it fit? Or is there genuinely something going on here? I can't rationalise it anymore Ryan, the more I think about it the more confused it is. His house was completely normal, just a regular bloke's house. No signs of extravagant spending, like corrupt staff always display.'

'That's what's bothering you?' Willis laughed. 'If Taylor is a crook, and I'm not saying that he is, of course, then he's not some part-time cashier on minimum wage, turning a blind eye for backhanders.'

'What are you saying?' Macgregor perked up a little, responding to Willis's input.

'Taylor's a *Payments and Processing* team leader. You saw his file before we left, economics graduate, worked in the City, god knows how he's ended up being stuck here for so long. Anyway, if someone smart like that was on the fiddle, then they're also, and I'm just guessing here, smart enough to not have their house packed with fancy TVs, gadgets, state-of-the-art PCs and the like. More likely he'd just tuck his earnings away in a hidden account somewhere.'

Macgregor looked at him for a while, chewing on her bottom lip.

'*You* can find hidden accounts, I assume? Being an auditor?'

'Certainly can. Part of the job.'

'Can we search Taylor's account records at the Hub?'

'Will you keep on nagging me until I agree?'

'Yes.'

'Then okay.'

Macgregor smiled and started the car.

71

Ben wasn't sure how long he'd been back at his desk.

He thought it might have been about fifteen minutes, but then again, maybe nearly an hour. He couldn't concentrate, his head was hurting so bad.

He had no recollection of the walk back to the Hub from the garden behind his house. He remembered a lady very kindly emerging through her patio doors to see if he was okay. She seemed to know who he was – she recognised him. He remembered telling her something about him standing on the fence to try and reach a kitten stuck in the tree, when he'd suddenly fallen off. It was all that he could think to say at the time.

He'd had retrieved some paper towels from the gents toilets. Some were wrapped around his left hand, trying to stop the blood. His left hand also held another wad of paper against the cut over his left eye where his head had connected with the stone paving in the lady's garden. The cut over his eye showed no sign of stopping bleeding as yet. The left side of his coat and suit was pretty muddy, where he'd lain on the ground for however long it was.

He was a man of two halves. The muddy, bloody, bruised left side and the reasonably clean and presentable, if a little moist, right side.

Ben took a palmful of painkillers from a packet in his top drawer, and popped them in his mouth. He had no drink to hand, and couldn't be bothered to walk to the water cooler, so he just started chewing the tablets, ignoring the dry, chalky taste in his mouth. After closing his eyes for a few minutes, he eventually managed to get himself together enough to log on to his workstation.

He needed to check the cash had been processed via the Cash Centre – and that the entry had hit the account. He keyed in the account number that he'd memorised.

The statement of account came up on the screen.

No Credits.

What? This should have gone through ages ago. His heart started to race, he felt sweat breaking out on his neck and back, running down the skin under his shirt. Keep it together he told himself, Helen said it was really busy down there, perhaps it was just in line to be processed.

It wouldn't have taken this long though. He was going to have to go down there and…

Ben Taylor Staff Account

He looked closer at the screen. He'd keyed in his *own* account number, not the new company account number. He was so *out of it* he'd used the only other account number that he had committed to memory. *Keep it together, Benny.*

'Concentrate.' He said out loud.

He took several deep breaths, then cleared the screens, before starting again with the correct number.

Credit £2,500,000

Thank fuck for that.

After the trembling in his hands had started to subside, he brought up another screen, the electronic transfer instruction. For all payments over a million pounds, the *HenleyStaffManual* requirement was that two members of staff had to co-authorise the entry. In reality, the Hubs had become so busy, and were so short-staffed, that complying with that would make it impossible to get through all the work in a day, so teams had for years taken to using generic passwords that everyone knew. Even *HenleyAudit* turned a blind eye to the practice, as to enforce the rules would cause chaos for customers.

Ben input the generic password *HenleyHub123*, and authorised the payment as '*First Official*'.

Then he went to screen two and started inputting his own password. This was it, the point of no return, so to speak, by taking the next step he would be creating the only tangible link between himself and the activities of the last couple of days.

Pointless dithering Benny, just get on with…

'Ben, you look awful!'

He jumped, so violently that his knee banged the underside of his desk. He retained the presence of mind, though, despite the pain, to hit the escape key and wipe his screen clear, cancelling the entry and removing it from view.

It was Janet, hovering near his desk, looking concerned.

'Just fell over in the car park, Jan. Nothing to worry about.'

Ben smiled at her, but as he looked up he saw that he was attracting attention from some of the other members of staff in the department, half turning in their chairs to have a look at him.

'I think you should go and have yourself looked at Ben. I really do.'

She wasn't going to go away, judging by her worried expression. He didn't like drawing so much attention from other staff, either.

'You're right Jan. I'm going to go over to the hospital. I'll get a taxi. If Greg Lamb is looking for me, will you let him know?'

'You just sort yourself out.' Janet took Ben's arm and walked with him down through the department. 'Greg Lamb is busy *hot-desking* it around the Hub with Mr Smyth. Your health is more important. I've got everything under control here. If I need to check anything Samantha has said I can phone her at home, so no worrying!'

'Thanks Jan, you're a star.'

'I know. Now go, you! And be careful.'

Ben walked across to the stairwell, thinking not of the hospital but of some place quiet where he wouldn't be disturbed for ten minutes or so.

The meeting and conference rooms didn't have terminals in them. And he didn't want to just start *hot-desking* at some random place in the building, it would look odd.

Hot-desking.

Lamby was off, *hot-desking* with Smyth.
His office would be empty.

A few moments later Ben tucked himself in behind Lamby's desk and powered up the workstation.
Five minutes and it would be done.
He waited for the screen to come to life.
Just repeat the process.

Find the account, the right one this time, Benny, and input the generic password, then authorise it yourself. Then relax.
Relax as much as you can when your staff number will be attached to a laundered payment, at any rate.

Then, as Lamby's workstation finally showed the log on screen, it dawned on him.
He couldn't believe he hadn't thought of it before.
He glanced at his watch. A bit last minute, Benny, to be changing the plan, but it was unlikely that Greg would be coming back to his office any time soon, and this would only take an extra ten minutes or so.
Ben decided to go for it.
He crossed his fingers, on his undamaged hand, and looked in Lamby's top drawer.
Then smiled.

72

'Andy' gazed out of the window from the IT Contact Centre.

It was a hot and humid evening outside and the air conditioning in the building was always playing up, but as a Senior Consultant he was allowed a window seat, so he didn't like to complain about conditions too much.

It had been non-stop since he'd started his shift this afternoon and he was glad of a few minutes' lull in the calls. Not that he didn't enjoy the role, particularly the programming work and assisting managers with spreadsheets and the like.

It was only the idiots in the UK banks who seemed to be forever forgetting their passwords that irritated him. His phone rang again. It was the Henleys Bank line. He glanced at his *Time Differential* chart.

'Good *afternoon*, Henleys IT. Andy speaking, how may I help you?'

'Hi Andy, this is Greg Lamb in the *HenleyEast* Hub in the UK. Sorry about this, but my log on password seems to be disabled and I've also forgotten my payments password.'

Andy tried not to let the caller hear the sigh that came out.

'Staff number please, Greg?'

'Ah, let me just read it off my payslip, make sure I quote it right. Err…*2721244*.'

‘Are you at your designated main terminal, Greg?’

‘Yes, I am in my office.’

‘Then I will reset you now, please bear with me.’ Andy processed the request and waited for confirmation to pop up, which it did. ‘There you go, your passwords are both reset to *Password123*. Is there anything else that I can help you with today, Greg?’

‘No. Thanks Andy.’

‘Andy’ went back to looking out of the window. It really was hot. He decided to treat himself to a chilled drink from the machine before settling in for another couple of hours of these password reset requests.

73

Ben sent the payment.

He felt an immediate, overwhelming, sense of calm.

Not relief, not excitement, not even satisfaction. Just calm.

Like he could go to sleep for a long time.

He powered down Greg Lamb's terminal, then started to stand up and leave. Except he couldn't be bothered. He was so tired now.

He sat back down, then propped his feet up on Lamby's desk and reclined in the chair. He pressed the paper towels in his cut, left hand hard against the wound on his head – and started to feel a slight easing in the pain. He stretched his legs a little and sank lower in the chair. It was getting almost comfortable.

He closed his eyes and kept the towels against his head. There was still blood trickling out, he could feel some getting through the soaked paper and running down his face to his mouth. It tasted strange, but he couldn't be bothered to alter his position in order to wipe it away.

Just five minutes rest, then he'd go home.

He started thinking about Abi. What she'd be doing. She should have been home a while by now. She hadn't said whether she was working tonight. He wanted to be with her, driving somewhere, talking, stopping for coffee, holding hands, she'd tell him about her plans, maybe she'd bought a house, then it started changing – her face started to morph into Sam's, the eyes stayed the same, *that's* why she looked familiar – the eyes. Sam was telling him off, like she had at the Charity Ball, then it was Abi again, then Sam, then…

…then nothing.

His hand slipped from his head and lay limp over the arm of the chair.

Blood started to seep through the saturated paper and drip onto the floor.

74

'That's what we're telling you. He isn't there!' Willis tried, again, to gain Lamb and Smyth's attention.

They were hunched over Smyth's computer screen, engrossed in a spreadsheet.

'He probably just didn't want to answer the door. Seeing as he's ill and all?' Smyth smirked, not looking up.

'We checked. He isn't there.' Macgregor glared at him.

'You checked? What the hell do you mean?' Greg Lamb enquired. He was being rather more attentive.

'That's not important. We just know he isn't there.' Willis confirmed.

'He might have gone over to Moran's house.' Lamb suggested. 'Her kids have the flu. If he *is* ill then he probably caught it off them, he's always over there, and maybe she's looking after the three of them?'

'Where does she live?' Macgregor demanded.

'Oh, for goodness' sake, you can't go round members of staff's houses like this!' Smyth started to raise his voice. 'Look, we'll have her home number listed. We'll go and phone her, okay? See if she's seen him? Then will you let us get on, please?'

'Her number is in my notebook. In my office.'

Lamb mumbled.

Macgregor nodded.

'Do you want to wait here, Marc?' Lamb asked.

'Oh, no, Lamby! I have nothing better to do here, I'm only the Retail Ops Director, after all. I can't wait to see if one member of your staff has seen another today. Lead on!'

Willis followed the others up to Greg Lamb's 'old' office.

Marc Smyth opened the door and walked in, followed by Lamb.

There was a long silence as Willis and the others took in the sight of the man in a muddy suit and coat, face half-covered in blood, feet on the desk, apparently collapsed in the chair.

'Is that him?' Willis leant across and whispered to Max.

She nodded.

'Ben?' Lamby was as white as a sheet, like he thought Taylor was dead.

'Taylor! Is that who this is?' Smyth blurted. 'Taylor!'

Ben Taylor opened his eyes a crack. His good eye at least. It was difficult to see what the other one was doing, underneath the congealed blood and the fresh stuff trickling over the top. He slowly raised a bloodstained wad of paper, pressed it to his forehead, and appeared to wake up a little more when he did so.

'Taylor, what the hell do you think you're doing?' Smyth demanded.

Taylor's good eye tracked around the room until it appeared to focus on the person that had just spoken.

'Are you Smith?' Taylor asked. He sounded barely

conscious. Like someone who was way beyond exhausted.

'Don't you know? I am Marc Smyth, Retail Ops Dir…'

'Mark?' Taylor seemed to be waking up, but his voice remained hoarse and dry.

'Yes?'

'You speak to me like that again and I will pound your fucking head against this desk until you stop breathing. Do you understand?'

Smyth's expression changed. He stayed quiet.

'Good.' Taylor's eye moved around to Willis and Macgregor. 'You the two that came to my house?'

Willis nodded. Macgregor said 'yes'.

'You're from the FCA?'

'I am.' Macgregor replied.

'Suppose you want to ask me some things?'

'If that's okay with you?' Macgregor responded, quietly and politely. Willis hadn't heard that tone from her previously.

Ben slowly lifted his legs off the desk and placed his feet down on the floor, bending forward as he did so. He remained doubled over for a long time, as if trying to get some feeling back into the lower half of his body. Then he slowly stood upright, still clutching the paper towels to his head.

When he finally managed to balance himself, Willis thought he looked totally out of it, like someone who was high, or completely inebriated. His good eye was dancing around, not focussing on any of them. At one point it briefly rolled back into his head.

'It's okay, Ben.' Lamby finally said, appearing to at last show some sign of concern for his colleague.

'Sit back down, we can do this here.'

Ben became more lucid, shaking his head.

'No. I'll only talk to *her*.' He started walking around the desk, heading towards Willis and the others.

Marc Smyth stepped in front of him, causing Ben to stumble to a halt.

'You're not calling the shots here Taylor. I am the Retail Ops Director and I am telling you that we will be sitting down to a meeting here to discuss your unprofessional conduct and…'

Smyth stopped speaking as Taylor slowly leaned forward, looking down at Smyth, until their eyes were an inch apart.

For a moment, Willis thought Taylor was going to aim a headbutt at the Ops Director, such was the look in Taylor's good eye. When he spoke though, it was very calm and quiet, although with sufficient force to send saliva and blood spluttering into Smyth's face.

'Are *you*? Seriously? Going to try my patience any further?'

Smyth stepped back. Willis didn't blame him.

Taylor stared at Smyth for maybe ten seconds. Smyth looked too frightened to look away, maybe thinking that Taylor would swing for him if he did.

Taylor walked past Lamb, then turned to Macgregor, inviting her to leave the room ahead of him. As Taylor followed her out, Willis watched him quietly close the door behind him.

75

He stood in front of her, trying to maintain his focus through the pain. He wanted to do this, so he could finally put today behind him.

He also wanted to do this as quickly as possible.

They were standing in front of the washbasins and mirrors in the ladies toilets outside the top floor Conference Suite. Where Taylor had taken her. The suite was not being used today and the area outside was completely deserted.

His head was pounding.

'Is this so they won't come and interrupt us?' Macgregor enquired.

'That too. Take off your clothes.'

'What? Dream on.'

'If you take them off I'll answer your questions.'

She just stood there staring at him. Looking puzzled, to say the least.

'I don't know anything about FCA work.' He continued. 'But I'm not prepared to take a chance that you have some means of recording this conversation. A phone or camera or something. You could just press a button. You want to talk? You get undressed. Otherwise I'll just be off home.' He turned to go.

'Does that door lock?'

It didn't, so Ben leaned his back against it. It was a position he actually found very comfortable.

He watched as Macgregor walked back to the far

end of the washbasin counter, quickly slipped out of her clothes, folding them neatly into a pile which she placed on the very end of the counter, as far away as possible from the washbasins and taps.

Then walked back over to him, maybe six feet away, and started removing her underwear.

'That's okay, you can leave those…' Ben said. But they were already off.

She threw her bra and briefs over onto the pile of her clothes and stood completely naked, apart from her shoes, in front of him.

'Want to cavity search me too?' She spat the words at him.

Ben slipped off his coat and wrapped it around her, covering her completely. She calmed down.

Ben leaned back against the door, holding his head again. Tried to get into as comfortable a position as possible.

'What happened to your head?" She asked.

'Fell over in the car park. It's just a scratch. So, what do you want to know?'

'I want to know what were you doing at that farm in Wales?'

'I'm not admitting to being at a farm in Wales.'

'Come off it, Taylor. Why bother with all this if you're just going to piss about? I saw you on Vladic's land and I saw you on the Severn Bridge.'

'I was in Wales, but I won't admit to being at any farm. I was just down that way visiting a friend.'

'That woman in the car, with the kids?'

'Yes.'

'Who is she?'

'Do you really need to know?'

'You're pissing me about again.'

'You promise it'll stay between you and me?'

'Okay.'

'She's Marc Smyth's wife.'

Macgregor's eyes widened.

'That guy downstairs? Fucking hell Taylor! You're having an affair with the boss's wife? Are you trying to tell me that's what all this is about?' She started to laugh. 'Bullshit! There's more to it than that.'

'No affair. She's just a friend. But he's started knocking her around – and she needed someone to talk to.'

Macgregor stopped laughing.

'How do you even know her?'

'She works in Premier Banking at *HenleyWest*. Hub staff talk to each other all the time, strike up friendships. I didn't even know who she was when I first spoke to her, she doesn't use the same spelling of 'Smith' as he does. Check the internal directory, you'll see.'

Macgregor chewed on her bottom lip for a while.

'Not buying it, Taylor. There's more to this. I'll still have to investigate it fully.'

'I didn't expect anything less. That's why I agreed to talk to you.'

'Go on then. I'm getting cold. And bored.'

Taylor reached into his inside jacket pocket and pulled out his wallet. He removed the two *HenleyCards* and placed them on the counter.

'I have a current account, a savings account and a staff mortgage. The details are on those cards. There are no hidden accounts, I swear. You can keep those. Investigate me fully. You won't find any earnings from money-laundering activity, anywhere.'

'Because they'd pay you cash.'

'You know where I live. You can search my house. Look for any signs I'm living beyond my means. What's more, you and *HenleyAudit* can keep checking my accounts, and keep coming back to search my house too if you like, for as long as you want, because the truth is that I have never, and will never, take any illegal earnings.'

'A very strange yet generous offer. Why would you suggest something like that?'

'Don't want to do fourteen years in prison.'

Macgregor shook her head.

'Still not buying this, Taylor. I saw you at that farm. I followed you across fucking *Wales*.'

Taylor pondered for a while. His head was getting worse and he wanted to conclude this discussion.

'I'll give you a *hypothetical scenario* if you like?'

'How very *Henleys Bank* of you.'

'I can just go home if you'd prefer?'

'No, I'm listening.'

'If, say, a professionally qualified banker at a Hub were to decide to have some fun at the bank's expense, then, maybe, he wouldn't necessarily want any financial gain from the enterprise, it would just be to stick two fingers up at the bank.'

'Why?'

'Maybe for proposing to make thousands of staff displaced for no justifiable reason?'

'How *very* noble of him.'

'Macgregor,' Ben leant his head back on the door, closed his eyes and took a deep breath, squeezing the towel tighter against his head. It helped numb the pain, 'I don't actually care about your opinion on that.'

'Fair enough.' She allowed herself a smile, knowing he wasn't looking at her. 'Can I get dressed now?'

Ben nodded. 'Carry on. Everything looks all blurry to me now, anyway.'

Despite this assurance, she got dressed under his big coat, using it as a sort of curtain. She'd given him enough of an eyeful.

She walked back, fully clothed again and handed him his coat.

He didn't move. Looked like he was sleeping.

'Taylor!'

His good eye opened. He looked less groggy than when he'd woken up in Greg Lamb's chair, but more tired. Exhausted.

'Thanks.' He took the coat from her. Then closed his eye again.

'Taylor, I still have to investigate you. It's my job. Even if you, sorry, your *hypothetical scenario*, didn't make any money out of it, the audit will still show whatever entries, hypothetically, were processed. I can't ignore that. I'd have to pursue a case anyway.'

'That's the thing.' His voice started slurring. He wasn't going to be awake much longer. '*No entries, did 'em under someone else's name . No evidence on Benny Taylor! Thought of that last minute – just between you and me – you'd prosecute wrong person, although he'd probably deserve it.*'

He started laughing. His teeth were covered in drying blood.

'Come on.' She took his arm over her shoulder and

moved him out of the way to open the door. 'We'll drive you to the hospital. That needs at least a couple of stitches. You should probably get your head scanned too – you sound delirious.'

Ben just continued giggling.

Macgregor assisted him to the lifts and pressed the call button.

'Taylor?'

'Uh-huh?' Still giggling.

'When I conduct my investigation, if I find out you've lied to me. Any lie at all. Or that you made a penny out of whatever you *hypothetically* did. I will do everything I can to make sure you serve a full fourteen years. Understand me?'

He stopped giggling. 'You're nice.' He told her, then started laughing out loud. Bloody spit running down his chin.

'Thank god.' She muttered as the lift doors opened. 'Let's get your head looked at, okay?'

Ben smiled.

76

He sat against the wing of his company car and waited for Vladic to arrive. It was a nice spot, under the trees at the edge of the car park, not too far from the main building of the motorway services – if you wanted to get yourself a coffee or sandwich. The trees were keeping the drizzling rain off him, although it looked like it would brighten up soon, the sun was peeking through the clouds over to the west.

After twenty minutes or so, Ben watched a gargantuan Mercedes off-roader pull into the car park and circle around. He gave it a little wave and it changed direction towards him, roaring across and pulling up next to his Volkswagen.

The passenger side window rolled down and the driver leaned across to speak to him.

'Ben! Get in my friend.'

Ben shook his head.

'We can talk out here. In the fresh air.'

'Really?' Vladic wrinkled his nose. 'Out there? Why'd you want to meet all the way out here anyway?'

'I like it here.'

'Okay.' Vladic shrugged, turned the engine off and got out.

He walked around and joined Ben, leaning against the company car.

'Huh.' Vladic looked around. 'This *is* quite a

pleasant spot for a motorway services! Peaceful.'

Ben smiled, but wasn't really paying much attention.

'I was worried about you, Ben, when I couldn't get hold of you. I even came round your house to look for you. By the way, you really should lock your back door, you know. There's dodgy people around, even on the Broadlands estate.'

'The hospital kept me in for a couple of nights. I had a concussion. My hand was infected.'

'What on earth happened to you? You've given your head a hell of a whack!'

Ben reached up and touched the stitches and the lump on his head. It made him wince.

'Fell off a fence into my neighbour's garden.'

Vladic laughed. 'Thought you were going to tell me you'd fought off a gang of carjackers to protect the cash.'

'No. You got my message about your Subaru?'

'All taken care of.'

'Who's the "Old Man"?'

'Pardon?'

'Who is he? I've risked going to prison for this deal. I just want to know what you're involved with.'

'Not your concern, Ben.'

He looked across at Vladic. Vladic kept his head down, avoiding eye contact.

'I always looked up to you, Tommi. You knew that. You knew I'd find it difficult to say no to a request for a favour. I just want to know how bad it is. What are you into? Drugs, guns, or something worse. People?'

'What kind of person do you think I am, Taylor?'

'I don't know any more, Tommi. Hence the question.'

Vladic leant back, resting his hands behind him on the bonnet of the car. He stayed like that for a long time. Eventually he sat up again.

'I don't benefit directly from any of the deals that are transacted on that land. I do collect rent, a very generous rent, from the tenants. I appreciate that is a fine distinction, but it is a distinction.'

'Really? You let land out to, what are they, modern-day *smugglers?* What the hell is that all about?'

'You can judge me all you want. But getting involved in this was not my choosing. It was a set of circumstances forced upon me.'

'Whatever. Give me my cash and I'll be out of here.'

Vladic didn't move.

'Okay. I guess you've earned the right to ask. Not that it's really any of your concern, but the Old Man is a…a sort of high ranking civil servant in the finance department of the government back home. He is one of the wealthiest men in the country. He uses my land for logistics – to manipulate resources in and out of the UK.'

'Are you telling me that your tenant is a foreign government?'

'Not really. They are companies set up at the bequest of the Old Man. I think some are used in matters of national interest, if they want to buy arms to support a local militia, they can get them out of the UK that way, or if they want to raise funds by getting narcotics, say, into this country, they could use that route. Other things the Old Man just does for his own personal gain. He has contacts all over Europe and the Middle East. He could be doing deals with all sorts of people. My people tell me that all sorts of unsavoury characters turn up down there from time to time.'

'I don't get it Tommi. Why be involved with someone like that?'

'Because I owe him. He saved my wife's life.'

Ben said nothing. He, sort of, realised where this was heading.

'Ten years ago,' Vladic continued, 'when I was still with Henleys, my wife went back to visit family over there. It was a time of much political unrest, and my family used to be quite high profile in local government. Anyway, an extremist group tried to capture my wife. If they had succeeded she…she could have…she still has nightmares about it, Ben. The Old Man was an associate of my father's. He agreed to find a safe place for her. He reckoned we had maybe two days before they tried for her again. In the end I acquired the services of a Security Consultant who had worked extensively in the area. He liaised with the Old Man and they got her out.'

'But the Old Man wanted a favour in return?'

'No. I *wanted* to do it for him. I felt I owed him more than could ever be repaid. There had been a lot of repossessed farms coming up all year across the Debt Management Team's desks. I knew a coastal farm may be useful to him, and as soon as a good one came up I did the deal. I was just going to give it to him, or maybe sell it, if he offered me anything, but he came up with this landlord and tenant idea and – and this is the thing that I regret – I was greedy at the time and I went along with it. I told myself that my hands were clean, that I was just the property company, like a landlord letting a property to a corrupt bank. I accept, now that I am older and wiser, that I took my thirty pieces of silver. But you can't turn back the clock, Ben.'

Ben stayed quiet. He wasn't happy about things and he wasn't particularly unhappy. He just wanted to be away from all of this now.

Vladic seemed to sense that the meeting was concluded and went around to the rear of his Mercedes and retrieved a heavy holdall from inside the tailgate door.

'Your earnings, Ben. Two hundred and fif…'

'Thanks.' Ben opened the boot of the Volkswagen and threw the green bag inside.

'Hey Ben, you ever need anything, you just…'

'See you around, Tommi.'

Ben got into his car, closed the door and drove out of the services, heading west.

77

She sat, staring at nothing in particular on her desk.

The phones were exceptionally quiet tonight. Only Melanie and Will were also in. Mel was reading another novel.

She'd told him not to contact her and he'd listened. She desperately wished that he hadn't. She had thought about him constantly for the last two days. She wanted so much to talk to him again.

A figure at the end of the department coming through the doors caught her eye and she looked up.

She smiled.

She watched each step as he crossed the department to her, past Mel and Will. Neither of them looked up.

He sat down next to her and she turned to him, taking his hands after he dropped his bag on the floor.

She noticed the cut on his head and she let go of his hands to run her fingers gently down his face. It was horrible seeing him damaged. She didn't want to think about what might have happened to him. Something to do with the deal he'd done, she assumed, or the people that he'd got himself involved with.

He took her hands in his then held them down low, out of sight of anyone else, though she didn't care anyway, then he started gently stroking her fingers, the backs of her hands and her wrists, where the faded bruises were. It felt lovely.

They watched each other for a while. Every so often he seemed to get embarrassed and look away, as if to check if anyone was paying them any attention, but she couldn't take her eyes off him.

Eventually, after a long time, she knew that she had to be honest with him. She wanted, so badly, to get up, walk away from her desk, go and get the twins and drive back to his house. They could stop for coffee on the way. She couldn't imagine anything more perfect.

At one point she very nearly did it. She was within a few seconds of standing up and dragging him out with her.

Then she stopped herself, thinking that tonight would be wonderful, maybe tomorrow and the next day. The next few weeks probably.

Then the trouble would start. Marc would get expensive lawyers involved, probably try and avoid paying any child support, claiming she'd walked out to live with someone else. He would try and get Ben in all sorts of trouble, maybe even try and jeopardise his job.

She was determined not to be selfish. It took all her remaining strength.

'I can't come with you.' She whispered. He smiled, like he knew she would say this. The tears started welling up. 'I can't come with you.' The words barely came out that time. He smiled again. It was physically hurting her, telling him this out loud.

'I can't come with you.' That time no sound at all came out, she just mouthed the words. Tears started to run out of her eyes.

He looked away. As if he didn't want to see her upset like this.

Then he squeezed her hands one last time, leaned forward and placed his lips on her forehead – just touched his mouth, very gently, against her skin.

Tears were pouring down her face.

She buried her head in her hands, desperately trying to compose herself. She didn't want to waste time getting emotional – she wanted to talk with him, tell him why she couldn't go with him yet. Talk to him about anything, about work if she had to, just to keep him here with her for a while longer. Maybe start devising a plan together.

When she looked up he'd gone.

She watched the door for minutes, hoping he'd come back, knowing that he wouldn't.

Eventually she looked down.

He'd left the green bag.

78

‘Where the hell have you been, mate?’

It had been two weeks.

‘Needed some time away. In the sun. To rest up.’

‘You *look* rested. Apart from that angry-looking fucking scar on your head!’

Sam was genuinely concerned by how painful it looked, although it appeared well past its worse.

She’d really missed him. Even more than she’d known she would have. She thought it would be good to have some time away from him (with him doing the away part). But it wasn’t. Every day she’d been thinking and worrying about him, not knowing what on earth was going on or why he’d suddenly disappeared. Last week, she’d spent one entire afternoon terrified that he’d done something stupid.

Then he’d called her, explaining that he’d been away on a couple of weeks’ leave. Asking if she’d meet him after work on Friday? She didn’t have the kids that night. She made her apologies to Kathy Hitchings, whose leaving do was scheduled for the Red Lion, and told him he could take her into the old town – there was a new bar open and she thought that the locals could do with the splash of glamour that they could provide.

She bought herself a new dress. She drove a hundred miles to the designer outlet park to get it in a sale. She told herself that she deserved it. The weather was still crap, hence the discount price, but she'd lost some weight, paid for a tan, and her hair was growing longer very nicely. That kind of effort deserved a designer look, even for a High Street wine bar.

She felt terrible about how she'd been acting. Stropping and sulking. She'd still tell him how she felt about him, but was determined to be fun and laid-back all evening, not the stressed-out psycho she'd been a couple of weeks earlier. He didn't deserve that. After she'd been pretty and fun, *then* she'd tell him. No work talk for now.

The wine bar was fantastic. Ben had driven them in to the town; the car park behind the high street would be a safe place to leave the company Volkswagen if they got a taxi home. The usual Friday types were there, before they headed to their brasseries and their posh restaurants for dinner. The middle-aged crowd, solicitors, surveyors and other professional *wannabes*, suddenly had the centre of attention shifted away from their overweight, second or third wives crammed into their outfits a dress size too small, by a made-over waif and a gym addict straying from the Red Lion crowd from the Broadlands estate.

She ordered a third bottle of Pinot Noir. They weren't going on anywhere, so why not. As the past-it crowd started to drift away for dinner, they ordered a soup and sandwich supper.

'You have so much to catch up on.' She decided that it was finally time to discuss a little *HenleyEast* gossip. Sport, TV, music and pretty girls could only sustain the conversation for so long.

'Lamb announced that the proposed *Phasedown*

had been indefinitely postponed. Or "car parked" as he called it. There was even a rumour going round that someone had uncovered a printout that implicated him in a money-laundering transaction, and he'd been pressured into withdrawing the proposal from the Board, but I couldn't find anyone who knew for sure if that was true.'

Ben smiled.

'Whatever happened, he and that Smyth guy are being moved elsewhere. We're having some new management. Proper, experienced ops managers apparently, not just career players.'

'That's good.'

'You should put your name forward.'

'For what?'

'Centre Manager at least. Why not Ops Director? You're better qualified than anyone else they could shortlist.'

'Not really my thing anymore.'

'Why? You'd be superb at it.' Her self-commitment to not talking about work had been abandoned. 'It could be the making of you. Big jump up in salary and grade.'

'Ooh! *Salary and grade!*'

'Grow up. Maybe you could, you know, get one of the exec houses, settle down a bit, start a family? Like normal people do?'

'Can't wait.'

His tone, his expression, his general demeanour, told her this wasn't a topic to pursue tonight. She wouldn't let it spoil her evening. She was enjoying his company too much, so she poked her tongue out at him and laughed.

‘What about you?’ He asked.

She stopped laughing.

‘What do you mean?’

‘Well, when you’re like this, like a *normal* person, without the sarcasm and the bad temper and all the other things you work so hard at to keep people at a safe distance, you’re fabulous company. You look amazing, you’re funny and charming. You’ve been my best friend for…actually, my only real friend for ten years. You should find someone who understands the real Sam Moran! Realises that the thorny exterior isn’t really you. Someone who appreciates your sense of humour – all that sort of stuff.’

‘Like you, you mean?’

‘Exactly, only, you know, that you fancy and whatever.’

‘You’re such an idiot.’ She shook her head. She was determined that his stupidity would not spoil her perfect night out. She excused herself and took a long, long bathroom break while she calmed down. If he was determined to keep pushing the idea that she should settle down with someone else, then so be it, but she was definitely going to tell him how she really felt about him. She just didn’t want to spoil everything by doing it so early. She’d leave it until the morning, she decided.

When she returned to their table he gave her a wonderful smile. She decided that she wanted to go back to her house, so after they’d finished the bottle she asked at the bar for someone to call them a taxi.

79

He'd been waiting all evening to bring the conversation around to their 'relationship'.

When it finally happened she'd made jokes, disappeared for twenty minutes, then wanted a taxi home.

He would have asked her to move in with him had she shown the slightest interest in discussing the matter. He knew it was a reaction to the last couple of weeks, but it was real nonetheless. She was lovely and she was his best friend.

But she would have said something.

At some point, over the last ten years, she would have given him some sort of indication if she'd had the slightest interest in him that way. Tonight just confirmed it – and he wasn't even sad about it. She was way out of his league. He'd always known that.

He wasn't going to let it spoil the night, though. She looked fantastic and they'd had a lovely evening.

He thought about it all the way home in the taxicab.

The emotionally exhausted state that he'd been in for two weeks.

The surprise at his own opening up of emotions with Abigail Smith, asking her to stay at his house, the heartbreaking feeling when she said no, even though it was obvious that she would. It was strange, but maybe understandable, how they'd connected so quickly and so strongly.

That had never happened to him before.

She'd probably patch things up with her idiot husband, but at least he knew she had another option now – her fault if she didn't take it. He'd check on her soon – to see how she was doing.

He genuinely wanted Sam to find someone better than her ex, though. He'd just have to find a better way of raising the subject the next time they went out for dinner.

They had one more glass of wine back at her house, but she was pretty sleepy. She'd changed into her pyjamas and spread out on her sofa before requesting a duvet, which he duly fetched for her.

'So?' She managed to mumble before she drifted off. 'Was this our first date?'

He smiled and pushed her hair away from her face, as she slipped into unconsciousness.

Ben found a notepad and paper in a kitchen drawer. It would have been better to talk to her earlier, but it wasn't fair to do it when she was drunk.

So he wrote it down. Not ideal, but he told himself that he'd make it up to her when they saw each other again.

Sam,

Thanks for last night.

I've resigned from Henleys so won't see you in work again. Look after the place for me!

I've let my house out for a few months - tenants move in tomorrow. I'll be selling it before the end of the year - going to use the equity to finance myself through a post-grad course. Maybe travel around for a while.

I'll miss you lots, of course - and will give you a call when I know what I'll be doing.

Sorry I made you so angry the other day. I'll regret that always. Forgiven me?

Take care mate.

Ben

P.S. Best first date I've ever been on!

He made sure she was tucked in and then he quietly let himself out of the house.

80

'Ben!'

He could barely move his head.

Last night's party had been an absolute shocker. Trying to keep pace with college students at his age was futile. He sometimes, often, wished he'd just got a place of his own, rather than share a house, but it was the best college of its kind in the south, and flats around here were scarce and expensive.

'Ben you old fart, get up! Phone call for you,' Zak, one of his housemates, shouted at him.

'Huh?'

'Some woman with a sexy voice on the house phone. Asking for you.'

Ben prised himself out of bed and, ignoring the blistering pain caused by the rays of sunlight piercing the ancient, dust-covered blinds, padded out into the hallway.

As soon as he heard her voice, he forgot about his headache.

'Hi…! How did you find this number…? No, I've been thinking about you too, of course I have, I just didn't want to, you know, I wanted to get myself sorted out before I rang you…I'd love to. No, bring the kids, it'll be fun. I'll book a room, somewhere half-decent, we can't stay in this hellhole…Yeah. I can't wait …'

Zak loitered by the kitchen door, waiting for ages for Ben to hang up.

'Is she the reason why you haven't looked at any of the student totty since start of term?' He asked Ben when the call finally ended.

Ben smiled. Then nodded.

'What's the best hotel around here?' He asked, hangover forgotten.

EPILOGUE

They were boxing him in on all sides, one to the right of him, one behind, and one cutting him off from the front.

This was a much better attempt than their last one. He resigned himself to the fact that this would be over soon.

He accelerated to the left. They weren't expecting that. It gave him some space.

If he could get to the outside then he might just get away.

He looked across just in time to see the collision. They'd worked out a strategy. At last.

They took him low and he went straight to ground. Blow the whistle, he told himself, frantically trying to get it to his mouth. They were getting savage if you didn't whistle them early – even in these training sessions.

Too late, they piled on to him, at least one of them hitting him with a knee on the way in. He eventually managed to untangle his whistle and gave it three blasts.

'Full time! Full time!'

One by one, in no particular rush, they rolled themselves off and started loping back to the changing rooms.

'Jennings! Was that you? With the knee?'

'No sir. Why would you assume such a thing?'

'You haven't handed in your no doubt original and insightful essay on Monetary Policy yet. Have you Jennings?'

'No sir.'

'Well don't expect a good grade after that cheap shot, okay?'

'Sir! What goes on, on the rugby field, should stay on…'

A buzzer sounded in the distance.

'Get a move on! Mummies will be waiting in their four-by-fours for their little darlings!'

Some of them accelerated from a lope into a shuffle.

He followed them back to the Sports Department buildings, before returning the bag of rugby balls to the metal cupboard in his tiny office. He ticked today's session, *Defensive Patterns*, off the planner. It was hard going a lot of the time, but when he'd first arrived three seasons previously they didn't have any senior rugby at all. Now they had four, well, three and a half, teams and the First XV were starting to win regularly – against the established schools. They may even make the league play-offs this season. He was also getting paid to coach part-time at the local professional club. The Head had been very good about that. Big rugby fan.

He threw his boots into the locker and stuffed his feet into his trainers. He didn't have time for a shower; he'd promised to take the kids to the park and he wouldn't keep them waiting – *their* school was just up the road and they'd be here any minute. He'd treat himself to a hot bath later, at home. He just pulled on a clean pair of track bottoms over the top of his kit.

The last few stragglers were walking down the drive as he headed for the main gates. He wandered along in their midst, enjoying the warm, early spring sunshine on his face.

Most of the 4x4s and other school-run tanks had gone by the time he got to the main road.

They were here already – he spotted them straight away. She waved to him.

He jogged along the pavement for a while before breaking into a run, impatient to see her, and their baby in her arms.

First things first though, he slowed down, flung the back door of the car open and, to a duet of protests, swooped in to plant noisy kisses on his step-kids' heads.

Then he ducked back out, closed the door and kissed the baby, before giving his wife his best tender, passionate embrace.

'Miss me today?'

'You smell of mud.' Her green eyes sparkled in the afternoon sun.